Kate Forsyth is the intern more than twenty books for *The Puzzle Ring*, *The Gypsy Dragon Gold*.

Since her first published book was named Novel of 1998 by *Locus* magazine, Kate has been shortlisted for numerous awards, including a Cybil Award in the US. In 2007, Kate became the first author to win five Aurealis awards in a single year when Books 2–6 in the Chain of Charms series were jointly awarded the 2007 Aurealis Award for Children's Fiction. Book 5, *The Lightning Bolt*, was also named a Notable Book for 2007 by the Children's Book Council of Australia.

Kate lives by the sea in Sydney, Australia, with her husband and three children, and many thousands of books.

the Starkin CROWN

KATE FORSYTH

PAN

Pan Macmillan Australia

First published 2011 in Pan by Pan Macmillan Australia Pty Limited
1 Market Street, Sydney

National Library of Australia
Cataloguing-in-Publication data:

Forsyth, Kate, 1966–

The starkin crown / Kate Forsyth.

9780330404044 (pbk.)

For children.

A823.3

Map by Jeremy Reston
Typeset in 11.5/15 pt Minion by Midland Typesetters, Australia
Printed in Australia by McPherson's Printing Group

Papers used by Pan Macmillan Australia Pty Ltd are natural, recyclable
products made from wood grown in sustainable forests. The manufacturing
processes conform to the environmental regulations of the country of origin.

For my own bold adventurers,
Ben, Tim and Ella

The Prophecy

Three times a babe shall be born,
between star-crowned and iron-bound.
First, the sower of seeds, the soothsayer;
though lame, he must travel far.

Next shall be the king-breaker, the king-maker,
though broken himself he shall be.

Last, the smallest and the greatest—
in him, the blood of wise and wild,
farseeing ones and starseeing ones.
Though he must be lost before he can find,
though, before he sees, he must be blind,
if he can find and if he can see,
the true king of all he shall be.

Royal Family of Ziva

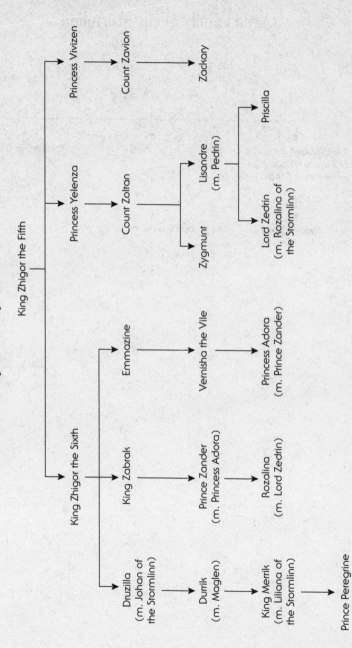

Royal Family of the Stormlinn

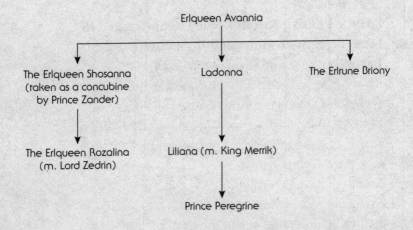

Erlqueen Avannia

The Erlqueen Shosanna
(taken as a concubine
by Prince Zander)

Ladonna

The Erlrune Briony

The Erlqueen Rozalina
(m. Lord Zedrin)

Liliana (m. King Merrik)

Prince Peregrine

Characters

At Stormlinn Castle, the stronghold of the wildkin in the Perilous Forest

PRINCE PEREGRINE (also called Robin)—aged 15
JACK, Peregrine's squire and royal taster—aged 16
LADY GRIZELDA of Zavaria—aged 15
KING MERRIK, Peregrine's father and rightful ruler of Ziva
QUEEN LILIANA, Peregrine's mother and queen-consort
LORD ZEDRIN, the king's third cousin and best friend
ROZALINA, the Erlqueen of the Stormlinn and
    Queen Liliana's cousin
SIR MEDWIN, the royal tutor
STIGA, an old servant
PALILA, a healer and one of the Crafty
TOM-TIT-TOT, an omen-imp

The Merry Men, the prince's bodyguards
LORD MONTGOMERY
LORD LEIGHTON
LORD HARTMANN
LORD MURRAY
LORD BAILEY
LORD GILBERT

At the Isle of Eels, stronghold of the Marsh King
LORD PERCIVAL, Lord of the Marshes
MOLLY, his daughter—aged 15
NAN, his mother
HAL, HANK, FRED, FRANK, BILL, BOB, WILL, WAT, GUS, GED,
    TY and TED: fen-men

At Swartburg Castle, the stronghold of the starkin in Zavaria
VERNISHA, the pretender-queen
LORD GOLDWIN
Lords and ladies of the starkin court
Starkin soldiers

Other members of the royal family
MAGLEN, King Merrik's mother (called Mags)
BRIONY, Queen Liliana's aunt, Erlrune of the Evenlinn
LORD PEDRIN, Lord Zedrin's father
LADY LISANDRE, Lord Zedrin's mother

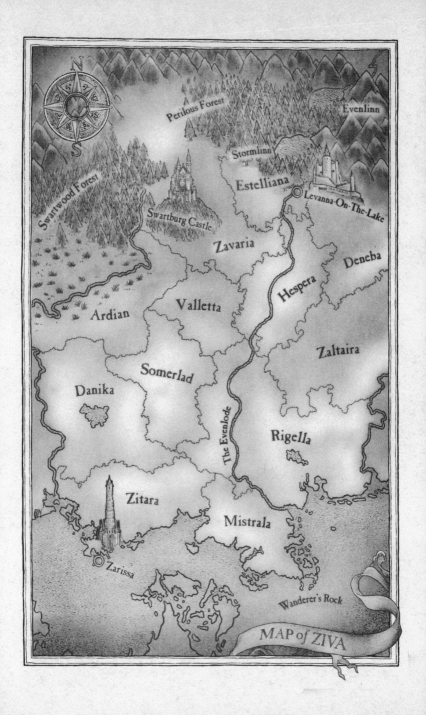

MAP of ZIVA

Are you in earnest? Seize this very minute—
What you can do, or dream you can do, begin it;
Boldness has genius, power and magic in it.

Goethe, *Faust*

CHAPTER 1

A Messenger

BEING A PRINCE WAS NO FUN AT ALL, PEREGRINE THOUGHT moodily, staring out through the arrow slit at the pine trees shivering in the snowy dusk. Especially when you're the son of a king without a kingdom.

Peregrine was meant to be memorising the rivers and forests of all the counties of Ziva, but he couldn't help thinking there was little point when he wasn't allowed to visit any of the other lands. It was too dangerous, his parents thought. He could fall into the hands of their enemies and be killed. Or worse.

At least there was the Midwinter's Eve feast to look forward to, the only break in the dreary round of lessons. It was Peregrine's fifteenth birthday and he was, for once, allowed to take part in the wildkin rituals. He was to be the Oak King and fight the Holly King for an end to the dark winter months.

'Your Highness, you are daydreaming again,' his tutor, Sir Medwin, said, tapping the atlas with his long pointer. A tall, thin man whose bones all seemed to jut at right angles to his body, he wore shabby black robes that flapped about his skinny

1

ankles and a pair of immensely thick spectacles that perched on the very tip of his long nose. He adored biology and geology and geography and chorography and all the other things that end in 'aphy' and 'ology', and could not at all understand why Peregrine did not enter into his enthusiasms. Sir Medwin was, however, also remarkably kind-hearted, always scooping spiders out of his bathwater and rescuing moths from candles, and he never ever told tales on Peregrine, even when the prince spent the whole day hawking instead of learning the alchemical tables.

Peregrine sighed and dragged his attention back to the atlas. Suddenly he heard the pounding of horses' hooves through the rush and swoop of the wind. He jumped up and ran to the arrow slit. By pressing his face right up to the narrow aperture, Peregrine was able to get a glimpse of a cloaked and hooded figure galloping across the drawbridge. At once he propelled himself away from the wall and caught up his fur-lined coat.

'Come on, Blitz,' he called. His small falcon spread his speckled wings and flew to perch on his wrist. Peregrine flung open the door and rushed outside.

'What is it, sir? What's wrong?' his squire cried, one hand flying to his dagger hilt.

'Nothing, Jack! At least, there may be . . . There's someone at the gates. Let's go and see.'

Peregrine raced down the corridor towards the stairs, then slid down the broad marble banister to the great hall below. Blitz was quick to take to the air, screeching in displeasure. Jack ran after Peregrine, taking the steps two at a time. Sir Medwin flapped behind them, calling, 'Your Highness! Sir! What about your studies? Your Highness!'

'What a noise!' Peregrine's mother looked up from her weather maps. 'Must you slide down the banister, Robin?'

'I'm in a hurry. Somebody's here! A rider, coming in from the storm!' Peregrine held out his arm for Blitz, who at once flew down and perched on his wrist.

'A rider? Who could it be?' Queen Liliana got to her feet at once, looking worried. 'It must be urgent if they're prepared to brave the winter storms.'

'I'll go see!' Peregrine cried. He did not wait for his mother but ran down the great hall. Jack, as always, was right behind him.

Peregrine flung open the doorway, letting in swirls of snow like a cloud of cold white butterflies. He bent his head against the arctic wind, so strong it threatened to force him back through the door, and fought his way through the storm to the inner bailey. He was in time to see the iron-barred gates creak open, letting in the mysterious rider.

By hanging over the battlements, Peregrine could see the horse limp in and the rider slip down to the ground, catching at the horse's stirrup. A tall hound was at the horse's heels; as the guards ran forward, weapons at the ready, the dog snarled. The rider uttered a quick command and the dog fell silent. Both horse and dog were white, the hound standing as tall as the mare's withers.

'Who are you? What do you want?' the guard demanded, his sword out of its sheath. Behind him, the portcullis slammed back to the ground.

'I must speak with King Merrik!' a clear, sweet voice rang out. As she spoke, the girl flung back her fur-trimmed hood to show a patrician profile and a fall of shining fair hair.

'A starkin girl?' Peregrine whispered. 'Here at Stormlinn Castle? She's brave!'

'Or stupid,' Jack responded, leaning beside him.

One of the guards rumbled something and the girl said imperiously, 'I will speak only to the king! Take me to him!'

Peregrine bounded down the stairs to the lower courtyard. Jack hurried behind, calling, 'Your Highness! Please . . . she may be dangerous.'

Peregrine ignored him. Bearing Blitz on his wrist, he strode across the cobblestones, saying, 'You want to see my father? He's in council, but I can send him a messenger.'

The girl gazed at him in surprise. She was dressed in a blue velvet mantle edged with white fur, which matched the voluptuous muff in which her hands were buried. Her eyes were an extraordinary colour, blue and translucent as aquamarines.

'I don't think that's wise, your Highness,' one of the guards said. 'She's starkin.'

'I know that,' Peregrine said impatiently. 'What else could she be with hair that colour? But I doubt she's here to assassinate me, not galloping up to the gate like that. And I've got my dagger.'

'And I've got mine,' Jack said, his hand again on its hilt.

'Are you . . . could you possibly be Prince Peregrine, the son of King Merrik?' the girl asked.

Peregrine nodded, and was dumbfounded when she dropped to her knees in the snow, seizing his hand and bending her head to kiss it. He snatched his hand away. 'Don't do that!'

Blitz shrieked his displeasure, spreading wide his speckled wings, and the girl flinched back.

'I'm sorry, your Highness, I didn't mean to offend you. It is just . . .' She rose to her feet again, one hand on her dog's collar to steady herself. 'Your Highness, I have come to warn you and your father!'

'Warn us? What about?'

'Can we not go inside? Please, sir? I'm so cold . . . and I've ridden so very far.' She swayed on her feet, and at once Peregrine was sorry. He reached out a hand to support her, and she crumpled against him, her muff falling to the ground. 'I feel rather faint . . .'

'Your Highness,' Jack said desperately, starting forward, but Peregrine waved him away with an impatient hand, helping her stand and asking anxiously if she was all right. She nodded and stood upright, keeping one hand on his arm for support. She wore crimson gauntlets with a flaring cuff, embroidered with gold thread and jewels. A heavy silver ring, set with a huge aquamarine the same colour as her eyes, was worn over the leather. Despite the heavy gloves, her hand was trembling.

'You're shivering,' he said contritely. 'Come in out of the snow.'

Jack bent and picked up her muff and she took it from him with a faint, sweet smile, cuddling it to her face. Gently Peregrine led the girl up the stairs towards the great hall, his falcon perched on his other arm. The tall hound slunk close behind them, his tail between his legs, a ridge of hair standing up stiff along his spine. Jack followed, scowling and gripping his dagger, while more men came to lead the horse away to the stables.

The girl slipped and almost fell on the ice. Peregrine put his arm about her back to support her. She leant against him, murmuring, 'Thank you, sir . . . I'm sorry . . . It's just I'm so tired. I've been riding for days, as fast as I could, to get here before them.'

'Before whom?' Peregrine asked.

'An army . . . sir, they seek to take you by surprise . . . attack you under cover of the snowstorm.'

'Jack, go and get my father, will you?' Peregrine said.

'But, sir . . .'

'I'm fine. Go on!'

Jack hesitated a moment longer, looking imploringly at the prince, but after another impatient wave of Peregrine's hand, he went running away across the courtyard.

Sir Medwin hurried towards Peregrine. 'Your Highness, that was most ill-considered! You must learn to think before you act. And walk, not run! Have I not told you a thousand times?'

Peregrine hardly heard him. He led the starkin girl across the snow-whirling courtyard. Queen Liliana was standing in the arched doorway, her old shawl wrapped close about her. 'Come on in, it's freezing!' She drew the girl inside, the dog staying close to his mistress, growling low in his throat. Peregrine followed, Sir Medwin scurrying behind him.

As the starkin girl pulled back her hood, Queen Liliana's old nursemaid struggled to her feet from her rocking chair by the fire. She pointed at the girl with two fingers spread wide in an age-old wildkin gesture against evil, her heart-shaped face grey with fear. 'Starkin!' Stiga hissed.

'Yes, I am of starkin blood, but that doesn't mean I'm your enemy,' the girl said angrily. 'I have ridden many furlongs here, through the snow and the storm, to bring you warning!'

'Venom in your heart and venom in your hand, to spill out across the land,' Stiga intoned, her eyes wide and blank.

The girl's face whitened. She clenched her hands into fists. 'How dare you!' she said in a shaking voice. 'I have come to warn you. How dare you accuse me?'

Stiga whispered, 'I see true.'

Queen Liliana frowned. She gestured to the guards, who at once drew their weapons.

'I can assure you I have no poison ... or weapon of any kind on me,' the girl said through her teeth. 'I've put my own life at risk to come here!'

'Nonetheless, I'm afraid we shall have to search you,' Queen Liliana said. 'We are at war with those of your kind, remember.'

'Is your king not of starkin blood too?' the girl demanded. 'Is that not why he seeks to seize the throne?'

'He is the rightful heir!' Queen Liliana cried. 'It is Vernisha who stole the throne.'

'Of course,' the girl said quickly. 'That is what I meant. Forgive me my clumsy tongue, I have ridden a long way today and am very cold and tired.'

What a difference a mere word can make, Peregrine thought. To *succeed* to the throne. To *seize* the throne. To *steal* it. To *win* it. Each side had their own rhetoric and their own justifications for what they did. Peregrine's father, Merrik, believed he was the rightful heir because he was the only descendant of the eldest child of King Zhigor the Sixth. When King Zhigor's son, King Zabrak, had died twenty-five years ago his niece Vernisha had snatched the crown, even though she was the daughter of King Zhigor's youngest child. Vernisha, however, was of pure starkin blood, while King Merrik had a wildkin grandfather and a hearthkin mother. The war was therefore not just about who wore the crown, but also about the rights and liberties of the hearthkin and the wildkin, kept in subjugation for so long by the ruling starkin.

'You must know we have little cause to trust those of starkin blood,' Queen Liliana replied coldly. 'Come, sit by the fire, try to warm yourself a little, and then tell us why you have come to Stormlinn Castle. Stiga, I know it distresses you to be near those of starkin blood. Will you go to the kitchen and ask one of the cooks to bring us some tea?'

The old woman got up and shuffled away, casting suspicious looks over her shoulder at the girl, who removed her ring so she could strip off her crimson gauntlets, dropping them all on the bench. She unfastened her rich, fur-lined mantle to show a riding dress in fine blue wool, trimmed at hem and waist and cuff in red velvet, over a flouncy red silk petticoat. Her feet were shod in crimson boots of the softest lambskin. Peregrine had never seen clothes so fine.

'See, no weapons,' the girl said angrily, letting her fur-trimmed cloak fall across the bench and spreading her hands wide. Indeed, her riding dress was so closely tailored it would have been difficult to conceal a weapon anywhere, but Queen Liliana made a swift gesture to Palila, an old woman of the Crafty.

Palila deftly searched the girl, then shook her head and said, 'Not even an eating knife, ma'am.'

'I would not be so unwise as to hide a dagger in my boot,' the starkin girl said, sinking down onto the bench near the fire and holding her hands to the blaze. Her ring lay with her gloves and she slipped it back on her finger, looking about her with undisguised scorn.

It was not a very grand room, the great hall of Stormlinn Castle. For years the castle had been a ruin, and had only been repaired when Peregrine was a baby. There was little time or money for major renovations, and so the tumbledown walls had been patched with whatever rock could be found, and hung with ancient tapestries to block the worst of the draughts. The few bits of furniture were old and shabby too, and grouped close about the fire, leaving a large stretch of empty floor where the men-at-arms slept at night. In an attempt to keep out the cold and the damp, the floor was strewn liberally with straw and dried rushes, mixed with rosemary and other winter herbs to mask the smell of the damp stone. Queen Liliana and her ladies had done what they could to patch and mend old cushions and rugs, and the men had built a tall screen for the fire which Peregrine himself had painted, with a picture of men and ladies riding out from the castle, hawks on their wrists.

Till now, Peregrine had always loved the old hall, with its massive oak rafters arching overhead, their ends carved with the faces of all kinds of birds and beasts, and its enormous fireplace with the secret door hidden to one side. Seeing the disdain on the girl's face made him look at it with new eyes, and squirm with embarrassment at its shabbiness.

'You must be half-frozen,' his mother was saying. 'What is your name, and what brings you here on such a bitterly cold night?'

'I have no time to exchange pleasantries with servants,' the girl replied. 'Do you not understand the castle is in danger? Summon the king at once!'

Queen Liliana stared at the stranger in surprise. 'My husband is presently occupied. Perhaps you could tell me what your business with him is?'

The girl stared at her. 'You . . . you are Queen Liliana?' Her incredulous gaze took in the queen's shabby gown, her old shawl and her wild, wind-ruffled hair.

'I am,' Queen Liliana responded, 'but I fear you have the advantage of me. Will you not give me your name and state your business, so I may judge whether or not I should disturb my husband?'

'I . . . My apologies, your Royal Highness, I did not know,' she said, flushing and stammering. 'I am Lady Grizelda ziv Zadira. I have come to bring the king a warning.'

Peregrine gave a silent whistle. One of the ziv! The mysterious rider was able to trace her lineage back to the first king of Ziva, just as Peregrine himself could do. What on earth was she doing at Stormlinn Castle? On his shoulder Blitz cocked his head and regarded the girl with curious black eyes.

'You can give the warning to me, my lady,' Queen Liliana replied.

'I was told to speak only to the king,' Grizelda said hesitantly.

Queen Liliana frowned.

Peregrine said, 'I sent Jack to get him, Mam. She says there's an army coming to attack us.'

'In winter?' Queen Liliana groaned and sat down on the nearest bench, her shoulders slumping. 'Couldn't we even have the winter months to rest and recuperate? Do they plan to besiege us?'

'It'll be a long, cold wait for them then,' Peregrine said. 'I wonder if they realise how bitter it is here in winter? They'll freeze their butts off camping out there.'

'Robin, language!' his mother said automatically. She raised both hands and pressed them against her eyes, and Peregrine knew she was thinking of the empty storerooms below. She dropped her hands and looked at Grizelda with calculating grey eyes. 'How many men? What equipment do they have? Siege towers? Trebuchets? Mangonels?'

Grizelda's eyes widened in surprise and new respect.

'Yet how could they bring such machines through the forest?' Queen Liliana demanded. 'Unless ... the river is frozen over. They could plan on bringing them, dismantled, on sleighs up the river and build them once they get here. Though I doubt they realise how high we are above the river, there's no mangonel that could reach us . . .'

'They have built a portable long-range fusillier,' Grizelda said.

'But what fuel do they have? We sabotaged their fuel storage depot seven years ago, and the marshes of Ardian are held by rebel hearthkins . . . unless . . . Has Ardian fallen back into the hands of the starkin?'

'No,' Grizelda said. 'Though not from want of trying.' Her face broke into a rueful smile. 'I don't know how they got the fusillier fuel, ma'am. I am only a girl, they do not take me into their confidence. All I know is they have tanks of it, wrapped in straw and sacking, and packed on giant sleds pulled by dogs. And all sorts of strange contraptions too, and many men, thousands of them, all dressed in white . . .'

'So they plan to take us by surprise,' a quiet voice said from the doorway.

Peregrine smiled at his father, who stood in the doorway wrapped in a long dark robe. King Merrik was a thin, rather stooped man, with a weary face and dark hooded eyes. His grey-streaked hair was scraped back into a messy ponytail and his chin was bristled. The only sign of his office was a chain about his neck with a small seal hanging at the end of it, engraved, Peregrine knew, with the sign of a swan floating under a coronet of stars. An omen-imp perched on his shoulder, and his councillors stood behind him, all looking tired and anxious.

Grizelda seemed startled to see the king. She sat motionless for a moment, staring at him, then rose and curtsied right down to the ground at his feet.

'Your Majesty,' she whispered, her head bent so her face rested against the ground.

King Merrik regarded her thoughtfully. 'You may rise.'

Gracefully she stood up, brushing straw from her skirt. 'Your Majesty, may I speak?'

'Please do,' King Merrik responded humorously. 'We are all most intrigued to have a starkin lady turn up on our doorstep in the midst of a snowstorm. What on earth are you doing here and where do you come from?'

She told him again the story of the starkin soldiers, coming up the river on sleds with tanks of fusillier fuel.

'How do you know this, my lady?' the king asked.

Grizelda hesitated. 'My brother travels with them, sir. He is the Count of Zavaria, and so they came to him for advice on how to penetrate into the mountains in winter. He breeds sled-dogs, you see, we are famous for them.'

King Merrik nodded. Even Peregrine knew that, from his mind-numbingly boring geography lessons. Zavaria was the county next to Estelliana and, like it, was edged by forest and mountains all along its northern border. It was snowbound in winter, unlike many of the lower-lying counties to the south.

'My brother has no great love for Queen Vernisha, I mean, for Vernisha sir,' Grizelda continued carefully. 'So far we have managed not to be drawn into the conflict, but he could not disobey her direct order, not without declaring himself rebel. So he sent me here, to warn you, while he does what he can to delay the soldiers' advance.'

'But it is midwinter!' Queen Liliana protested. 'It is against the code of chivalry to fight during the midwinter festivities. For twelve days, all must be at peace.'

'I doubt Vernisha cares much for the code of chivalry,' King Merrik said dryly.

'They probably hope to catch us by surprise, all befuddled with midwinter ale,' said his third cousin and best friend, Lord Zedrin. A tall, fair-haired, blue-eyed man, he walked with a pronounced limp, the result of a dreadful fall when he was a young man.

There was a murmur of agreement and comment from the other councillors.

'I am still sadly puzzled,' Queen Liliana said. 'Why should the Count of Zavaria risk being branded a traitor in order to warn us? And more puzzling still, why send his *sister* as messenger? Why put her in such danger?'

'Perhaps because he knows that King Merrik at least remembers the code of chivalry,' Grizelda replied coolly. 'He was sure his Majesty would not harm me.'

'There are other dangers in the Perilous Forest,' Queen Liliana flashed back.

'I had to rely on my horse's swift hooves and my dog's sharp teeth to protect me,' Grizelda said. She patted the hound's white head and he thumped his tail on the floor.

'Still, it was an odd thing to do,' King Merrik said slowly. 'He must have known we would act chivalrously to any messenger, not just his sister'.

Grizelda lifted her head. 'Yet if my brother had sent a servant, no matter how trusted, you would have thought it some kind of trick. I am only a girl, I am unarmed, and I am of true value to my brother.'

'He has sent you as a hostage!' Peregrine cried, feeling a surge of anger at the Count of Zavaria for gambling with his sister's safety.

'Yes,' she answered. 'I have come to warn you all to flee. There is no hope you can survive Vernisha's long-range weapons. This castle shall fall, and you shall all die if you do not flee now!'

CHAPTER 2

The Yuletide Feast

ILL-LIT AND SMOKY, THE CAVERNOUS HALL WAS CROWDED with people and all sorts of strange creatures. Some were tiny, as small and noisy as bees. Others were enormous, with heads like boulders and limbs like tree trunks. Some had stubby horns, others were covered with green scales; yet more had eyes that glowed like orange coals from under heavy grey brows. Grizelda could only clutch her goblet of wine and stare.

She sat alone on her bench. The guests that shared her table were all huddled together at the far end, as far away from her as they could get. Grizelda could only be grateful. She had no desire to share her meal with a monster with scales and webbed fingers like a frog's.

Sipping her wine and pretending to be cool and poised, Grizelda studied the throng. She was not very impressed with the court of King Merrik. Everyone had obviously made an effort to dress up for the feast, yet for most this was simply a matter of plaiting their hair with ribbons or making a wreath of green weeds.

Some of the women had changed their everyday sleeves for ones made of brocade or velvet; others had tied a pretty scarf around their waist or slung a vivid shawl about their shoulders. That was it. No jewels, no cloth-of-gold, no mantles of rare fur. Most of the men had done little more than lay aside their armour and weapons, though many wore holly pinned to their jackets.

The royal table had made a little more effort. King Merrik had changed into a robe of blue velvet, trimmed with gold embroidery and edged with fur. Queen Liliana sat beside him, wearing a sumptuous gown of blue brocade, sewn with jewels, with hanging sleeves of forest-green velvet lined with golden silk.

The same green velvet made up the dress worn by her cousin Rozalina, Erlqueen of the Stormlinn, who sat on the other side of King Merrik, wearing billowing sleeves of blue brocade sewn with jewels. By wearing each other's sleeves, Grizelda thought, the two queens were making a public statement about their bonds of kinship and friendship. Clever, she thought, and wondered if it was done for her benefit.

On Queen Rozalina's sleek black head was a garland of golden-green leaves. Grizelda stared at it in contempt. What kind of queen wore a crown of weeds?

Beside Queen Rozalina sat her husband, Lord Zedrin, dressed more simply in a dark brown velvet coat over black breeches, a red sash tied over his chest, a holly sprig in his buttonhole. Grizelda knew that he had put aside his own claim to the throne in favour of his third cousin and best friend, Merrik, and wondered at him. With his thick fair hair, laughing blue eyes and broad shoulders, he seemed a much better candidate for king.

Prince Peregrine sat beside his mother, dressed for the feast in dark green velvet. It made him look a little more princely than the skinny boy who had come bounding down the stairs to meet her in the courtyard. Grizelda felt his eyes on her and let herself droop sadly, her chin in her hand, her head tilted so the candlelight shone on her hair. She tried to look forlorn and neglected. It must have worked, because she saw the prince get up and walk down towards her. Grizelda bit back a smile.

'Is everything all right?' Peregrine asked, coming up beside the starkin girl. The white hound at her feet growled menacingly and she shushed it with a gesture of her hand, looking up at Peregrine with enormous blue eyes that looked as if they might brim over with tears at any moment.

'Oh yes. I mean . . . well, you can't blame them, can you?' She gestured to the rest of the table, where everyone was laughing and talking and paying her no heed at all. 'I mean, I *am* a starkin.'

'It's not very polite though. You are a guest in our house.' Peregrine stepped forward, ready to have a quick word with Lord Montgomery and the rest of the table, but Grizelda laid her slim hand on his sleeve.

'Please don't. I'm fine, really. Lucky not to have been thrown into a dungeon!' She gave a wan smile.

'My father would never throw anyone in a dungeon!' Peregrine cried.

'Really? Not even a starkin?'

'He's a starkin too,' he reminded her. 'Perhaps not full-blooded like you, but starkin nonetheless. His grandmother was Princess Druzilla, elder sister to King Zabrak.'

'I know,' she replied softly. 'Do you think we are not aware that he is the rightful king? Why else do you think I am here?'

'I'm really not sure,' he answered. 'It was either a very brave or a very foolhardy thing to do.'

'I could not let you be taken unaware,' she said, gazing up at him. 'You are our only hope. Vernisha is a tyrant!'

Peregrine nodded. 'We hear terrible things about her. She is even worse than King Zabrak was, and that's saying something.'

'Will you not sit awhile with me?' Grizelda asked, shifting over on her bench invitingly. 'I'd so like someone to explain everything to me.'

Peregrine hesitated, glanced at the high table on its dais, and then sat down on the bench. Jack at once came down to stand behind his shoulder, bringing Peregrine's cup with him and a ewer of apple cider. Peregrine could feel his squire's disapproving gaze but ignored him, saying, 'What do you want to know?'

'So that's the wildkin queen?' Grizelda demanded. 'The one sitting next to your father?'

'Yes. She's my mother's cousin, you know, and my father's second cousin. Their grandparents were brother and sister.'

She nodded in understanding, and he grinned and leant a little closer. 'It gets even more complicated than that. Lord Zedrin, Queen Rozalina's husband, is also my father's third cousin. That means . . .'

'Yes, I know,' she cut in impatiently. 'Lord Zedrin's great-grandmother was Princess Yelenza, sister to King Zhigor the Sixth who was King Merrik's great-grandfather. Do you think you are the only one made to study genealogical tables?'

'Sorry.' Peregrine brooded for a moment then said, 'Do you know the genealogical tables of all the counts of Ziva, or only our family?'

'All of the families, of course,' she replied haughtily, but Peregrine did not think she was telling the truth. He wondered if she had studied up on his family before being sent here as hostage, and thought it would be no surprise if she had. He would have done the same.

'Why does she wear a wreath of weeds? Doesn't she have a proper crown?'

Peregrine was flabbergasted. 'They're not weeds! It's mistletoe. Can't you see the little white berries? Mistletoe is sacred to the wildkin. It's the winter crown. In spring she will pick and weave herself a new crown of hawthorn, and the summer crown is made of elderflowers. In autumn she wears a crown of autumn leaves and berries.'

Grizelda shook her head in amazement. 'So strange.'

'Nicer than wearing a hard crown of metal and jewels,' Peregrine said defiantly.

She gave him a sideways glance, then dropped her lashes. 'Is it true that her own curse rebounded on her, so that all her children have died?'

Peregrine nodded. 'Yes, it's true. Though whether it's the curse rebounding no-one can tell for sure. Except that Princess Adora lost six babies, and so now has Aunty Rozalina. I think she blames herself. We have a saying, you know, that curses are like chickens, they come home to roost.'

'Who is *we*?' Grizelda asked. 'I mean, you're a starkin, aren't you? Like me? Yet that's not a starkin saying.'

'I have the blood of all three races in me,' Peregrine said proudly. 'That is why I will one day be the true king of prophecy. *Born between star-crowned and iron-bound . . .*

in him, the blood of wise and wild, farseeing ones and starseeing ones.'

She stared at him, and he gazed back, his jaw set, his head held high, trying to read her expression. He wondered if she felt the revulsion that many of the starkin felt about his mixed blood. Mongrel blood, Vernisha the Vile called it, and swore that no-one with such tainted ancestry would ever wear the crown. For twenty-five years she had sat on the starkin throne and worn the starkin crown, and Peregrine's father, the true king, had not been able to wrest it from her.

A roar of excitement went up as a hobhenky carried in a huge oval platter with a roast boar proudly displayed upon it, its head garlanded with ivy and mistletoe. He carried it up to the high table, and Peregrine stood up, saying, 'I must go. My parents will be wondering where I am.'

'I don't understand it!' Grizelda burst out. 'Why are they not packing? Don't they believe me?'

'Oh, they believe you,' Peregrine answered. 'Though my father will have sent out scouts to verify your tale.'

'But they must flee before the army gets here!'

Peregrine looked at her scornfully. 'My parents won't just abandon the castle. We have old and sick and wounded who couldn't manage to struggle through the snow, and besides, we're better staying here where we have food and shelter than freezing our bums off in the forest. We'll enjoy watching the starkin do that instead.'

'But . . . everyone's feasting and having fun! Why aren't they getting ready?'

'We are always ready,' Peregrine replied in exasperation. 'My family has been fighting for years, you think they don't plan for surprise attacks? They're not stupid! Besides, it's

Midwinter's Eve. This is one of the most important dates for the wildkin. To leave the rituals undone would be a very bad omen indeed.'

Grizelda gave a superstitious shudder. 'I just can't understand it. Don't they realise an army's coming to annihilate them?'

Peregrine cocked his head. 'Can you hear the wind?'

Grizelda shrugged her shoulders impatiently. 'Well, yes, of course. It's howling like anything.'

'That army of yours will barely be able to take a step out there. Their best bet is to hunker down and wait it out, and it won't be stopping any time soon.'

'How can you be so sure?'

He stared at her in amazement. 'Surely you know one of my mother's Talents is whistling the wind? She's a weather-witch. That army of yours will be buried in snow come morning time.'

'I thought that was just a story.' Grizelda gazed at Queen Liliana, who was trying to coax Queen Rozalina to eat some of the roast boar. At Peregrine's snort, Grizelda said stubbornly, 'Well, at least an exaggeration.'

'It's no exaggeration,' he said shortly. 'She can call wind and thunder and lightning and rain.'

'What else can she do?'

Peregrine hesitated. Grizelda smiled winningly and he said reluctantly, 'She can heal too, with the touch of her hand. That's what makes her one of the Crafty, you know, having two Gifts. Most people only have one.'

'What's your Gift?'

All her questions were making him feel uncomfortable, but Peregrine could not see how to avoid answering her without being rude. He was opening his mouth to reply, when Jack barged forward to fill up Grizelda's glass of elderflower wine and accidentally spilt it all over her skirt.

'Idiot!' she flashed and mopped up the golden liquid with her napkin.

'Sorry, my lady,' Jack answered stonily, and filled up Peregrine's goblet, all the while waggling his thick eyebrows meaningfully.

Peregrine bit back a grin. 'If you will excuse me, Lady Grizelda, I must go. I have only a short time to eat before the battle begins.'

'The battle? I thought you said my brother and the army will be hunkered down, freezing their . . . backsides off.' The starkin girl sounded disgruntled.

'Oh, not that battle,' Peregrine replied. 'Much more exciting than riding out against a few goose-pimply starkin lords. No, I'm talking about the battle I must fight tonight, against the implacable forces of darkness and death!'

She stared at him, amazed, and he grinned and walked away.

CHAPTER 3

The Oak King

PEREGRINE CLIMBED THE STEPS BACK TO HIS SEAT AT THE high table. His mother turned and smiled at him, lifting one eyebrow. Peregrine shrugged slightly and took his seat.

Jack took up his position behind him. 'I think she was sent here to spy,' he whispered as he carved Peregrine some meat and served him from the various jugs and platters on the table. Jack then drew his eating knife from the sheath on his belt and delicately tasted everything on Peregrine's plate before placing it back before his master.

'Maybe,' Peregrine whispered back. 'Yet what does she hope to gain? She'll be watched closely the whole time. It's not as if we'd let her eavesdrop on any council meetings, or send messages in secret code.'

'She wants something,' Jack said darkly.

'Maybe she and her brother really do want to help overthrow Vernisha,' Peregrine replied. 'Imagine what it must be like having that horrible woman ruling over you! We can't just assume that Lady Grizelda means us harm simply because she's a starkin.'

'You can't trust a starkin!' Jack protested.

'My father's grandmother was a starkin, remember,' Peregrine answered rather sharply. Jack looked mutinous, but said, 'Yes, sir, I'm sorry, sir.'

He stood back, sliding his knives and carving fork back into the sheaths at his waist.

Peregrine waited a few moments, to make sure Jack had suffered no ill effects from the food, then began to eat. Jack was his taster as well as his squire, and so sampled all Peregrine's food and drink in case of poison.

It was not a purely symbolic gesture. Jack's father had been the king's taster for many years and had died horribly three years ago from poison smuggled into the royal gravy jug. Jack, who had then been just thirteen, had begged for the right to inherit his father's position. King Merrik had appointed him taster to the prince and, when Jack had proved loyal and handy, promoted him to the prince's squire. King Merrik had his own taster, Jack's uncle Liam.

The feast continued for several hours, though Peregrine knew just how difficult it must have been for the cooks to stretch out their scant supplies. He knew his mother had led a hunting party into the forest every day for a fortnight, shooting numerous deer, wild pigs, hares, beavers, rabbits and game birds for the feast, while his father's men had cut holes in the ice to fish.

It was close to midnight when two lines of men ran in, spinning flaming torches in their hands so the dark hall was filled with giddy whirligigs of fire. Peregrine closed his eyes, shielding them behind his hand, till Jack bent and touched his shoulder gently.

The men had taken up ceremonious positions all along the

wall, their torches now still and smoking fiercely. Peregrine stood up, allowing Jack to unfasten his short cloak and lay it aside. Jack passed him an oaken spear, carved beautifully with runes all along its length, and a shield woven from willow twigs. He jumped down the steps to the stone-flagged floor, where six pretty girls were sweeping an area free of straw and rushes. Queen Rozalina brought him a crown made of brown oak leaves which rustled as she placed it upon his brow. She kissed him and smiled at him. 'Fight well, my prince!'

He smiled back at her then took the mask she passed him, made from the hide and antlers of a stag. A low thunder of drums announced the arrival of his opponent. A tall man, twice Peregrine's weight, bounded into the lit archway. He was dressed in red and wore a holly crown upon his bushy dark hair, the red berries glowing like droplets of blood. He carried a spear made from the wood of a holly tree and wore a mask fitted with stag antlers.

Peregrine and the horned man saluted and then ran forward to clash their spears together. It was a ceremonial battle, so neither wished to hurt the other. It was as much a dance as a battle, each attempting to leap higher or twirl faster. The crowd cheered and called encouragement, but no-one laid bets. The outcome of this battle was always the same, and had been for centuries. Peregrine, acting the role of the Oak King, the ruler of the summer months, at last laid low the Holly King, ruler of the winter months, and wrested his crown from him. Everyone cheered and toasted him and, panting slightly, Peregrine went and laid the crown of holly leaves at the Erlqueen's feet, sweeping off his own crown.

'Thank you,' Queen Rozalina said in her low, sweet voice. 'Well fought! And happy birthday, Peregrine.'

'Fifteen now and old enough to fight a real battle,' he replied exuberantly.

She smiled wistfully and drew him close so she could kiss his cheek. 'Don't be in too much of a hurry to grow up,' she said, then ruffled his hair affectionately.

A toast was called for Peregrine's birthday and his victory over the King of Winter, and everyone stood up, clanking their horn cups together and shouting a huzzah. Grizelda stood up too, and raised her cup to him. Peregrine grinned and returned the gesture, and then lifted his cup to the high table and the crowd.

Servants marched in with platters of midwinter pudding, blazing with blue fire. Oohs and aahs sounded all around the room. Peregrine bounded back to his place, stripping off his heavy antlers with relief.

Jack took his spear and shield and mask from him and stowed them away neatly in their chest, then cut him a slice of pudding with his knife. Before placing it on Peregrine's plate, he tasted some, then stood waiting to see if he would fall writhing in pain as his father had done. Nothing happened, so he offered the pudding to Peregrine on bended knee.

Peregrine ate with pleasure, knowing they would not eat so well again for a very long time. When his bowl was half-empty he mentioned to Jack to eat the rest. Apart from the small mouthfuls he had tasted, his squire had been on duty all night and so had had no chance to eat any supper of his own. By the time the feast was cleared away, there would be only scraps left and very little pudding. Peregrine knew Jack loved midwinter pudding.

The servants scrambled to clear away the dirty plates, and the trestle tables were dismantled and put outside in the corridor, leaving everyone to stand against the walls. Only the royal family stayed seated, and Stiga, who huddled in her rocking chair by the fire. Peregrine looked for Grizelda and found, as he had expected, that she looked outraged to be treated like anyone else in the crowd. His father noticed too, and beckoned one of his squires, who ran to find her a stool.

The Yule log was brought in, garlanded and beribboned. Young men danced all around it, leaping and cartwheeling. As the huge oak trunk was carried around the hall, the glowing ashes of the fire in the hearth were smothered with a heavy blanket, sending smoke billowing out into the room.

When the smoke had cleared, a fire was laid with the charred remains of last year's Yule log, and the new green log was arranged upon it and anointed with salt and wine.

At midnight, the candles were snuffed and the torches quenched, so that chill darkness descended on the great hall. The wailing of the wind sounded very loud.

After a long moment of silent contemplation, standing quietly in the pitch blackness, Queen Rozalina struck a piece of flint with her steel file. A single bright spark flew out, and she caught it adroitly with a tinderbox filled with a small handful of dried moss draped with charred cloth. A red spot sprang to life on the cloth, slowly unfurling like a glowing flower, and the wildkin queen bent and blew gently on its golden heart. At once a small flame leapt up, and everyone cheered.

Ceremoniously Queen Rozalina carried the tiny dancing flame to the fireplace, and knelt on the hearthstone. Very carefully she lit the tinder under the Yule log. Everyone held their breath, and released it in a communal whoosh as flames began to lick up the sides of the great oak trunk. People cheered and clapped, and one by one came with their candles to light them from the newly kindled fire.

Jack stiffened as Grizelda came to the dais, looking up at Peregrine to ask, 'What does it all mean? Why do they put the fire out and then relight it again?'

Peregrine shrugged. 'It's the custom. We do it every year.'

Grizelda watched as everyone took their lighted candle and walked out of the great hall in groups of two and three, smiling and talking. 'Where is everyone going? Is the feast over?'

'They're all going to light their own fires again,' Peregrine explained. 'Every fire in the castle is extinguished, and relit again from the Yule fire.'

'That explains why it's so cold,' Grizelda said with an exaggerated shiver.

'Most will go to bed now. Only the Erlqueen will stay up, to watch the fire and make sure it doesn't go out. Normally we'd all stay up too, drinking mulled apple-ale and telling stories till dawn, but Father thinks it's best if we all get some sleep while we can.' Peregrine stood up and picked up his own candle, set in a beautifully wrought silver holder with a handle shaped like a swan.

'Why? Why does the queen have to stay up? Can't a servant do it?'

'No,' Peregrine answered curtly.

'I'm sorry, I didn't mean to pry. It's just all so strange. I'd like to understand.'

Her words disarmed him. Peregrine came down the steps to her side. 'It's the Erlqueen's duty and her honour to kindle fire for her people. One day it'll be my job. I have to practise lighting fires so I can do it with a single spark. It's harder than it looks.'

'I have never lit a fire in my life,' Grizelda said.

'You can start now. Jack, get Lady Grizelda a candle. She can kindle her own fire and share in the Yuletide luck.'

Glowering, Jack went across to the side table and picked up two of the hundreds of candlesticks laid out neatly in rows. He brought them back, and Grizelda took one with a quick smile of thanks. Then she and Peregrine joined the long queue of people filing past the Erlqueen, who gave them all small gifts of scented candles, or candied fruit, or a little pot of rosemary or winter hyssop.

Peregrine bent and kindled his candle, with Grizelda and Jack following after, then went to make his bow before the Erlqueen. She bowed her head and gave him the midwinter blessing, then offered him a sprig of mistletoe from her crown. He stared at her, his heart sinking, and she nodded her head and tried to smile. He stepped back and Grizelda gave a perfunctory bob, then stared as the Erlqueen passed her a small pot planted with trailing ivy.

'Ivy is symbolic of fidelity and friendship,' Peregrine explained to her as, carrying their lighted candles and their gifts, they moved towards the door. Jack accepted his gift—a pot of heal-all salve—and hastened after them.

'So it's like a message to me?' Grizelda asked.

Peregrine nodded. 'Everything has a deeper meaning for the wildkin. The Erlqueen is offering you a hand in friendship, but she expects loyalty and friendship in return.'

'What does your gift mean? It's just a mistletoe twig,' she said contemptuously.

'It means many things,' he replied slowly, trying to think how to explain. 'It's sacred to the wildkin. It is their winter crown. The Erlqueen cuts it with a silver knife and does not allow it to touch the ground. A sprig from her crown is a great honour and shows that I am her heir.'

'Yet you looked surprised when she gave it to you,' Grizelda said. 'Surely you've always known you were her heir.'

'Well, since her last little boy died, yes, I have.'

'So why so surprised?'

'She always gives me mistletoe when I'm about to go on a journey. It's protection against misfortune and illness and lightning. See how the twig grows, in a forked shape like a lightning bolt?'

Grizelda gave him a sharp glance. 'So you think you're being sent away from the castle? I want to go too!'

'I don't know . . .'

His parents were standing together at the far end of the hall, both looking tired and worried. King Merrik had flung open a window and was looking out into the storm-swept night. There was a gust of wind that made the heavy curtains billow and the hundreds of tiny candle flames flicker like snakes' tongues. Snow whirled in, bringing with it a small bat-winged creature with smouldering orange eyes. 'Wake up, wake up!' the omen-imp shrieked, swooping through the crowd, knocking off wreaths of flowers, tweaking ears and pulling beards. 'Get your spears and swords, time to fight starkin lords!'

'So it's true?' Queen Liliana cried.

'Are you sure, Tom-Tit-Tot? Did you see them? What do they plan?' King Merrik asked.

'Through the storm, soldiers creep, hoping to kill you while you sleep,' Tom-Tit-Tot replied.

'How many?' the king demanded.

'Many as trees in a wood, many as plums in a pud,' the omen-imp answered, flinging wide his hairy arms.

'Where are they? How far away?' Queen Liliana wanted to know.

'Not as far as I can spy, not as close as I can spit.' The omen-imp came to rest on the stag-horn chandelier, causing it to swing madly and shadows to hop and skip over the walls.

'That close? There's no time to waste.' King Merrik glanced at Peregrine, then issued a quick order in an undertone to the head of his bodyguards, who went out of the hall at a run.

Peregrine stepped up to his parents, gripping the mistletoe so sharply its barbed leaves cut into his palm.

'I don't want to go,' he said. 'Please, may I not stay with you?'

His father answered wearily, 'I know you'd rather stay, Peregrine, but we need to know you're safe. You're too precious to risk. You'll leave for the Erlrune's just as soon as we can get you out the door.'

'Out the door, what a bore!' Tom-Tit-Tot shrieked, swinging on the chandelier so wildly half the candles blew out.

Peregrine's protest was drowned by Grizelda, who flung herself down on her knees before the king, her candle spraying hot wax. 'Please, your Majesty, let me go too! I beg of you! My brother thought you would flee the castle and take me with you. If I am found here, it will prove my brother a traitor and we will both be killed. Let me flee before they arrive.'

King Merrik bent and raised her from the ground. 'Very well. You must ride out before dawn.'

'Before dawn, what a yawn,' the omen-imp jeered.

'Go and prepare,' Queen Liliana said to Grizelda. 'And wrap up warmly. It'll be a cold, hard journey through the winter forest.'

Grizelda nodded, excitement kindling in her cerulean-blue eyes. King Merrik detained her with a gesture. 'I must warn you, Lady Grizelda, that you will be gagged and bound. If you make any attempt to draw the attention of the starkin, any sound or sign at all, you will be killed. My men will not hesitate for a second. Do you understand?'

Grizelda nodded, white to her lips.

CHAPTER 4

Child of Storm

'I'M SORRY, ROBIN, YOU HAVE TO GO,' QUEEN LILIANA SAID, methodically packing a satchel with everything she thought her son might need. She trusted no-one else with the task, even though this was not the first time Peregrine had had to flee in the middle of the night. 'You'll be safe with Aunt Briony.'

'Oh Mam, why? Why can't I stay with you and Father? I haven't seen you in months.' Peregrine sat cross-legged on his bed, sharpening his dagger. His mother's old nursemaid, Stiga, padded softly back and forth from the wardrobe, bringing his mother what she thought might be required.

'It's too dangerous,' Queen Liliana replied.

'Then why are you staying?'

Queen Liliana sat down next to him, drawing up her knees under her skirt so she could hug them close to her chest. 'You know why, Robin.'

Peregrine did know why. The best defence against fusillier fire was wind, to blow it back into the shooter's face, or a deluge of rain to snuff out the flame. 'If I could work weather magic, would you let me stay?' he asked sullenly.

She drew him close, kissing his forehead. 'I'd still want to keep you safe.'

'I'm not a little boy anymore,' he protested.

She sighed. 'I know, darling. But your father and I will be better able to fight if we're not worrying about you all the time.'

'But I spent all summer at the Evenlinn, studying spell craft with Aunty Briony and war craft with Uncle Pedrin and court etiquette with Aunty Lisandre. When can I actually *use* all the stuff I have to learn?'

Peregrine loved his great-aunt Briony, who was the guardian of the Well of Fates, a magical pool in which could be seen visions of the past, present and future. He loved her best friends, Pedrin and Lisandre, who had lived with her ever since their home, Estelliana Castle, had been seized by Vernisha's soldiers. Pedrin and Lisandre had raised King Merrik while his own mother Mags had been busy leading the rebel forces in the long war for freedom from the starkin, and had adopted Peregrine as their own grandchild. Peregrine also loved the Erlrune's old house on the shores of the Evenlinn, the vast lake which glimmered quietly in a secret valley deep in the mountains. However, he felt a deep frustration that he must always be sent away whenever danger threatened, instead of helping his poor, worn-out parents like he wished.

'There's so much you need to know,' his mother replied, looking harassed. 'And we are in the midst of a war, Robin. Your people are suffering cruelly. They are hurt and hungry and ill. There is no justice for them, no-one to protect them or keep them and their children safe. How can you be a good king to them if all you care about is having fun?'

'It's not all I care about!' Peregrine said. 'I'm not asking to stay because I want *fun*! I want to fight! I want to help you win this war. I know I can help. Just let me stay, Mam, please.'

She held up one hand. 'Don't even try that with me, Robin. It's not safe. You're to go to the Erlrune's.'

'Could I go in search of the Storm King's spear instead? Please, Mam! I'm sure I could find it. You know the Erlrune thinks I have the Gift of Finding. She has spent ever so much time teaching me how to find things that are lost, I'm sure she . . .'

'It's too dangerous,' said his mother flatly.

'Why? Why is it dangerous? I could go in disguise, no-one need know who I am. I could pretend to be a minstrel.' He picked up his flute, playing a few sweet notes.

His mother took the flute away and laid it down again. 'Vernisha thinks all minstrels are spies, and all pedlars and travelling scribes too. And you know what would happen if you played in a village square, or at a manor house. Every animal for miles would come galloping along to hear you play.'

'Oh, Mam, they wouldn't! Not anymore. I've got really good at calling them only when I want them.'

'Really?' His mother pointed at a corner of the room where two mice had crept out of a crack, their beady eyes fixed on him in wonder. Blitz moved restlessly on his perch, turning his hooded head towards the tiny sound their claws made on the stone.

'Oh, blast it!' Peregrine said, thumping his fist into the eiderdown. Then he grinned reluctantly. 'I wasn't really paying attention,' he confessed. 'Honestly, Mam, I can control it if I want to.'

'So you say,' she answered dryly, pointing now to a spider

that had dropped down from the ceiling on a long thread and was dangling in front of Peregrine's face. He swatted it away irritably.

'Please, Mam! You know you always said I could go in search of the spear once I had come into my Gift. Well, I'm fifteen now, practically a grown man! And I could find the spear, I know I could. The prophecy says we shan't be able to defeat the starkin until we have the spear.'

His mother sighed and looked at him with worried eyes. Peregrine gazed back, willing her to say, 'Yes! Of course you must go! Ride forth with my blessing, my son!' After all, it was his mother who had sworn to find the lost spear of the Storm King when she was just his age, and who had told him so many tales about the spear that he could imagine exactly how it would feel in his hand.

'*A child of storm shall raise high the spear of thunder, and by the power of three, smite the throne of stars asunder,*' Stiga mumbled. She brought Queen Liliana a packet of needles, pins and coloured threads, then came to stand before Peregrine, patting his face with her tiny gnarled hands. 'Child of storm, find the spear, it is time, do not fear.'

'See, Mam, Stiga says it's time.'

Queen Liliana smiled wearily at the old woman who, murmuring the prophecy to herself again, went to the wardrobe and brought out Peregrine's grey travelling cloak.

'Robin, the spear was lost when your grandmother was very young. It was thrown into a bog and must've surely rotted away by now.' Queen Liliana took the cloak and checked its pockets, removing a handful of flints, a broken quill, some knucklebones and a wrinkled apple core that looked like it had been there for months. Holding it distastefully by the stem, she flicked it to the mice, who seized their bounty and disappeared.

'But . . .'

'No buts, Robin-boy.'

'But, Mam, I have the Gift of Finding, just like your father did.' Peregrine jumped to his feet, seizing his mother's arm pleadingly.

'My father died looking for the Storm King's spear and so did my mother, and the world is far more dangerous now than it was then.' Queen Liliana gave his hand a pat and then hefted the bulging satchel in her hand. 'It's a bit heavy,' she said anxiously. 'Do you think you'll be able to carry it?'

'I've been carrying a travelling pack since I could crawl,' he said impatiently, taking it from her and swinging it onto his shoulder. 'Stop fussing, Mam.'

'All right. I'm sorry. It's just that I so hoped we'd have the winter together. I've hardly seen you in ages.'

'That's because you keep sending me to the Erlrune any time there's a battle,' Peregrine said, taking up his flute and tucking it safely inside his pocket. 'If you'd let me stay and fight with you . . .'

'If you were killed or captured, we'd lose everything.' Queen Liliana's voice was drained and weary.

Peregrine huffed out his breath. 'All right, all right, I'll go.' He slid his dagger into its tooled leather scabbard, and took up Blitz from his perch, the falcon's bells chiming softly.

'Blood is blood and duty is duty,' his mother said. 'Right now it's your duty to keep yourself safe. Never forget that you are heir to two thrones, and so our only hope to bring peace to this poor land of ours.'

'I said all right!' A moment later he was sorry. He laid his cheek briefly against her shoulder, keeping his right arm still so as not to disturb the hooded bird. 'I do understand, Mam. It's just I wish—'

'Don't wish!' Queen Liliana threw up her hand.

'You're afraid it'll come true? That's Aunty Rozalina's Gift, not mine.'

'Robin, we don't yet know what Gifts you have. You're always talking people into doing what you want, so it wouldn't surprise me at all to know you've inherited the Tongue of Flame from her.'

'Oh, that's no Gift, Mam, that's just my natural charm,' he said cheekily.

She sighed. 'You know how much grief Rozalina's Gift has brought. I just wish you to take care.'

'Take care, child of storm, do you dare?' Stiga said. 'Find the spear, be of good cheer.' She brought Peregrine his longbow and quiver of arrows, and stared into his face intently.

He thanked her absently, shouldering his bow and saying to his mother, 'But Aunty Rozalina herself said the spear of thunder would be found, and so surely that means—'

'Robin, my boy, please, can we just get through this battle? You'll be safe with the Erlrune, she can teach you to control your Gifts, and then, maybe, when you're older—'

'Yeah, when I'm ninety.'

'Please, Peregrine, don't argue with me.'

Peregrine, startled by the use of his real name, glanced at his mother in surprise. She had always called him Robin, ever since he was a newborn baby and far too small, she said, for a grand name like Peregrine.

Queen Liliana looked close to tears. At once he was sorry again. He said so contritely, and she ruffled his hair and kissed him and said, 'You're the last of the Stormlinn, Robin. If you should die, the wildkin throne will be left without an heir, and all our hopes would perish. Remember, you alone carry "*the blood of wise and wild, farseeing ones and starseeing ones*".'

'I know, I know.'

She said nothing more, going out the door in a rush and banging it shut behind her. Peregrine sighed.

'She fears the lightning in your head,' Stiga said.

He frowned in response, staring at the still-quivering door.

'No need to fear.'

'I'm not afraid,' he assured her, and he wasn't. A secret escape through the dead of midwinter was far more exciting than having to study geography and cartography, and he loved galloping through snow. He only wished the quiet house of the Erlrune was not his destination.

Peregrine pulled on his thick leather coat, lined with beaver fur, and caught up his heavy gloves and his beaver-fur hat. He already wore so many layers he felt like a swaddled baby, but he knew he would be glad of them once he was outside. Stiga brought him his travelling cloak, woven for him by the Erlrune, and then he followed her down the stairs, his falcon perched on his wrist.

Peregrine thought about what his mother had said about his Gifts. What would it be like to have the Gift of Telling, like Queen Rozalina, so that every word he spoke had power beyond the ordinary weight of language? To have every wish, every curse, every prophecy he spoke come true? Queen Rozalina had told her stepmother, Princess Adora, that no child of hers would ever live to sit on the starkin throne, and that had come true. She had told her father, Prince Zander, that he would die by his own hand, and that had come true. She had told her grandfather, King Zabrak, that he would die on the day she was set free, and that also had come true. Peregrine felt a little superstitious shiver. No wonder Queen Rozalina was so quiet now. No wonder she was afraid to speak.

It was Queen Rozalina's wildkin mother, Shoshanna, who had first foretold that the throne of stars would be broken by the spear of thunder. To prove her wrong, and to assert his power over her, Prince Zander had taken the spear and thrown it in a bog, and taken Shoshanna in chains to the royal palace, where he had made her his concubine. Shoshanna had died there, giving birth to Rozalina, who had, in time, inherited her mother's Gift of Telling and pronounced her own dire prediction.

'This palace shall fall into desolation and none shall dwell here but owls and bats. The spear of thunder will be found and your throne shall be smote asunder. The rivers will run red and the sun shall turn black. Only when a blind boy can see and a lame girl walk on water shall peace come again to the land, and the rightful king win back the throne.'

Was it a curse or a prophecy? Not even the Erlqueen knew. In the twenty-five years since, the royal palace had indeed fallen into ruin and the rivers of Ziva had run red with blood. Vernisha, Prince Zander's cousin, had seized control and proved to be the most ruthless sovereign in starkin history.

Seeing the devastation her words had caused, the Erlqueen had sworn never to curse again. She had become a quiet, gentle woman who spent her free time writing songs and stories that were sung and told in secret all over the land.

Meanwhile, Peregrine's parents searched out blind boys and lame girls in an attempt to help the final part of the prophecy come true. Some Queen Liliana had been able to heal; others were beyond help. Many had become healers themselves, or scribes in the library, or spinners and seamstresses in the royal service. One had been Jack's father, his sense of smell and taste so acute after a lifetime without the ability to see that he was able to detect poison with a single sniff. Until someone had found an odourless, tasteless poison . . .

Jack was waiting for them in the great hall, dressed for the bitter cold, a short sword and two daggers strapped to his waist. His pack was far larger and heavier than Peregrine's, and he carried a shuttered lantern in one hand.

King Merrik was standing before the fire, Queen Liliana beside him, her head against his shoulder. He looped an arm about her waist.

'Why couldn't they just let us have the winter to rest?' she said bitterly. 'Fight, fight, it's all we ever do.'

'It's fight or die,' King Merrik replied gently. 'And we have achieved a lot in these past twenty-five years, you know we have. Don't lose heart now, darling.'

'I'm afraid,' she whispered. 'Do you think it's wise to let this starkin girl ride out with Robin? What if it's a trap?'

'What could she do?' Peregrine demanded. 'She's only a girl. I have my bow and arrows, and my dagger and my flute. And we're safe here in the Perilous Forest, the wildkin would never let harm come to me.'

'Stiga does not trust her,' Queen Liliana said.

'It took Stiga a long time to trust me too,' King Merrik reminded her. 'You know Stiga fears all those with starkin blood.'

'Yes . . .' Queen Liliana drew out the word, her dark brows knotted. She looked at Peregrine. 'Be wary of her, Robin. We know nothing of what is in her heart. I fear she means you harm.'

'I'll have the Merry Men to guard me, and Jack, and Blitz,' Peregrine said buoyantly. 'And we only have to get to the Erlrune's. What could one slip of a girl do between here and the Evenlinn?'

CHAPTER 5

The Door to the Underworld

GRIZELDA STARED HAUGHTILY AT THE HEALER. 'I WILL NOT wear that ugly old thing. Take it away!'

Palila stood resolutely, a heavy grey cloak draped over her arm. 'You must wear it, my lady. It has spells of concealment and camouflage woven through it by the Erlrune. It will help hide you from watching eyes.'

'It's magic? You want me to wear a thing of magic? I shall not!' Grizelda shuddered at the thought.

'If you will not wear it, you cannot ride with the prince.'

Grizelda eyed the old woman speculatively. She was only small, with a hunched back and hands so crooked and swollen she could not button Grizelda's mantle. She had told Grizelda to button it herself, but when Grizelda refused she had had to call a serving-maid. She walked with such evident pain that Grizelda wondered she did not take to her bed and stay there.

Yet there was strength there. Grizelda had no doubt Palila meant what she said. She bit her lip. Her skin crawled at the thought of allowing a thing of wildkin design to come anywhere near her body, but she had no intention of staying here at Stormlinn Castle, soon to be reduced to ashes and rubble. She had to stay with the prince.

'Very well.' Palila turned to go.

Grizelda flung up a hand. 'Wait! I'm sorry. Of course I will wear it. I do not wish to bring danger to Prince Peregrine.'

Palila turned back, her eyes steady on Grizelda's face as she held out the cloak. The material shimmered slightly in the candlelight, like water in the grey light before sunrise.

Grizelda took the proffered cloak, glad she was wearing her gauntlets so she did not have to actually touch the material with her bare hands. She draped it about her shoulders as gingerly as if it were a snake. 'There. Satisfied?' she said tartly.

'You do know, don't you, that Prince Peregrine has wildkin blood in him, inherited from both parents?' Palila said softly. 'He is heir to the wildkin throne. He has the gift of magic.'

Grizelda struggled not to let her distaste show in her face. 'Of course I know,' she said loftily. 'I'm not an idiot.'

'Do not underestimate him,' the old woman went on. 'Yes, he is young and not very strong. No doubt you think you can wrap him around your little finger as easy as blinking.'

Grizelda turned away, giving a light laugh. 'What are you talking about? Of course I don't think that!'

Palila continued as if she had not spoken. 'His wit is keen, though, and his heart is good. He's as valiant a prince as you'll ever find, and he has talents he has hardly discovered yet.'

'He is lucky to have such a loyal subject.' Grizelda spoke frostily, wanting to stop the old woman from saying any more.

'He has many loyal subjects, you will find,' Palila responded.

Grizelda showed her teeth in a smile and swept to the door. 'I assure you he can count me among them.'

Palila made a gesture with her crippled hands and the door opened. Grizelda tried not to flinch. She thought she had been prepared for anything, but the wildkin stronghold was even more strange and uncanny than she had expected. That feast last night, with its barbaric customs, all that leaping and jabbering with spears, all the horrible creatures with bulging eyes and horns and weird glowing eyes. She had been so uneasy it had taken all her strength to smile and chatter away, let alone use her wiles to entrance the prince.

As Grizelda swept down the staircase, she considered the prince. She had been disappointed in him to begin with. He was so thin and so pale, so ordinary looking. His squire was twice his size and three times as handsome.

Yet he had been kind to her, and surprisingly lithe and bold during the strange ritual dance he had performed. And she liked his eyes. They were a beautiful colour, grey-blue in some lights and grey-green in others, and filled with light. If only he were taller!

Peregrine shifted from foot to foot, eager to get on his horse and ride out into the frosty night.

His father was giving a few last-minute orders to Lord Montgomery, the captain of Peregrine's bodyguards. Meanwhile, people scurried about the great hall. Some carried racks of spears and pikes out to the battlements, or dragged baskets filled with rocks and boulders to throw down the murder holes. Old women sat tearing linen sheets into strips and rolling them into bandages, while others pounded herbs to make new batches of healing lotions and ointments. Although Peregrine's mother could heal simple wounds with a touch, she could not heal too many in a row without exhausting herself. More complex injuries took time since she drew upon the strength of the patient themselves as well as her own, and too hurried a healing could drain the injured to the very point of death.

'Time to go,' Lord Zedrin said, coming into the hall, dressed in armour, his helmet under his arm. 'It'll be dawn in less than three hours. Are you hungry, Peregrine?'

He shook his head. 'I'm still full from the feast.'

'You need to make sure you eat properly and get plenty of rest,' said King Merrik. 'Jack, can I trust you to make sure his Highness doesn't get too tired?'

'You can, your Majesty.'

'I'll be fine, Father,' Peregrine sighed. On his wrist, Blitz shifted, his bells chiming gently.

'Well then, let's get you out of here before they start throwing their blasted fusillier fire,' Lord Zedrin said. 'Where do you think they got it, Merry? I thought we'd blown up all their gas mines.'

'I don't know, Zed,' the king answered. 'Tom-Tit-Tot has flown out again to see what he can learn. He plans to change shape into a louse so he can sit on the commander's ear and hear all their plans. Hopefully they don't have too much fusillier fuel. I'd like to destroy it all before they even have a chance to try and fire it at us.'

'How will you do that?' Peregrine asked.

'I have a few ideas. A flock of birds bombarding the tanks with rocks is just one of them.' King Merrik had the Gift of the Tongue of Heavens, which meant he could communicate with birds. Vernisha the Vile had, in retaliation, ordered all birds in the land of Ziva to be shot on sight. Here in the Perilous Forest, however, birds were still free to fly and sing as they wanted.

King Merrik slung his arm about Peregrine's shoulder and they walked together towards the stables. 'What would you suggest?' his father asked.

'Shooting them with arrows of flame?'

'We would have to get a lot closer before we could try that, but it would certainly create a pretty blaze,' his father said. 'We might just try it.'

'Father, please, can't I stay and help? You know I'm a good shot. I could creep out across the ice with Jack and—'

'I'm sorry, Peregrine, it's just too—'

'Dangerous,' Peregrine finished glumly. Blitz cocked his hooded head at the tone of his master's voice and gave a soft chirrup.

'You're only just fifteen,' his father said gently. 'None of us wants you to see too much of war yet, my boy. It's something you can never forget. In truth, I hope you never have to see it. If we prevail in the next few days, maybe you won't have to. Maybe we can break the back of the army and be able to march on Vernisha.'

'I hope so,' Peregrine said sombrely.

It was snowing heavily outside and the wind was cold, stabbing at Peregrine's lungs with every breath he took. He and his father hurried across the dark courtyard into the warm, dim stable, Jack and Lord Zedrin close behind. The two queens were already there, inspecting the saddlebags and giving last-minute instructions to the guards. Stiga waited quietly, perched on the edge of a bundle of hay.

Half-a-dozen of the king's bodyguards were standing by six tall horses, their hooves and harnesses swaddled to prevent any noise. Officially called the King's Troop of Gentlemen at Arms, they were more often referred to by their nickname, the Merry Men. Like Peregrine and Jack, they wore long grey cloaks over their heavy buff jackets, woven for them by the Erlrune with spells of camouflage and concealment. Sir Medwin was already hunched on his sturdy grey mare, his long ungainly legs sticking out at what Peregrine judged to be an obtuse angle. His saddlebags bulged with textbooks and bristled with scrolls.

Peregrine's black stallion, Sable, was being held waiting for him. The stallion was well prepared for a long journey through a snowy forest, with two long panniers packed with oats and grain hanging on either side of his saddle. Under his saddle, he was draped in a long embroidered blanket, both to keep him warm and help protect him from arrows. Another bag was slung behind the saddle, with a water bottle, camp axe and other tools hanging from it. Peregrine had his own supplies in the pack he carried on his back, in case he and Sable were accidentally separated, as well as his longbow and quiver of arrows.

The king himself boosted Peregrine into the saddle. 'Keep safe,' he said. 'Tell the Erlrune to send us a message to let us know you are safely arrived.'

'I will, Father,' Peregrine answered. He put Blitz on the wooden saddle-perch so he could bend down to embrace his father.

King Merrik hugged him close. 'Keep safe, my boy,' he said huskily.

As the king stepped back, Lord Montgomery came forward with a safety harness for Peregrine.

'Oh no, do I have to?' Peregrine cried. 'Father!'

'Please, Robin,' Queen Liliana said. 'I know you hate it, but it'll be a dangerous ride, we can't risk you falling.'

Peregrine was silent, his jaw thrust out mutinously.

'Please, for your mother's sake,' King Merrik said gently. 'Just to stop her worrying.'

'It's not that I don't trust you,' Queen Liliana said, dashing away tears. 'I know how well you can ride. It's just in case.'

Sullenly Peregrine let Lord Montgomery buckle the leather straps about his waist. The harness was then attached to Sable's girth.

'Thank you,' his mother said, stepping forward to clasp his hand in hers. He nodded and she pulled him down so she could kiss his cheek and ruffle his hair. 'Don't forget to take your medicine.'

He huffed an exasperated breath. 'I won't.'

'Well, you do, all too often. Jack, will you remind him?'

'Yes, your Highness.' Jack bowed deeply, and then mounted his brown gelding.

'I'll be fine, Mam,' Peregrine said in long-suffering tones. 'It's only a few days' ride. That is, if we ever get going!'

'Take care out there, look after yourself,' Queen Liliana said anxiously.

He nodded and said farewell to Queen Rozalina and Lord Zedrin, who had their own messages of advice and warning to give him.

'Stiga will guide you,' Queen Liliana said. 'You've never made the journey in winter before and the forest will look very different covered in snow.'

The old nursemaid stood up and came to stand at Peregrine's stirrup, wrapped in her old shawl, her heart-shaped face turned up so she could look at him. 'Do not fear,' she whispered. He smiled and shook his head.

'Where is this starkin girl?' demanded Lord Montgomery, the leader of the bodyguards. He was a tall, strong man with dark eyes and iron-grey hair, carrying a heavy crossbow. 'If we do not get moving soon, the horses will take cold.'

'She's coming,' Lord Zedrin said.

A few minutes later, they saw Grizelda being led across the courtyard. Her eyes were blindfolded and her mouth was tightly gagged. She was wrapped in a long grey cloak. Only the high red heels of her boots could be seen. Her tall dog slunk behind her, growling softly in his throat. Her horse was led out of the stable and she was lifted up into the saddle. She gripped the pommel with both gauntleted hands as her reins were passed to Lord Leighton to hold. Her back was rigid.

'Lady Grizelda, you must keep quiet,' King Merrik told her. 'You are to be led through a secret passage. Its entrance and exit are closely guarded. Any attempt to leave a sign or communicate with the starkin army in any way and Lord Montgomery shall shoot you without mercy. Do you understand?'

She nodded her head.

'Very well,' the king said. 'I would like to thank you for putting yourself in danger to bring us news of the starkin soldiers. It may be some time before we can return you to your home. I am sorry for that. You will be safe at the Erlrune's. She is a wise and kind woman. You need have no fear.'

Grizelda inclined her head, her spine very straight.

King Merrik stood back. 'Goodbye, Peregrine!' he said. 'Please take care.'

'Bye, Robin!' Queen Liliana's voice cracked with tears. 'Look after him, boys.'

'We will.' Lord Montgomery bowed, one hand on his chest, and the other five bodyguards followed suit.

Stiga went to the far end of the stable, towards the outer wall of the castle. On the other side, the wall plunged several hundred feet down to the frozen lake. A dusty old carriage was parked in the far stall. On Stiga's gesture, the grooms harnessed two huge carthorses to the carriage and dragged it out, backing it into another stall. Stiga went in and crouched by the manger, which was carved with the eagle emblem of the Stormlinn. She pressed the shield and a part of the floor slowly sank away, revealing a steep ramp that led down into darkness.

'The Door to the Underworld,' Peregrine said with satisfaction. 'Come on! Let's go!'

CHAPTER 6

The Escape

DOWN AND AROUND, THE SMALL PROCESSION WOUND, DEEP into the bowels of the earth.

Stiga's lantern shone like a small red eye in the darkness, winking out as she disappeared around the curve of the wall and then reappearing as the horses followed her quiet footsteps. Jack kept close to his master, all his senses on high alert. His breath hung frostily in the air, and the dank cold seeped through his jacket, making him shiver.

His gelding, Snapdragon, snorted a little uneasily and Jack at once quietened him. Sound travelled far at night and he had no desire to draw the attention of any starkin scouts. He knew how important it was to keep Prince Peregrine safe.

The ramp beneath their horses' hooves was steep and slippery and so they moved slowly, leaning back in the saddle. At last it began to level out, and the horses came to a halt as Stiga fumbled somewhere to one side. With a low rumbling noise, a crack widened in the blank walk before them, and fresh air stung their faces. Lord Leighton passed

Grizelda's reins to Lord Murray, another of the bodyguards, and rode out cautiously to scout the surrounding area. After a few long, tense moments he came back, lifting his hand to show all was well.

One by one they rode out into the dark snowy forest, and Stiga closed the stone gates behind them. Once they were shut, there was no sign of any crack between the two sections. It was simply a massive grey boulder, surrounded by snow-laden bushes and trees, and ghosted over with grey lichen. Jack stared in amazement. After three years in the prince's service he still had not grown used to the uncanny ways of the wildkin.

Grizelda made a whimpering noise, deep in her throat, as if struggling to speak. Lord Leighton hushed her softly. Her dog whined and pressed himself close by her crimson boot, and she stretched out her hand to him, circling one gloved finger. The dog ran and lifted his leg against the stone, sending a stream of hot yellow liquid splashing down into the snow.

'The poor dog was bursting,' Prince Peregrine whispered to Jack, who grinned and nodded. Lord Montgomery turned and lifted a finger to his lips.

Jack stared around, orientating himself in the landscape. Behind him reared the massive bulk of Stormfell, its bare rocky crown wreathed as usual in clouds. Ahead was the steep pinnacle on which Stormlinn Castle was built. They were in the broad ravine that ran between the two. The trees in the ravine were bare as twigs, while those on the flanks of the mountain were sombre-green and dusted in snow like icing sugar. It was dark, the moon swathed in clouds. Cold stabbed with every breath Jack took.

Stiga hunched down in the snow and shuddered. In the blink of an eye, she flew up from the ground in the shape of a white owl. Jack had seen her change shape many times before but it never ceased to astound him, how easily she shed her human shape. In her owl shape she flew through the forest. The horses and their riders cantered after her, muffled hooves almost soundless on the soft snow. Grizelda's dog bounded after them, the snow up to its belly.

Beyond the tracery of bare black branches, the sky was low and ominous, and snow whirled in the wind, quickly filling their tracks. They came around the base of the pinnacle and saw, stretching before them, the frozen expanse of the Stormlinn. They would have to cross the lake if they were to make their way to the Evenlinn, the next great lake up the river, for there was no way to cross Stormfell in winter, on horseback.

They hesitated in the shadows under the trees for a long moment, listening and watching. The white expanse of the lake was visible even in the darkness, patched with shadows where the ice was thin. Even camouflaged as they were in their grey cloaks, it would be possible for any keen-eyed watcher to see them as they crossed. They could not ford the river further down, where it was narrower, because the starkin soldiers were tramping up the river towards them.

'We'll take the risk,' Lord Montgomery whispered. 'Jack, keep close to his Highness. If we are attacked, get him back to the castle as fast as you can or, if the way is blocked, ride for the Erlrune's. I know I can trust you to keep him safe.'

Jack nodded. He felt immense pride that the captain trusted him so well. He had taken an oath three years ago to serve his prince and guard him with his life. That oath was the most important thing in Jack's life, the only thing that made any sense of his father's agonising death. His father had died for the king; Jack was ready and willing to die for the prince. He drew his dagger and moved Snapdragon as close to the prince's horse as he could.

Peregrine sighed.

With Jack and his men riding so close about him, he could not see a thing. Peregrine had never ridden across the lake before at night. He'd have liked to have galloped, Sable's hooves kicking up shards of ice, the frozen lake glimmering in its bowl of icy peaks under a starry sky. Instead he was so hemmed in by broad backs that he could see nothing but the faint outline of Sable's ears, laid back in displeasure. He urged Sable to go a little faster and at once Snapdragon lengthened his stride as well, Jack leaning forward in his anxiety to keep pace with his master.

Peregrine sighed again. He clamped his right fist a little closer to his chest, keeping his falcon tucked within the shelter of his cloak. Blitz was showing signs of unease, his back humped, his hooded head turning from side to side. Peregrine crooned a lullaby under his breath, and Blitz quietened.

Lord Montgomery led the way across the ice. Snow whirled and Peregrine lifted his face to the wind, feeling the touch of the snowflakes like tiny freezing kisses. The snow would have been sent by his mother, he knew, to help hide their escape. He glanced back at the castle and saw just one light, still burning in one tower.

Far away, in the forest, a dog bayed loudly. At once Grizelda's dog bayed in response. Lord Montgomery reined his horse back on its haunches and reached over to drag away Grizelda's gag and blindfold. 'Quiet that dog, else I'll shoot it!'

Grizelda gasped air into her lungs. 'No, Oskar, quiet,' she managed to say. At once her hound fell silent, though the other dog continued to bay in the distance.

'If it barks again, I'll not have mercy,' Lord Montgomery warned her. She nodded, her breath uneven, and clicked her fingers. Oskar at once slunk close to her left heel.

'I fear the howl of the dog was a signal, your Highness,' Lord Montgomery muttered to Peregrine. 'I think we should ride as fast as we can.'

Peregrine nodded. He unhooded Blitz and flung the bird up in the air, knowing his falcon would fly after him. He was then able to spur Sable into a gallop, the other riders racing after him. It was a wild and dangerous ride across the ice and then veering through the stark black trees, leaping over mounds of snow that masked fallen logs and boulders. Stiga led them well, though, and soon the place where Oskar had barked was far behind them.

Peregrine was just beginning to relax when he heard a loud yammering and baying in the distance. Lord Montgomery uttered a low curse and beckoned them on to an even faster pace. One of the horses misjudged the leap over a fallen log and went crashing down. Lord Gilbert, the rider, was on his feet in an instant, sword drawn, but Lord Montgomery did not slow or turn back. On he galloped, the other riders quick on his heels. Peregrine followed, sick with worry for Lord Gilbert. He shot a look at Lord Montgomery's grim face and did not speak. Peregrine knew the captain would never have left one of his men behind if it had not been for the necessity of getting Peregrine himself away safely.

By dawn the flurries of snow had thickened to a storm, and they could gallop no more. Peregrine whistled to Blitz, who flew down to his wrist, his feathers fluffed against the cold. Peregrine hooded the falcon and tucked him inside his cloak, keeping his fist near his heart so that Blitz would hear his heartbeat and be warmed and comforted by it.

He was well wrapped in his cloak, but the wind seemed to cut through the heavy layers of his clothes like a broadsword. Lord Montgomery roped them all together so no-one would be lost, and Stiga stayed close, stopping often on snow-laden branches so that the riders would not go blundering off the narrow pathway into the uncharted depths of the forest. They did not stop to rest all day, eating as best as they could in the saddle from supplies each rider carried in their saddlebags.

The storm punched and bit and dragged at Peregrine, like a gang of bullies wielding clubs of ice. He gritted his jaw, pulled his hood about his face and endured. No-one had ever said adventures were comfortable.

Queen Liliana stood by an arrow slit, gazing out at the snow-whirled darkness. She could see nothing, but she knew that the starkin army was even now creeping close about Stormlinn Castle, making camp on the frozen lake and among the dark pine trees.

She whistled a few rising notes, and at once the high-pitched whine of the wind rose even higher. Snow hurtled from the sky. Queen Liliana clenched her hands together. Should she have waited till Robin was safely away before whistling up the wind? Although if she had waited, perhaps the starkin soldiers would have arrived sooner and caught him before he could escape. Peregrine had his bodyguards, all skilful at surviving in the wintry forest, and he had the Erlrune's cloak, woven with all the magic at her disposal. He had his own wildkin Gifts, and his falcon and his bow and arrow. Surely he would be safe?

Yet Queen Liliana could not rest. She worried about Stiga's warning. Stiga had said the starkin girl had venom in her heart and in her hand. Lady Grizelda and her luggage had been searched carefully. Nothing apart from a few expensive follies had been found: silken underwear, pots of rouge and face powder, a vial of perfume, a set of jewelled goblets, a silver mirror and comb, rolls of the finest vellum, a long feathery quill and some ink, and belladonna eyedrops that Queen Liliana knew were used by court ladies to make their eyes seem bigger and brighter. The belladonna eyedrops had been thrown away, for they were made from the flowers of the deadly nightshade family and were indeed poisonous. The entire bottle would have to be drunk before it was dangerous, and even then probably would not do more than make the drinker very ill, but it was better to be safe than sorry.

Perfume and powder, silk underwear and jewelled goblets. Who would pack such things for a dangerous ride through the Perilous Forest in winter? Lady Grizelda had not even packed a spoon or an eating knife. The girl was either a fool, or thought Prince Peregrine was one. Queen Liliana could only trust to her son's own good sense, and to Jack and Stiga to keep an eye on him.

'I have wished for him to stay safe,' Queen Rozalina said softly behind her.

'Thank you,' Queen Liliana replied, turning to look at her cousin. They smiled wearily at each other.

'I am not happy in my heart, though,' Queen Rozalina went on. 'I have such a sense of black foreboding.'

Queen Liliana nodded, her face bleak. 'I do too.'

Queen Rozalina came to stand next to the arrow slit, tucking her hand through her kinswoman's arm. 'For us or for Peregrine?'

'For us all,' Queen Liliana answered.

CHAPTER 7

The Ambush

AN EARLY DUSK WAS FALLING WHEN SUDDENLY, WITHOUT ANY warning whatsoever, an arrow whizzed out of the twilight forest and pierced Lord Leighton through the heart. He fell, his horse rearing in terror. Peregrine gasped in shock, and wheeled his horse about, searching the trees for their attacker.

'Careful, your Highness!' Jack called and spurred his horse in front of Peregrine, who had thrust Blitz onto his perch so he could unhook his own bow and notch an arrow to it.

'Out of my way, Jack!' Peregrine cried. 'Do you want me to shoot you?'

He spurred Sable forward, catching a flash of movement from the corner of his eye. He raised his bow and shot it, quick as a thought, and there was a hoarse cry and someone fell heavily in the forest. More arrows were zooming past him, though. One caught Lord Montgomery through the throat. Blood sprayed, black against the white and grey landscape. Lord Montgomery fell, the bolt from his crossbow shooting uselessly up into the clouds. Grizelda screamed.

Lord Hartmann immediately had his last two men crowding around Peregrine and Grizelda, protecting them with their bodies as they began to fire into the trees. More arrows zinged past, one grazing Lord Murray's arm, another piercing Lord Bailey's eye. Lord Murray swore, clapping his hand to his arm, while Lord Bailey fell with a dreadful scream, his horse bucking as the reins were tangled and dragged. Another arrow would have caught Peregrine in the breast if his tutor, Sir Medwin, had not urged his old mare in front of him, his elbows at right angles, his long robe flapping. The arrow took him straight through the heart. He fell without a sound.

'Sir Medwin!' Peregrine fired another arrow blindly and heard a satisfying scream, but their attackers were mere darting figures in the gloom and he could not see to aim. Tears stung his eyes and he dashed one arm across his face, looking for someone to shoot. The once pristine snow was stained with blood and churned with mud, as the horses reared, trying not to step on the bodies of the fallen men.

'Lord Murray, ride on with his Highness! Get him out of here!' Lord Hartmann shouted. 'I'll hold them off.'

At once Lord Murray spurred his horse forward. Peregrine and Grizelda followed him, Jack galloping behind, his reins in one hand, his dagger in the other. Oskar raced after them, with Stiga soaring ahead. On his perch, Blitz spread his wings, shrieking and almost falling. With a quick jerk, Peregrine untied his jesses and his hood so he could fly. The falcon shot up into the black sky, shrieking with rage and terror.

Down a steep slope they galloped, snow spraying up from the horses' hooves, then wove through the black swaying trees, peering ahead and behind. Branches slapped Peregrine across the face. Behind them the sound of battle faded away. On they rode into a night whirling with snow, heads down, hearts sick with grief and misery at the loss of their companions. At last they could ride no longer. Lord Murray dug them an ice cave, where they lay huddled together, prince, soldier, squire and starkin girl, with no thought at all of decorum.

Peregrine woke in the morning with a heavy heart and aching limbs. He lay silently for a moment, the shadow of dark nightmares pressing hard upon his spirits. As sleep ebbed away, he realised the nightmares were memories. He heard again the screams and shouts and horse whinnies, the whine of arrows, the clash of arms, the gurgle of Lord Montgomery's last, dying breath. He saw again anonymous shadows darting through the crystal lattice of snow and trunk and twig and icicle, and the explosion of red against the whiteness as the arrow pierced Lord Leighton's heart. He felt again the freeze of his own heart as Sir Medwin tumbled back from his horse like a broken marionette, his limbs crossed and tangled and limp.

Peregrine moaned in pain.

Jack immediately sat up, reaching for his dagger.

'It's all right,' Peregrine said, his voice sounding strange and unsteady. He smiled at Jack, but his mouth would not work properly. To his dismay, Peregrine realised his lips were trembling and his eyesight was blurred with tears. He got up awkwardly, his legs so stiff from their long and desperate ride that he could barely move them. He pushed his way outside and stood in the snow, taking deep breaths of air. It was so cold his lungs were stabbed with pain, and the bones behind his ears ached. But Peregrine welcomed the pain. He was alive. He was still breathing. The Merry Men had given their lives for him; he must go on.

Jack crawled out of the ice cave, his square face unusually sombre.

'Comets and stars, it's freezing!' Peregrine said, stamping his feet and rubbing his gloved hands together. Jack nodded, his arms crossed about his body.

Snow drifted lightly in the air, looking like giants were having a pillow fight. The sky was low and dark and menacing. Peregrine's breath streamed white in the frosty air.

'Ow, I'm sore!' he said, trying to speak lightly. 'What a ride! We were lucky none of the horses broke their leg.'

'Those starkin must've been looking out for us, your Highness,' Jack said in a low voice. 'Yet how did they know we would be trying to escape? We weren't meant to know the starkin were coming.'

'Scouts?' Peregrine suggested. 'I think they were well camouflaged, I could hardly see them at all in the dusk. Those arrows seemed to come from nowhere.'

'Yet how could they have picked up our trail so quickly, sir? Even if they were on the lookout for someone trying to escape the castle, they can't have known where the secret passage came out,' Jack protested.

Peregrine remembered how Grizelda's dog had barked. Had the baying of the hounds been a prearranged signal to lead the soldiers straight to them? Or had it simply been an unlucky chance, the dog acting as his nature demanded?

'I think it was planned,' Jack said grimly when Peregrine told him his thoughts. 'I think that starkin girl came to try and lure us out into the open. Remember how insistent she was that everyone flee?'

'Maybe,' Peregrine said. 'Or perhaps the dog was just answering those of his kind. She certainly didn't try to get away from us, or leave any signal. I was watching to see if she dropped one of those crimson gloves accidentally on purpose, but she didn't.'

As he spoke, Peregrine was scanning the dawn sky for any sign of his falcon, but there was no distinctive scythe-shaped wings soaring high above. He felt an immediate twinge of disquiet, for he had raised his falcon from a downy chick and was used to carrying him everywhere.

Peregrine pulled off his gauntlets and thrust one numb hand into his pocket, withdrawing his flute of bone. He lifted it to his lips and played a single high, long note. Far away he heard a falcon screech and smiled in relief. Blitz had heard him.

Behind him, the dog whined, his tail between his legs. Grizelda came out of the cave, grasping her heavy fur mantle close about her.

'Oskar, piddle,' she said and made a rotating gesture with one finger. At once the dog lifted his leg against a tree and relieved himself.

'Is the poor dog not even allowed to pee without your permission?' Jack demanded.

She gave him a haughty glance. 'No, he may not. I suppose you allow your dogs to do their business any old place they like. We of Zavaria prefer to control our hounds properly.'

'I bet you do,' Jack muttered.

Lord Murray was already up and attending to the horses, who had been hitched under some trees nearby. They stood in snow to their fetlocks, their breath steaming gently in the cold air. Lord Murray looked white and tired under the dark bristle on his chin, and Peregrine suspected he had slept only a little, despite the silent guard of the owl who sat hunched on a branch nearby. The guard had wound a bandage about the wound on his arm, but it was stained dark with blood.

'Good morning, your Highness,' Lord Murray said. 'We must ride on as soon as you have broken your fast. I dare not light a fire, so I'm afraid it's cold rations this morning.'

He had laid out a repast of bread and cheese and preserved fruits on a wooden tray nearby, and Jack tasted it all, before standing back and saying, 'I think it's fine, sir.'

Peregrine sat down to eat, spreading his cloak over the tree stump and taking the tray onto his lap. 'Will you not eat with me?' he said to Grizelda, who was busy trying to tidy her hair with the help of a silver comb and mirror. 'And you too, Jack. No need for court manners when we're in the wilds, surely.'

Jack hung back, saying, 'Oh, no, sir, I'd much rather wait,' but Grizelda came forward at once, saying, 'Is this all there is? Surely we are not to eat like peasants?'

'I'm so sorry, my lady, I seem to have mislaid our baggage train,' Lord Murray said with heavy sarcasm.

'Along with most of our escort,' Grizelda answered, laying some cheese on the hard, dark bread and nibbling at it daintily.

Lord Murray went white, while Peregrine laid down his food, suddenly unable to eat a mouthful. 'Do you think Lord Hartmann is all right?' he asked Lord Murray anxiously. 'Perhaps he beat off the attackers and is trying to catch up with us.'

Lord Murray shook his head. 'There were too many of them, sir. I saw at least six. I can only hope that he managed to stop anyone from following us. We must've left a pretty trail behind us, crashing through the forest like that. We must take care today, particularly now the snow has stopped.'

'You think the starkin will still be on our trail?' Peregrine stared at him in dismay.

Lord Murray nodded. 'They must know by now the prize that slipped through their fingers. If any of those starkin scum are still alive, they'll be hot on our trail, I assure you, sir.'

Grizelda said, 'It is hardly polite of you to refer so to those of starkin blood, particularly when I am present!'

'I'm afraid I'm not feeling very polite this morning,' Lord Murray replied, beginning to buckle the packs to the horses' saddles.

'I know how you feel,' Jack growled, casting Grizelda such an accusing glance that she dropped her bread and cheese.

'You cannot suspect me?' she cried. 'But I came ... I was the one who warned you of their approach! You must believe me, I did not know of any ambush, nor how they found us so fast.' She looked from one face to another with imploring blue eyes, her hands clasped at her breast.

Peregrine found it hard to meet her eyes. He stood up, gesturing to Jack to come and eat his fill. Jack made himself a hasty sandwich, while Lord Murray carefully packed away the remnants, throwing the crumbs under a bush.

'Please believe me. I am sorry for the loss of your companions, but it is not my fault!' Grizelda cried, her own bread and cheese forgotten.

'Your dog barked,' Jack said.

'Dogs do,' she answered swiftly. 'I did not tell him to.'

'He won't even pee without you telling him to!' Jack pointed out.

'But that's different. He's been trained to never piddle inside, or anywhere we don't want him to. You've got to do that if you live in a castle! Particularly if you have as many dogs as we do. Your Highness, don't you agree?'

Peregrine shrugged. 'I guess so.' He lifted his flute to his lips and called to Blitz again.

'And he's been trained to stop barking when I tell him too, but I was gagged, I couldn't tell him to stop, let alone to start!' Grizelda's colour was up, her eyes were brilliant with anger, and she stamped one small crimson boot for emphasis. Oskar raised his hackles and growled, obviously sensing his mistress's anger.

'Just don't let him bark again,' Lord Murray said, leading Sable to Peregrine. 'We must try to keep ahead of any pursuit and leave no trail. Do you understand, my lady?'

She nodded, looking mutinous. Lord Murray bent and cupped his hands for Peregrine to put his foot into, but Peregrine leapt up into the saddle without any help, saying, 'Watch your arm, my lord! I would not want you to start bleeding afresh.'

Lord Murray nodded and carefully harnessed Peregrine to his saddle. Grizelda watched in surprise, but was cast such a warning look by Peregrine that she asked no questions, though her fine golden brows drew together in a calculating look.

Peregrine heard the faraway tinkle of the falcon's bells. He held out his arm and Blitz came plummeting down, his feathers all ruffled by the wind, landing heavily on Peregrine's wrist. Peregrine stroked his head lovingly and gave him a lump of raw meat from the wallet at his waist. 'I was worried about you,' he murmured. 'Where've you been?'

Blitz replied in his own harsh falcon language, and then Peregrine hooded him and tied his jesses to the perch. Lord

Murray and Jack both mounted and began to ride out of the clearing.

Grizelda looked at her own horse, left standing hitched to the tree, and then crossed her arms and tapped her foot angrily.

'Jack,' Peregrine said softly.

His squire sighed noisily. He dismounted, unhitched the white mare and brought her to Grizelda. With an expression of stoic suffering, he cupped his hands and lifted her into the saddle. He then leapt nimbly back up into his own saddle, without even putting his foot in the stirrup.

'Which way?' Peregrine said to the owl, who had sat unblinking on her branch, watching them eat and pack with round, golden eyes.

Stiga hooted softly and flew away through the forest. The four riders cantered after her, the tall white hound loping tirelessly behind.

CHAPTER 8

Lightning Attack

THE ICY WIND RATTLED THE BARE BRANCHES AND SNOW whirled from the sky, but Peregrine could only be glad, for it quickly filled the deep impressions left by their horses' hooves.

It was the second day after the ambush in the forest. They had ridden as long as they could the previous day, only stopping when it was too dark to see. Lord Murray had made them a tent out of his cloak, and he and the two boys had taken turns in standing guard all through the endless hours of the night. No-one had trusted Grizelda to stand watch. They had risen before dawn, their makeshift tent so deeply covered in snow it was just a white hump in the winter landscape. Oskar sank to his stomach when he tried to go outside. The only way he could keep up was to leap and bound as if running through waves.

It had kept snowing all day. The wind was so strong it buffeted against Peregrine, piercing through the wool of his cloak and leaving it dusted with frost. He could not see more than a few feet in any direction, and was glad of the low hoot of the owl guiding him safely through the trees.

He kept Blitz pressed close to his heart, for the falcon would not wish to fly in this howling wind.

Sometime during the afternoon, the wind began to die away. They rode through an immaculate landscape, the trees all wearing hats and scarves of snow, the bare twigs in white mittens. Peregrine unhooded Blitz and untied his jesses so the falcon could hunt.

'Where are we?' Grizelda asked, quickening her pace so that she rode beside him. Her eyes were very blue in her face, the tip of her nose pink.

'Somewhere in the Perilous Forest,' Peregrine answered rather tartly.

'But don't you know?'

'It's a very big forest. And I only know small parts of it—the forest around the castle and near the Evenlinn.'

'That's where the Erlrune lives, isn't it?'

He nodded.

'You're related to her too, aren't you?'

'Yes. She's my great-aunt.' Peregrine spoke rather tersely. He could not be sure whether Grizelda's many questions were mere curiosity or if she was really a spy, pumping him for information.

She did not seem to notice any restraint in his manner, saying, 'Is she very terrifying? We have heard such stories of her! Is it true she cuts the throats of children in order to see into that well of hers?'

'Of course it's not true!' Peregrine would normally have explained that the Erlrune cut herself to get the blood necessary to see into the Well of Fates, so that her palms were crisscrossed with scars, but he wished to give nothing away. The starkin had been seeking for centuries to find some way to undermine the enigmatic power of the Erlrune, and he certainly did not want to be the one to say that she was in fact the most gentle and kind person he knew. Her reputation for fearsomeness did a great deal to protect her.

'I must admit I'm rather apprehensive about meeting her,' Grizelda said. She smiled at Peregrine. 'You'll protect me, though, won't you, your Highness?'

Peregrine contented himself with a stiff, formal bow.

'How long until we get there?' she asked.

Peregrine had been scanning the sky as they rode, looking for Blitz, but he had not been paying much attention to the landscape. Now he looked about him in some surprise. They should have been heading north, the ground growing steeper and harsher, pines and firs casting a deep green gloom over them. Instead they seemed to be heading west, towards the setting sun, and the ground was gentle and rolling, covered with bare-branched beeches and larches, with the occasional towering oak tree still hung with a few brown leaves.

He shrugged. 'I'm not sure. I think Stiga is taking us the long way around, just to be safe.'

'Stiga? You mean that funny little old woman who kept hissing "starkin" at me? Didn't we leave her at the castle?'

Peregrine glanced at her in surprise, but then remembered that Grizelda had been blindfolded when Stiga had changed shape, and the old woman had not changed from her owl shape since.

'No, Stiga came with us, didn't you realise? She's been with us all the time, in her owl shape. That's her, flying ahead of us, showing us the way through the forest.' Peregrine pointed to the white owl, flickering in and out of the trees ahead of them. She was almost invisible against the white banks of snow. 'That's Stiga.'

Grizelda peered at the owl, then looked at him in disbelief. 'Are you having a jest with me?'

'Of course not.' Peregrine called to Stiga and she wheeled about and came down to rest on a low branch nearby, staring from one to the other with round golden eyes. 'Stiga, will you change, please?' he asked.

The owl ruffled up her feathers in displeasure, but stepped off the branch and into the form of an old woman wrapped in a pale mottled shawl.

Grizelda screamed. She flung herself back so violently in her saddle she almost fell off, and had to clutch at her pommel to steady herself. 'What . . . what the blazes . . . ?'

'No time to waste, we're on the chase,' Stiga said scoldingly. 'Let us flee, come follow me.' She hunched her back, spread her shawl-fringed arms and flew up in the shape of an owl again, hooting commandingly.

'She changes shape into an *owl*?' Grizelda cried.

Jack clicked his tongue. 'Really, starkin are so unobservant.'

'She's our guide,' Peregrine said. He would have explained more about Stiga's uncanny magical powers, but at that moment there was a shrill cry and Blitz came plummeting down from the sky. Peregrine braced his knees and held out his gauntleted wrist, and the falcon landed heavily, scolding him, his feathers ruffled. He carried a dead white hare in one claw. Peregrine rested his wrist on the wooden perch, holding his reins in that hand so he could scrabble for some gobbets of raw meat in the pouch at his belt. Blitz tore hungrily at the meat and, when he had finished, Peregrine hooded him again and tied his jesses to the perch so the bird could ride in comfort. He threw the hare to Jack.

'Fresh meat for supper tonight!' he said exultantly.

'Oskar needs to hunt too,' Grizelda said. 'He hasn't eaten since we left the castle, and he'll be hungry. He can bring down a deer or even a wild boar if need be. We can hunt together and feast afterwards!'

Peregrine glanced at her, a little surprised, and she laughed at him, her eyes bright and clear. He smiled back, quite involuntarily.

A dog bayed mournfully behind them, and then another. Their smiles were extinguished at once. Lord Murray gestured to them, his horse breaking into a gallop. Peregrine untied Blitz deftly, loosening his hood and throwing him into the air. The falcon screamed, high and shrill, and soared away as Peregrine pressed his heels into Sable's satiny black sides. At once the stallion leapt forward, Grizelda's white mare easily keeping pace beside him. Snapdragon was not so swift, but galloped gamely in the rear, Jack drawing his sword.

They galloped through the brown tracery of trees, the dogs baying for blood behind them. Down a hill, along a broad slope, in and out of trees, through a copse of mossy birches, up a steep and stony slope and down the other side they galloped, pursued by the howl of the dogs. The owl swept sideways. Through a shadowy gateway of stone and along a deep, fern-hung gorge they raced, horses sweating and labouring. Still the dogs bayed at their heels.

Along a small, rocky brook the horses cantered, icy water splashing their riders' legs. The dogs clamoured behind them. The brook plunged down in white cascades into a deep green pool. Lord Murray did not hesitate. He urged his horse down the waterfall and into the water, kicking his legs free so he floated alongside, gripping his pommel. Peregrine followed close behind. The shock of the cold water was like an iron clamp on his lungs and heart, but he kicked his feet free of the stirrups and let Sable tow him towards the far shore.

Grizelda hesitated on the bank. 'It'll be cold . . . my boots will be ruined . . .'

'Suit yourself,' Jack said as his horse plunged past her, sending up a spray of glittering droplets that drenched her to the skin.

'Lady Grizelda, if you don't come now we will leave you,' Lord Murray called back. 'My responsibility is to get his Highness to safety!'

'Come on,' Peregrine called.

Grizelda kicked her mare forward. She cried out in shock as she was plunged up to her waist in the freezing water, but she did not immerse herself as the others had done, making her mare carry her weight so her upper body remained dry. Oskar swam after, his head held high.

Two enormous hounds burst out of the ravine, baying loudly. They were far larger than Oskar, with bloodshot eyes and drooping eyelids and flabby red lips that hung away from teeth as sharp as icicles. They looked strong enough to tear a man apart in seconds. Behind them rode a man dressed all in grey, with hair and beard the colour of dust.

Peregrine had only time to snatch a quick impression, for the man was raising a longbow even as he spurred his horse into the pool. The string twanged, the arrow sang straight for Peregrine's heart. He kicked Sable forward, feeling strangely as if time and space had turned to honey. Stones slid and rattled. Lord Murray flung himself forward, his face distorted, his mouth stretching, ugly as a scream. Peregrine could not hear him. Everything seemed very far away. Sable reared, and the pommel caught him in the chest. He heard the thud as the arrow meant for him pierced the thick leather of Lord Murray's coat. The bodyguard groaned and fell from his horse, which galloped away with a wildly rolling eye. Lord Murray lurched to one knee.

'Go! Go!' he mouthed. 'I'll hold him back. Go!'

Lord Murray drew his sword, leaning on it for a moment, fresh red blood leaking down his leather coat, the arrow deeply embedded in his chest. He rose to his feet with a great effort as the grey man on the grey horse thundered through the pool towards him, the two bloodhounds swimming close behind. Peregrine looked back at his bodyguard, tears burning his eyes, even as he let Sable gallop forward through the freezing water. Jack and Grizelda were close behind, the white owl hooting ahead. Peregrine bent over the reins, hearing with unnatural clarity every blow and clang and grunt of the duel behind him.

The pool fell away behind them, ice-cold spray dousing them from head to foot. The forest blurred past. Peregrine's head swam. He held out a hand. 'Jack,' he whispered. He felt the lightning in his head surge up, bringing a green taste, euphoria, dread, darkness. Then there was only the sensation of falling.

'What is wrong with him?' Grizelda whispered.

'Nothing!' Then, 'It's the falling sickness, my lady.' Jack's voice was sombre.

Peregrine could hear their voices, but they sounded far away. His head ached, his mouth tasted awful, and there was a faint tinny ringing in his ears. He felt he had to anchor himself to the earth, as if his body was so insubstantial it would blow away in a puff of breath.

Jack saw his hands groping out. He said with a gasp of relief, 'He wakes! Pass me the medicine.'

Someone rifled through his pack. Peregrine realised he was lying on the ground. It felt like ice below him, seeping through his wet clothes. Jack must have unbuckled his harness and lifted him to the ground. He wondered how long he had been unconscious. He felt as if he had been beaten with iron-studded clubs and kicked with hobnailed boots. Peregrine groaned and tried to open his eyes. Snow drifted down through black branches, swirling in eddies that made his vision swim. He shut his eyes again.

'What's in it? It smells awful,' Grizelda asked.

'I don't know. The healers make it. I know it has mistletoe in it, for Queen Rozalina cuts that herself for him. And skullcap and valerian too, I think, for I can't count the times I've been sent to gather them from the garden.'

Peregrine heard the gurgle of liquid, then he was lifted and a cup held to his lips. An all too familiar smell assaulted his nostrils. He turned his head away. Jack said hoarsely, 'You know you must drink it, sir, please?'

Peregrine obeyed. For a moment he gagged. Then his muscles began to relax. Jack laid him back down in the snow. Peregrine became aware of being very, very cold. His wet clothes were white with frost, his fingers so stiff he could not bend them. Each breath hurt.

'We need fire,' he said.

'Too dangerous. That hunter is still out there somewhere. Keep your cloak wrapped tight about you, it seems to help.'

'Lord Murray?'

'I'm so sorry.' Jack's voice was clogged with grief.

Peregrine struggled to sit up. 'Lord Murray? Lord Murray is dead?' The thought filled him with horror and sorrow and fear. Lord Murray had been his bodyguard all of his life. Lord Murray had played pig's-bladder-ball with Peregrine, taught him to fight with dagger and sword, and had stayed up with him when Blitz was a fledgling, helping him feed the baby falcon all through the night. It seemed impossible that someone so tall and strong and indomitable could be dead.

Tears suddenly overwhelmed him.

'Why does he weep?' Grizelda demanded. 'What is wrong with him?'

'A man has died in his service,' Jack said harshly. 'Would you have him laugh?'

'No, of course not! But Lord Murray died valiantly. It was his duty. And while his Highness weeps, we are in danger.'

'Sir,' Jack whispered. 'I hate to say it but she's right. We must go on. I've done my best to hide our trail. We rode through water as far as we could, and then, when we came ashore, I made sure we rode on the rocks awhile so as not to leave hoof prints. But he'll be following us, we must ride on. Can you rise?'

'Of course,' Peregrine said. In trying to rise, he fell again. 'Help me up. I'll be fine. Help me, Jack.'

His squire heaved him to his feet and lifted him across to where Sable stood, ears twitching uneasily. Jack hoisted him into the saddle and buckled the harness about him. Long years of training asserted themselves. Peregrine sat straight, his heels down, his hands lifted. With a screech and a whirr of wings, Blitz exploded from the trees, landing on his saddle perch, scolding Peregrine for his neglect. Once again tears overwhelmed him. He whispered his bird's name.

Just at the edge of his hearing he heard Grizelda whisper, 'He's weeping again. What ails him?'

'It leaves him worn and sad,' Jack said defensively, then more sharply, 'Look to your own horse and dog, my lady. Let's ride!'

They rode for the rest of the long day, Peregrine aware of very little beyond the jolting of the saddle, the blur of the white and black forest, the thudding of his head. If it had not been for the harness about his waist, he would have fallen from the saddle. Peregrine hated that. He hated the harness, and he hated the brief storm of lightning in his brain that always shamed him and made of him a child again. Sometimes it came often, when he was tired or ill, or when battle came close to him with all its heart-wrenching, blood-jolting terror. Sometimes there were long months of peace, when even his parents stopped worrying over him and people began to forget. Peregrine thought his mother felt it the worst. She was a healer. She could stop blood with a touch of a finger, she could heal grazes with a stroke of her hand, she could knit bones and steady heartbeats and soothe tortured gasping lungs, yet she could not save her own son from the sickness that stalked him.

Peregrine did not know what he did when the lightning storm came upon him. He often felt it approaching, a strangely golden, lucent glow that flooded his inner landscape with extraordinary warmth and beauty, like a field of buttercups at sunset under a stormy sky. Even as he shrank away and thought, *Oh no! It comes*, part of him welcomed it because the world, for a moment, was so bright and beautiful: a harp sang tremolo; he smelt something like rain on roses; he felt brave and splendid and lovely, as if he could cut the air with a sweep of his hand, lead legions to the stars. Then came the stench of refuse, dark spots swarming into his eyes, the sensation of falling, worse than utter failure.

Afterwards Peregrine was exhausted, like a child after a storm of crying. Often he slept for hours and could not eat. He could not sleep today, though, he could only cling to his pommel and try to stay upright, as the miles jounced away under his horse's hooves.

Twilight fell on them. Peregrine swayed and would have fallen from his saddle if not for the harness. Jack gently unbuckled him and lifted him down. Peregrine staggered and dropped to his knees under a tree. He ached all over, and the cold was like a vice trapping his legs. Jack wrapped him in his cloak. It was soft and warm and smelt of home. Peregrine nestled his cheek into it and fell again into darkness.

CHAPTER 9

Lost

PEREGRINE WOKE WEARY AND SORE THE NEXT MORNING, but returned to himself. He sat up and looked around.

It was early morning and Jack and Grizelda still slept, wrapped in their cloaks, in the shelter of a massive log. Beneath them were soft brown needles; above them drooped a tumble of dry ferns and brambles that gave them some shelter from the cold. He got stiffly to his feet and ducked under the brambles.

He was standing in a long, narrow forest glade. Snow lay thickly along the floor of the glade and mantled the top of the fallen tree trunk. A few stray flakes drifted down from clouds as low and menacing as a bully's brow. Sable stood nearby with the other horses, head hanging, one of his hind legs relaxed. Snow lay over their backs like white caparisons. The hound raised his head at the sight of Peregrine, growling softly. Oskar had obviously been hunting, for a well-gnawed rabbit carcass lay between his paws.

Peregrine heard a familiar whirr of wings and held out his

arm for Blitz, who landed heavily, claws digging through the thick buff of his jacket.

'Good morning, Blitz,' he whispered. 'Have you eaten? Do you want me to try to get some of that rabbit away from the dog?'

Blitz gave a low chitter in response and Peregrine said, 'Well, I can try, but to be honest I don't think I have a chance.'

Peregrine bent and stretched out one hand but the dog's growls intensified, and he withdrew his hand. 'You'll just have to hunt for yourself,' he told the bird.

He looked round the clearing for Stiga. The owl sat in an oak tree nearby, her eyes shut, her head sunk down. Peregrine whispered her name and the enormous golden eyes at once opened, focusing on him.

'Stiga, where are we?' he asked. 'I can't see one single landmark I know. There's not a mountain in sight. Are we lost?'

The golden eyes stared at him unblinkingly.

'Stiga, please, come down and talk to me.' When the owl did not move, Peregrine crossed his arms, tapped his foot, and said, 'I'm waiting.'

The owl sighed, ruffled her feathers, then flew down to the ground. As her claws touched the ground, she transformed into a tiny, white-haired old woman with a heart-shaped face and a shabby shawl tied over a ragged brown dress. Peregrine always found it amazing that Stiga somehow carried her clothes with her during her transformation. It was as if they were as much a part of her as an owl's feathers. He had certainly never seen her dressed any other way, even at festival time.

'Where are we, Stiga? Are we lost?'

She gazed up at him, obviously puzzled.

'Aren't we moving south instead of north? Look where the sun is.'

'It is time to find the spear, you said you did not fear,' she answered in her strange cryptic way.

He stared at her, an odd tingling sensation spreading throughout his body. It was trepidation and anticipation together.

'You are leading me to find the spear of thunder?' he asked slowly, and she bobbed her head.

'You know where it is?' he demanded in excitement.

She cocked her head to one side, then spread her hands and shrugged.

'Stiga, this is important! I need you to answer me. Do you know where the Storm King's spear is?'

'He threw it into the blue. I see from the tree.' Her words, as always, had the hooting rhythm of an owl.

'You saw ... who? Prince Zander? You saw him throw the spear into the bog? What did you do, fly after them?' At each question she bobbed her head, and Peregrine's excitement grew.

'Can you show me where?'

She shook her head.

His spirits deflated. 'You can't? Why not? Can't you remember?'

'Long long time ago. Road gone, trees grow.'

He grasped at a word. 'Road?'

She made a sweeping gesture with her hand. 'The soldiers strode along a road, to Stormfell, rang death's knell.'

Peregrine pondered for a moment. He remembered being told, at some point during an extremely boring geography lesson, that the starkin soldiers were great road builders, constructing straight, flat thoroughfares wherever they went, to enable the fast, efficient movement of troops, messengers and supplies. He knew that Prince Zander had somehow travelled all the way to Stormlinn Castle, where he had betrayed all the laws of hospitality by massacring everyone in the castle—everyone but Princess Shoshanna whom he had dragged back to the royal palace at Zarissa. By all accounts, Prince Zander had been fat and lazy and rather too fond of brandywine. It seemed entirely possible that his troop of soldiers had built a road for him to travel on, particularly since the starkin had only just begun to breed the huge white sisika birds the lords rode upon.

'Road?' He asked Stiga if this is what she meant.

She nodded and waved one hand to the south. 'Through glade and glen, forest and fen, all the way to the fox's den.'

'Do you mean back to where Prince Zander lived? Back to the old palace at Zarissa?' After years of living with Stiga, Peregrine had grown used to her oblique way of speaking. It was only a small stretch of the imagination to see Prince Zander as the fox, and Queen Rozalina's mother, Shoshanna, as the wounded bird.

'Do you think you could find this road again?'

'Here, there, everywhere,' Stiga said anxiously, waving her hands about.

Peregrine bit his lip, frustrated. On his wrist, the falcon shifted from foot to foot, turning his head to look at his master. His bells chimed softly.

'Perhaps I can find this road,' Peregrine said slowly. He put Blitz down on his wooden perch and rummaged through his saddlebags until he found a small silver bowl. He filled it with snow, and then gathered together kindling and built a small fire. His hands were so numb with cold it took him two strikes of the steel against the flint before he could make a spark, and he cursed under his breath. 'What kind of wildkin prince are you?' he said to himself. 'Sloppy, Robin, sloppy!'

The fire was soon burning away merrily, though, and he was able to melt the snow in his silver bowl. He perched on a small, upright boulder nearby, first brushing away its nightcap of snow, and held the bowl steady between his palms, looking down into its lucent depths.

Peregrine had spent years studying with the Erlrune and the spell for finding lost things was just one of many that she had taught him. He took a few deep breaths, then said softly, 'What is lost must now be found, take my luck and turn it round, show me the vanished road, where long ago Prince Zander rode.'

The soft reflections in the water swayed and shifted and slowly re-formed into a vision, diaphanous as a dragonfly's wings. Peregrine saw a broad road running through the forest, built of paving stones carefully fitted together. The trees and bushes had been cut back on either side, and there was an immense tree trunk thrown down on one side. Soldiers marched along the road, and then came a litter carried by two hobhenkies with iron collars about their necks. Reposing in the litter was a plump young man with bulging blue eyes and blond hair as fine and colourless as a baby's. He was yawning behind one ring-laden hand.

The vision faded in a moment, but Peregrine was on his feet, spilling the water wildly. He stared all around the valley. The fallen tree trunk still lay to one side, though now it was ancient and mossy under its mantle of snow. He dropped to his knees and dug through the snow, heedless of the sting of ice on his bare skin. He found a cracked paving stone, and then another. Sitting back on his heels he stared about in wonder. He was actually sitting on the old starkin road. That is what Stiga had meant when she said, 'Here, there, everywhere.' The old wildkin woman had led them to the very road that Prince Zander had once travelled along.

His eyes were caught by a strange shadow on the boulder on which he had been sitting. He bent forward and rubbed away the dirt and brown lichen. The shape of a Z was carved upon it, and then a few numerals and an arrow. Fifteen hundred miles to Ziva. Peregrine thought of the ruined palace, cursed long ago by Princess Rozalina. Nothing but owls and bats dwelled there now, just as she had predicted.

He jumped to his feet in excitement and went running across the valley to the fallen log, catching up his silver bowl as he went.

'Jack! Wake up! Guess what?'

'What?' Jack sat up, his black hair sticking up on one side. He rubbed his eyes, yawned and stretched. Then, realising who was speaking to him, he cried, 'Your Highness! What's wrong?'

'Nothing's wrong,' Peregrine said jubilantly. 'We're going to go in search of the lost spear.'

Jack stared at him. 'I don't understand. What lost spear? You mean the Storm King's spear? But it's been missing for ages. Years and years.'

'I know,' Peregrine said. 'Since my great-aunt Briony was a baby. But just because something is lost doesn't mean it can't be found.'

'But we're meant to be going to the Erlrune's.'

Jack was so bewildered and bothered that Peregrine had to smile. 'We're miles and miles away from the Evenlinn. Stiga has been leading us in the wrong direction.'

'What?' Grizelda screeched, sitting bolt upright. 'What are you talking about?'

Peregrine began to explain, but Grizelda did not wait for

him to finish. 'She's been leading us *away* from the Erlrune? Well, she'd better start leading us back there right now!'

'But we've already come so far,' Peregrine said. 'We're on the very road that Prince Zander travelled all those years ago. This might be our best bet to find the lost spear.'

'But we're meant to be going to the Erlrune's!' Grizelda wailed.

'Well, what do you care?' Peregrine was taken aback by her vehemence. 'I thought you were scared of the Erlrune.'

'I'm not *scared* exactly,' Grizelda answered, looking down and fiddling with the ring on her finger. 'It's just . . . well, that's what we're supposed to do.'

'We can't just turn around and ride back,' Peregrine said. 'We've got a hunter on our trail, with those enormous baying dogs. We'll ride straight into their jaws.'

She bit her lip. 'Isn't there another way? Can't we circle back?'

'We could, I suppose, except I certainly don't know the way through the Perilous Forest from here, and I'm not at all sure Stiga does either.'

'But she's meant to be our guide!'

'Stiga doesn't know all the paths through the forest, no-one does. I think we must have been travelling by the old road for much of the way, for certainly we were able to gallop our horses quite easily yesterday, weren't we?'

Jack had been sitting quietly, his thick brows drawn together, his gaze moving from Peregrine's face to Grizelda's. 'Your Highness, I don't think your parents would want you to risk yourself.'

'It's a stupid idea! Ridiculous!' Grizelda cried, scrambling to her feet.

'It is not!' Peregrine began to get angry. 'Stiga—'

'She's just a stupid old woman. What does she know? She's half-crazy anyway. You're the prince, order her to take us to the Erlrune.'

'I won't,' Peregrine said. 'Why should I? I wanted to go and look for the spear in the first place. If my mother wasn't so protective . . .'

'She just wants to keep you safe,' Jack said quietly. 'You are the heir to two thrones, remember, your Highness.'

'How could I ever forget?' Peregrine retorted. 'Well, I wish I wasn't! Locked up all the time, made to do lessons, not allowed to do anything fun. Being a prince is a bloody bore!'

'Blood is blood, duty is duty,' Stiga said from behind him. Peregrine ignored her. He had heard that particular saying of hers enough times that it made him want to scream.

Grizelda stamped her foot. 'I tell you, we need to turn around! Surely you can find the way. Haven't you been there before? Don't you know the way?'

'Well, I know the way from the Stormlinn, of course, but that's miles behind us,' Peregrine said. 'I have no idea how to get there from here. Besides, there are only two, maybe three, passages into the Erlrune's valley.'

'Only two or three ways in,' Grizelda repeated, narrowing her eyes.

'What's it to you anyway?' Jack demanded.

She flicked him a look. 'You think I *want* to be lost in the Perilous Forest? The queen said we'd be safe with the Erlrune.'

'But if we're headed southwest, then we're headed straight towards your home,' Jack said, his voice hard with suspicion. 'I'd have thought you'd be begging us to take you home, not to head straight back into the Perilous Forest.'

Grizelda stared at him. 'Oh, goodness! Are we really almost home? How can you tell? I thought we were lost.'

'Don't you have any sense of direction?' Jack sneered. 'How like a girl!'

She put her nose in the air. 'I'm sure I have a perfectly good sense of direction, thank you very much. Except how I'm supposed to use it when we've been galloping through a forest, I don't know.'

'Haven't you noticed how flat the land is, and how few pine trees? There are no mountains in sight at all,' Peregrine said. 'And the rising sun is behind us.'

She glanced at the long rays of early light striking through the bare branches, then shrugged. 'I'm sure I would've noticed if I'd had time. I'm sorry if I lost my temper. I'd just woken up and it was a shock. There's no need for your lackey to get cantankerous with me.'

Jack scowled at her words but Peregrine said, 'That's all right. I should've thought.' He bent and picked up his pack and thrust the silver bowl away inside, before slinging his pack onto his shoulder. 'We should get on our way, we can eat in the saddle. I'd hate for that hunter to find us. If he's managed to kill off all of my bodyguard, I'm sure he'll make short work of us!'

Although he spoke lightly, Peregrine felt a dull ache in his chest at the thought of the bodies of his brave and loyal bodyguards strewn through the forest behind him. He had known most of the Merry Men since babyhood and he was shocked and deeply grieved at their deaths. The death of Sir Medwin, his tutor, was an even sharper grief. Peregrine had loved the kindly old man, and was tormented with guilt that Sir Medwin had sacrificed his own life to save his prince's.

Grizelda stepped closer to him. 'We will go now to the Erlrune's, won't we?' she asked pleadingly. 'I hate the thought of your Highness riding into danger.'

He looked at her in surprise. 'No, I told you. Stiga brought us here for a reason. She thinks it's time to search for the lost spear and so do I. It feels as if it's meant to be.'

'Child of storm, find the spear, it is time, do not fear,' Stiga repeated.

Grizelda cast her an irritated look. 'But sir,' she protested through clenched teeth. 'Surely that is not wise. What is this lost spear anyway? Surely a child's plaything is not worth risking your life for?'

'It's not a plaything,' he said, walking to where Sable was tethered. His saddle rested nearby and he hoisted it up.

'Your Highness, let me do that!' Jack cried.

Peregrine waved him away. 'Saddle your own mangy hack! Oh, and that's something else. You'll have to stop calling me your Highness, Jack, it'll give the game away in an instant. Just call me . . . I don't know . . . Call me Robin like Mam does.'

Jack's face was sober. 'You are sure about this, your Highness?'

'In truth, I have never been more sure about anything,' Peregrine replied, returning his gaze steadily. Jack bowed his head.

'You can't be serious! Jack, tell him! It's a crazy idea. We should do what the queen commanded and go to the Erlrune.' Grizelda stamped her foot and glared at Jack.

'I do what my Highness commands,' he said woodenly.

'Robin! Call me Robin!' Peregrine mounted his stallion and held out his arm for his falcon, who flew down at once.

'I do what Robin commands,' Jack repeated, a very faint grin quirking his mouth as he jumped up into his own saddle.

'But it's stupid! It's foolhardy. We'll get into trouble.'

'You can go home if you want,' Jack said. 'It's really not that far. Keep the sun on your left in the morning and your right in the afternoon, and you'll be there in no time.'

'But I don't know the way! I'll get lost!' Grizelda wailed.

'Come on, Grizelda. I promise we won't do anything dangerous. Well, not too dangerous anyway. We'll see where the road leads and then, if we can't find the spear in a week or so, we'll go back. I promise.' Peregrine smiled at her.

After a moment she sighed. 'Oh, all right then. But someone's going to have to help me up onto my horse.'

'Jack!' Peregrine called.

'I thought I wasn't a squire anymore,' Jack grumbled but got down from his horse and cupped his hands for Grizelda's boot. She allowed him to lift her into the saddle, and then dug her heels deep into her mare's side. The horse reared, neighing loudly, then took off, showering Jack with clods of icy mud.

CHAPTER 10

The Storm King's Spear

'RACE YOU!' GRIZELDA CALLED TO PEREGRINE. HE GRINNED and wheeled Sable about, the stallion leaping forward into a gallop.

Jack cursed under his breath and brushed the mud away. By the time he had swung himself back into his saddle, Grizelda was racing away down the valley, Peregrine in close pursuit. Jack sighed and urged his gelding into a canter. The owl swooped past him, and Jack grinned. He loved the way Stiga turned from an old woman into a snowy-white owl in the merest blink of an eye.

Ahead, the white mare slowed just enough that Peregrine was able to gallop past Grizelda with a whoop of excitement, waving his hat. 'Oh, well done, sir!' Grizelda cried.

Jack came cantering up behind them, wishing his horse was as swift as the other two. It was hard to guard a prince who kept galloping off.

Grizelda said to Peregrine, smiling, 'What a beautiful boy you have! It's not many that can beat my Argent!'

'Argent? Is that your mare's name?' Peregrine answered. 'What a coincidence! My boy's called Sable.'

She laughed. 'No, really? That's quite uncanny. We obviously think along the same lines.'

'Jack, listen to this! Both of us named our horses after the heraldic colours. Black is *sable* in heraldry and silver or white is called *argent*. Isn't that a coincidence?'

Sure, Jack thought to himself. *I'd wager a week's wages that she found out what his Highness called his horse and named hers accordingly.*

He glowered at Peregrine, willing him to see it for himself, but his prince simply trotted on with Grizelda by his side, talking as comfortably as if he had known the starkin girl all his life.

'So tell me more about this crazy plan of yours,' Grizelda said. 'Where are we going and why?'

'We're going in search of the lost spear of the Storm King,' Peregrine said. 'I've always wanted to but my parents are so protective of me, they never let me do anything.'

'Is that because of the . . . you know. The falling sickness?'

Jack felt grim satisfaction. His prince hated anyone to refer to his ailment. He was pleased to see Peregrine draw himself up, moving his stallion away from Grizelda.

'No,' Peregrine answered shortly. 'It's just because there have been so many attempts to get rid of me.'

'People have tried to kill you?' Grizelda leant towards him. 'But who? Why?'

'Isn't it obvious? I'm heir to both my father and to Queen Rozalina. And so many stories have been told about me. You know, that I'm the one who will smite the throne of stars asunder and bring peace to the land.'

'Do you believe those stories?' she asked curiously.

Peregrine looked at her in surprise. 'Of course! Aunty Rozalina is a Teller of Tales, she speaks true. So many things she predicted have happened.'

'But the future has not happened yet, how can she possibly know?'

Peregrine hesitated. 'Aunty Briony . . . I mean, the Erlrune . . . says that we can never truly know what is to happen, that visions in the Well of Fates or prophecies uttered by a Teller only forewarn us of what *may* happen. Often it is impossible to tell the future until some action has been taken that will set off the chain of consequences leading to a particular future.'

He paused for a moment, thinking. This was why the Erlrune had never been able to tell him if he would find the spear of thunder or not. Even though they had looked for the spear in the Well of Fates, the whirl of possible futures had been too difficult to read. There had been blood and poison and death, and a wild ride of storm-racked creatures, and a blazing crown, and his mother, sobbing. The memory of the visions he had seen made Peregrine shudder.

'But?' Grizelda prompted.

'But . . . a Teller's words have weight. Once spoken, they tip the balance of fate in that direction.' He spoke slowly, trying to explain the inexplicable.

'So their words are like a curse.'

'Yes.' Peregrine was quiet for a long moment.

'So tell me about this spear. Who was the Storm King?' Grizelda asked.

'It's an old, old story. The Storm King was the first king of the wildkin, hundreds of years ago. It was a time when dark magic and wild magic still stalked the land, battling each other for supremacy. But the Storm King made a magic spear and used it to bring peace. His spear never misses its mark. It returns to your hand once you've thrown it, and it can be used to heal as well as to kill. It also has power over the storm, raising it or quelling it, and it can unbind Lord Grim and call up the Wild Hunt, or bind him again under the hill.'

'Who is Lord Grim?' asked Grizelda.

'One of the great lords of wild magic,' Peregrine answered. 'The Storm King made the spear to overcome Lord Grim, for he refused to abide by any law or rule and caused much grief and havoc in the land.'

'And this is the spear you intend to find?' Grizelda raised one well-shaped eyebrow sardonically.

Riding silently behind, Jack was filled with a fierce gladness. If she knew Peregrine better, she would never mock him like that.

His prince nodded. 'Yes. I don't believe it can have been destroyed, it's magic. And Aunty Briony says magical objects hate to lie unused, that it will want me to find it.'

Grizelda laughed disbelievingly. 'The spear *wants* you to find it?'

'Mock me all you like. It makes no difference to me. I know the spear wants me to find it, I feel it in my heart.' Peregrine urged Sable into a canter, riding ahead. Grizelda glanced back at Jack quizzically. He said nothing, just kicked Snapdragon into a canter to follow his prince.

Grizelda frowned and urged her horse forward. She thundered past Jack, calling, 'Your Highness, stop! I'm sorry. Please stop.'

Eventually Peregrine slowed and turned his horse to wait for them. His eyes were stormy.

'I'm sorry. I didn't mean to laugh. It's just ... well, we starkin are taught differently. I've never heard of anyone speaking about a spear as though it was ... I don't know, a person. Please, don't be angry. Tell me more.'

Jack had to admit Grizelda was very beguiling when she wanted to be. Peregrine nodded and let Grizelda fall into place beside him. They rode on through the forest, the sky the colour of old pewter. Stiga flew on ahead, almost invisible in the gloom.

'The Storm King's spear was always wielded by the Erlking or Erlqueen—' Peregrine began.

'*Women* could wield the spear?' Grizelda interrupted, surprised.

'Of course. Why not?'

'I don't know. I've never heard of women being allowed to use a weapon.'

'That's just your peculiar starkin custom,' Peregrine teased her. 'Wildkin women can do anything a man does. Well, almost. They can't have peeing competitions.'

Grizelda laughed despite herself. 'I doubt they want to!'

'Anyway, the spear was passed down through the generations until the day Prince Zander came to Stormlinn Castle.' Peregrine's expression sobered. 'Do you know the story of the massacre at Stormlinn Castle?'

Grizelda shifted uncomfortably in her saddle. 'Well, I know the wildkin queen insulted him and he took the castle in retaliation.'

'Queen Avannia fed her baby when it was hungry,' Peregrine said quietly. 'Some insult.'

'Surely it was more than that? Though I must admit I think she could have had the manners or the sense to retire somewhere private. We of the starkin do not do such things in public.'

'We of the wildkin do.' Peregrine's voice was cold.

She shrugged one shoulder. 'Oh well, I'm sure that was not the only thing that sparked the battle.'

'There was no battle!' Jack spoke up, startling her. She looked back at him as he went on, 'The starkin scum waited till all were sleeping and then they murdered them in cold blood, every man, woman and child. Do you wonder you were not welcome at Stormlinn Castle?'

'I'm sorry,' she said, faltering. 'I didn't know. Are you sure?'

'Sure as eggs,' Jack replied coldly.

'No wonder the wildkin hate us starkin so much.' Grizelda gazed at him with tear-bright eyes and Jack swallowed and looked away.

'That's all right,' he answered gruffly. 'You're not responsible for all that your people did. It was a long time ago.'

'I can try to make things better, though, can't I?' she said. 'That's why I'm here, really.'

Jack nodded, smiling faintly.

'So what happened to the spear?' Grizelda turned back to Peregrine.

'Prince Zander took it when he left. He took Princess Shoshanna too, Aunty Rozalina's mother, and made her his concubine. He threw the spear into a bog and woke Lord Grim and hung him in bells, knowing those of wild magic cannot bear the sound. It must've been torture for Lord Grim, tied up with bells for so many years. My parents freed him from the starkin palace when they rescued Aunty Rozalina.'

'But why would Prince Zander throw the spear into the bog if it is such a thing of power?' Grizelda frowned in puzzlement.

'I guess he meant to prove to Shoshanna that he was stronger than the wildkin and that it was no use resisting him. Or perhaps he did it to make sure the prophecy would never come true.'

'What prophecy?'

Together Jack and Peregrine chanted: '*A child of storm shall raise high the spear of thunder and by the power of three, smite the throne of stars asunder.*' They glanced at each other and laughed.

Jack's heart warmed. How many times had he and Peregrine pretended they had found the spear? They had battled each other all through the halls, up and down the stairs and onto the battlements, Peregrine always being the valiant prince and Jack taking whatever role he was given. For the first time Jack forgot his doubts and worries about this quixotic quest of Peregrine's and thought that perhaps he really did have a chance of finding the lost spear.

'Aunty Briony has looked in the Well of Fates and seen where Prince Zander was when he threw away the spear. She says he was near a tall hill with an oak tree on top.'

'Well, I'm guessing there's only a few thousand of those in the land,' Grizelda said caustically. 'That really helps narrow things down.'

'The oak tree had been blasted by lightning.'

'Still!'

'And mistletoe hung in its branches. Do you know how rare that is?'

'So how come no-one has been able to find this rare oak tree?'

Peregrine shrugged, making Blitz's bells chime out. 'Maybe it was not yet time? Maybe the spear is waiting for me.'

Grizelda said nothing for a moment, then flashed him a smile. 'Maybe!'

The road stretched before them, straight as an arrow, immaculate as a newly washed sheet. Glancing behind them, Jack saw the deep tracks made by their horses' hooves, punctuated by the small tracks of the white hound Oskar, who ran tirelessly at Argent's heels.

'I wish it would snow again, your Highness,' he said uneasily. 'I'm worried about leaving such a clear trail through the forest. Do you think that hunter is still on our trail?'

Peregrine glanced back and frowned. He put Blitz onto his wooden perch and took out his flute, playing a few sweet, soaring notes.

Grizelda watched him in surprise. 'What are you doing?'

Peregrine did not answer her, too busy playing his flute. After a minute or two, Jack heard a rattle of twigs and a rustle of fir needles. Oskar growled, lifting one foot and staring into the forest. Wood-sprites came swinging through the trees. Tall, slim and agile, they had long supple limbs and wild hair all matted into elflocks. Oskar barked and, wide-eyed, Grizelda silenced him with a gesture. The wood-sprites called to Peregrine in their own tongue and he called back, waving his hand towards the tracks behind him. Laughing, the wood-sprites seized the snow-laden branches of the trees and shook them till the snow showered down and filled in the hoof prints. Peregrine called out his thanks, and they swung close to him, hanging upside-down from the branches or leaning out from the trees, grinning wickedly and pointing at Grizelda, who shrank close to Peregrine. One leant down and tried to tug her ring off her finger, and she slapped him away. He slapped her back, but not hard enough to knock her from her horse. She gasped and put her hand to her cheek, and the wood-sprite swung away, laughing mockingly.

'It hit me! Do something! Shoot it!' she cried.

'Shoot a wood-sprite? I'd not be so stupid!'

'But he hit me!'

'You hit him first.'

'He was trying to steal my ring!'

'Wood-sprites like flashy things. All you had to do was tell him no and he'd have let you be.'

Grizelda breathed quickly, holding her reins so tightly her mare shied and cavorted. 'You ... you ...' She sucked in a breath. 'You are the crown prince! You must not put up with such insolence.'

Peregrine shook his head, his mouth set firmly. 'I'm not a murderer! I'm sorry he slapped you but you did hit him first. The wood-sprites have helped us by hiding our trail. How could I possibly repay them by shooting one of them?'

'But ... but it's just a wildkin.' Grizelda's cheek flamed red and her eyes shone brilliantly. 'Would you put a creature like that before me?'

Peregrine took a moment to answer. 'I'm grateful to you for warning us about the ambush, but the wood-sprites are faithful subjects of the Erlkings of Stormlinn and have helped my family more times than I could count. I know they are undisciplined and, well, wild.' He grinned briefly. 'I guess that's why they're called wildkin! But I could not shoot one.'

Grizelda stared at him, her breast rising and falling rapidly with her angry pants. 'I'm sorry. Of course you couldn't shoot it ... him, I mean. I'm afraid I have rather a quick temper. I do hope you'll forgive me.'

'Of course,' Peregrine said courteously, though his guarded expression did not relax.

She nodded curtly and wheeled her horse about, whacking Argent's neck with her reins. Argent took off like a bolt from a crossbow. Peregrine grinned at Jack. 'She is rather testy, isn't she?'

'That's an understatement,' Jack replied with a grin, adding belatedly, 'sir'.

'Stop with the "sirs",' Peregrine cried, giving Sable his head. 'We'll be away from the forest soon! We'll have to travel in disguise. Call me Robin!'

Then he was gone, his stallion's hooves churning up great chunks of snow. Jack sighed and once again spurred his trusty old gelding to follow. Prince Peregrine seemed to be revelling in his newfound freedom, but did he not realise the danger? How could Jack ever keep his Highness safe?

Behind him the wood-sprites whooped with glee as they threw snowballs at each other, obliterating the marks of horses' hooves in the snow.

CHAPTER 11

Nightmare

IT WAS DUSK WHEN STIGA FLOATED DOWN FROM THE SKY LIKE a great soft snowflake. She landed lightly before the exhausted horses and shook off her feathers. In a second the owl was gone and a small hunchbacked woman was in her place, her heart-shaped face lifted to Peregrine's enquiringly. 'Sun is gone, shadows creep, time to find a place to sleep?'

'Yes.' Peregrine dismounted and led his horse to Stiga. 'Is there somewhere safe where we can sleep?'

'Somewhere deep and hollow, where no-one can follow,' Stiga murmured, waving one small hand towards the thick evergreen shrubbery crowding close on the side of the road.

Peregrine parted the branches and looked through. 'There's a kind of depression here where we could sleep,' he reported. 'It's so thickly sheltered there's no snow on the ground at all.'

'Is someone still following us?' Jack asked anxiously, dismounting and leading Snapdragon off the road.

Stiga nodded. 'Sniffing and snuffling behind, seeking and searching to find.'

Jack screwed up his face. It was almost dark and the horses were barely able to plod any further. They had to rest. Prince Peregrine would fall sick if he got too tired.

'I guess we'd better stop for the night,' he said. 'We can't light a fire, though, it's too dangerous.'

'But it's freezing!' Grizelda clambered awkwardly down from her horse's back, scowling at Jack who had made no move to help her. 'And I'm hungry. What are we meant to eat?'

'I think I have some cheese left,' Jack said dubiously.

'This is not how I expected to be treated!' Grizelda cried.

'Mmmm, let me think about that. Was his Highness expecting to have all his bodyguards murdered and our supplies lost? I don't think so!' Jack snapped back.

'Was that my fault?'

Jack opened his mouth to answer and Grizelda pointed her finger at him. 'Don't say it, I'll scream!'

He shut his mouth ostentatiously and spread his hands.

'I wish it would stop snowing,' Peregrine said, huddling his arms about him. 'I feel as though I'll never be warm again.'

'I don't want you getting sick,' said Jack with a worried frown. 'It's just, well, a fire out here in the forest would guide the hunter straight to us.'

'Light us a fire! I swear I'm dying of cold.' Grizelda lifted her gloved hands to her mouth and blew in them, then tucked them back in her white fur muff. 'We've ridden so fast we must've left that hunter far behind us.'

'Tell you what,' Peregrine said. 'I've got some rabbit that Blitz hunted today. Why don't we make just a little fire, roast up the rabbit, and have something hot to eat, then douse the fire to sleep? Our cloaks will keep us warm.'

'If you so command, your Highness,' Jack said stiffly.

'It'll only be a little fire, Jack. I'll make it, I need to practise my fire-making. Maybe you could find us some acorns we can grind up for meal. It'd be good to make some bread.'

'Guess who'll be doing the grinding,' Jack muttered under his breath.

They ate a sketchy meal. All were tired and cold and cross. They smothered the small glow of the fire with snow, then wrapped themselves in their cloaks to sleep. Jack's breath puffed white before his face; his nose felt like an icicle. He buried his head in his cloak and was instantly warmed. Blessing the Erlrune's magic, he fell asleep.

At some time during the night, Jack woke from sleep and raised himself up on his elbow, looking about uneasily. All was dark and bitterly cold. Snow was blowing through the branches, dusting their cloaks with frost like icing sugar. Beside him, Peregrine was crying out, 'No, no, Mam! Watch out.'

'Shhhh.' Jack knelt beside him, trying to comfort him. 'It's all right, sir. Go back to sleep. Shh now.'

Peregrine twisted restlessly in his sleep then cried out, 'No!' He sat up abruptly, his eyes wide and staring. 'The castle! The castle has fallen!'

At the same moment Jack heard an unearthly shriek. Again and again it echoed through the night. He stumbled to his feet. A great white shape swooped down, screaming in his ear. Jack ducked, arms over his head, and felt icy air whoosh past him. 'Stiga?' he called, but the owl was gone, soaring away into the night. 'Stiga?' Jack called again.

'What is it? What's happened?' Grizelda's voice sounded scared.

'Stiga,' Peregrine sobbed.

'I don't know what's wrong,' Jack said. 'His Highness had

some kind of nightmare and then Stiga began shrieking and flew off.'

'Something's wrong,' Peregrine said. 'Terribly, terribly wrong.'

'It was just a dream, sir,' Jack said. 'You just frightened Stiga, crying out like that.'

'It was the most dreadful dream,' Peregrine said, his voice shaking. 'I dreamt the enemy was inside Stormlinn Castle, soldiers pouring through, and hacking and killing . . .' His voice broke and he pressed his arm across his eyes.

'It doesn't mean anything, it's just a nightmare,' Jack said, though his insides were knotted with fear.

'A dream is never just a dream,' Peregrine said. 'You should know that, Jack! Oh, what can have happened? Has Stormlinn Castle fallen? What should I do?'

'You're cold. Let me light a fire.' Jack began to grope in one of his pockets for his box of tinder.

'What about the hunter? He might see the glow,' Peregrine protested.

'We've not heard the dogs for days now,' Grizelda said.

Jack thought he could hear her teeth chattering.

'All right. Just a little one. We'll get warm and wait for Stiga to come back,' Peregrine said.

But the owl did not come back. The three companions sat shivering by their little fire till dawn.

'I say we go on,' Grizelda said.

'But you didn't want to go looking for the spear in the first place!' Jack objected.

'Well, I didn't know what the spear was,' she said. 'And I'm sick of this forest. You said we were almost into Zavaria.

We could go home, have a bath, sleep in a real bed, get some supplies.'

'I don't think that would be wise,' Peregrine said. 'I don't mean to cast doubt upon your family's loyalty to my father, but I believe we must remain hidden. If we went to your castle, there would be grown-ups there telling us what we should do. They'd probably forbid us to leave. I think we should go and find the spear, and then get back to the Stormlinn as fast as we can.'

'There's no blazing way I'm going to a starkin castle!' Jack said.

'But that's so stupid! My brother's not even there.'

'No, he's besieging Stormlinn Castle right now!' Jack shot back.

'Well, yes, but he did warn you about the ambush so you were at least prepared,' she pointed out.

'Probably to set up a trap for us all!'

'Whether or not his intentions were good does not matter,' Peregrine said placatingly. 'It would be a disservice to the count to take shelter in his castle. If Vernisha found out about it, she would name him traitor and have him fed to her lapdog, limb by limb.'

Grizelda bit her lip and said nothing.

'We'll need to be careful not to draw too much attention to ourselves,' Peregrine said. 'What disguise shall we adopt? What can be our excuse for riding through?'

'Strangers are frowned upon,' Grizelda said. 'You may not travel without a licence, and the penalty is to be whipped through town. Each town you come to will do the same.'

'That doesn't sound too pleasant,' Peregrine said. 'I don't particularly want my tail whipped. How do you get a licence?'

'From the bailiff, but he doesn't give them out lightly. Only to royal messengers, or merchants of the guild who must travel for trade.'

'This isn't getting any easier. Whatever happened to the good old days when a minstrel could stroll from town to town, singing for his supper?'

Peregrine spoke lightly, but Grizelda answered him seriously. 'Minstrels and troubadours are banned by law, for spying and spreading sedition. It's even against the law to sing a song in a tavern, or any public place. The penalty is really quite nasty.'

'Why? What happens?'

'They strip you naked and tie you to a table and then they turn an iron tub filled with rats upside-down on your stomach.'

'That is nasty,' Peregrine said.

'Oh, the nasty bit happens after they light a fire on top of the iron tub. As the iron gets hot, the rats get agitated.'

'Urrgh.'

'The rats try to gnaw their way to freedom through your entrails.'

'That's disgusting!' Jack cried.

'How barbarous,' Peregrine said, creasing his brow. 'Is that true? That's the penalty for singing?'

'Yes,' she answered. 'I beg you not to bring out that flute of yours where anyone can see you or hear you.'

'We shall have to travel at night,' Peregrine said decisively.

'But what about food?' Jack said. 'What shall we eat?'

'I doubt there are many wildkin to bring us food,' Peregrine said wryly.

'And your bird may not hunt,' Grizelda said. 'The penalty for poaching is—'

Peregrine held up one hand, wincing. 'I don't want to know!'

'They cut off both your hands,' she finished. 'That is if you hunt by day. The punishment for poaching during the night hours is immediate death by hanging.'

'We will not get far without food.' Peregrine frowned. 'Let me think.'

After a few moments he pulled out his flute. He began to play a soft lilting tune that sounded like wind through leaves, water over stones.

Grizelda stared at him in amazement, then smothered a scream as the undergrowth rustled and out crept a line of tiny brown mice, each carrying food to lay at Peregrine's feet. Some brought seeds and grains, some brought chestnuts; two rolled a wrinkled apple, only a little nibbled around one side. Then a squirrel scampered out, carrying an acorn in its paws, another two making its cheeks bulge. It left the acorns at Peregrine's feet.

A white-tailed deer tiptoed out fearfully, with a mouthful of tiny mushrooms. A kingfisher flew down with a silver wriggling fish. Another fish was brought by an otter. A wild pig brought some black truffles, smelling richly of the soil from which they had been dug. A red fox brought a lean mountain hare, its coat white as the snow. A weasel dragged in a pheasant. Slowly the pile of food at Peregrine's feet grew.

Although the day was bright and still, they risked lighting a fire and cooking the hare, making a kind of stew from the grains and mushrooms and truffles. The fish they cleaned and gutted, and then smoked on sharp sticks. The pheasant they cooked and wrapped up in flat bread they made from grinding up the chestnuts and mixing the meal with water.

There were enough chestnuts left to roast a handful in the coals.

'We have enough food here to last us days,' Jack said exultantly. 'Well done, your Highness!'

'I'd like to know why you didn't do it days ago,' Grizelda said, gnawing happily on a bone.

'I didn't think of it,' Peregrine admitted. He stroked Blitz's head and fed him another shred of roast hare. The falcon was perched on Peregrine's knee, his eyes keen and fierce as he tore the meat to shreds with his sharp beak. 'Besides, I'd feel bad about taking *all* the animals' winter hoard. I wouldn't like them to starve.'

'So what's our plan?' Jack felt much better now he was warm and full.

Peregrine got up and kicked snow into the fire, extinguishing it. 'We ride on, as swiftly and silently as we can. We'll ride till dawn, then find somewhere to hide during the daylight hours.'

'You mean, ride all night?' Grizelda was not impressed. 'But I'm so tired. I ache all over.'

'Jack has some heal-all salve,' Peregrine said sympathetically. 'Aunty Rozalina knew what she was about when she gave it to him.'

Rather crossly Grizelda retired behind a tree to rub the salve into her saddle sores, taking her bag with her.

Peregrine gazed through the sunlit forest. He felt uneasy and restless, his nightmare weighing heavily on his spirits. 'If only Stiga was here to guide us!'

'Maybe she'll come back,' Jack said.

Peregrine shook his head. 'It's probably better that she doesn't. Birds are shot down elsewhere in Ziva, remember. I must keep Blitz close to me at all times.'

'So if we are not going to my castle, where are we going?' Grizelda demanded, coming out from behind the tree and tossing the tub of salve at Jack's head. He caught it easily.

Peregrine looked at her in surprise. 'Ardian, of course.'

'Ardian?' Grizelda cried, her face blanching. 'But Ardian has been taken over by the rebels!'

'No,' Peregrine said sternly. 'Ardian has been won for the true king. It is the pretender Vernisha who is the rebel, not my father.'

'Yes,' Grizelda said stiffly. 'Of course. Forgive me.'

'And don't forget that Ardian is a land of bogs and marshes,' Peregrine said. 'It's the most logical place for Prince Zander to have got rid of the spear. Perhaps Lord Percival will know where the lightning-blasted oak is.'

'Is that the Marsh King?' Jack asked in lively interest.

Peregrine nodded but said, 'He must not be called king. There is only one king and that is my father. He has thanked this rebel leader for his loyalty and allegiance and named him lord of the fenlands, but no true treaty has yet been signed. Still, I believe Lord Percival will help us if he can.'

'They say he is a law unto himself,' Grizelda said in a shaking voice. 'That he has destroyed all the causeways into the marshes, and shoots anyone who comes near the fens. What is to stop him shooting us?'

'He shoots any *starkin* that comes near,' Jack said with satisfaction. 'So his Highness and I should be safe enough. I guess you'll just have to pretend to be a hearthkin.'

'After a week without a bath, I'm certainly filthy enough to be taken for a hearthkin,' she answered bitterly. 'I guess my smell will have to be my disguise.'

CHAPTER 12

Fallen to the Blade

BLACK FOREBODING CAST A PALL ON PEREGRINE, DESPITE the brightness and beauty of the day. Snow should have been falling, wind should have been howling, if all was well with his mother. What did this sudden sunshine mean?

He kept glancing behind, sure eyes were watching him. Once he thought he could hear horses' hooves behind them, though Grizelda said it was only an echo.

By the day's end, they came to the edge of the forest. Patchwork meadows, brown and grey and white, rolled away to the horizon, edged with low drystone walls and thorny hedges. Small cottages could be seen nestled among small copses of bare-branched fruit trees. Far away, a white castle stood on a hill, its banners flourishing in the breeze, its thousands of windows shining golden in the last rays of the sun.

'That's my home,' Grizelda cried, pointing in delight. 'Look, it's only a day's ride away!'

'The old road leads straight towards it,' Peregrine said gloomily. 'We'll wait till it's dark before we ride out.' He dismounted stiffly and stretched, his whole body aching. Blitz flew down to his wrist and Peregrine stroked his head. 'Did you have a good fly, boy? Catch us any dinner?' Blitz rubbed his master's hand with his beak, then flew to a branch nearby, grooming his ruffled feathers.

Jack dismounted too, and came to take Sable's reins. Oskar whined and twitched his ears, glancing back into the forest. His tail wagged. Grizelda sat still in her saddle, staring at the castle. 'I want to go home,' she said firmly.

'You can if you want,' Jack said. 'We're not stopping you.'

Suddenly there was an unearthly shriek. A huge white owl hurtled out of the twilight-grey forest, talons extended, straight for Grizelda. She screamed and flung up one arm, trying to protect her face. A bow string twanged from the shadows. An arrow sped out, piercing the owl through the breast. She tumbled down to land awkwardly on the ground, one wing bent and broken.

'Stiga!' Peregrine screamed. He flung himself on his knees beside the owl, who groaned and shimmered, changing shape into a frail old woman, an arrow protruding from her chest. Blood ran down and stained the frosty ground.

'Your Highness, we must flee!' Jack cried. 'Get up, sir! Mount! I'll pass Stiga to you.'

Peregrine obeyed at once, numb with shock. He leapt into his saddle and bent so Jack could pass Stiga up to him. She was light, no heavier than a child. One arm dangled helplessly. Peregrine dug his heels into Sable's sides. The stallion bounded into a gallop, Jack only a few seconds behind him. Blitz screeched and flew after them.

'Ride, Grizelda!' Peregrine shouted. 'Quick!'

She was close behind them, her hair tumbling free of her

hood and whipping behind her. Heedless of any watchers, the three companions galloped down the old road, straight towards Swartburg Castle.

Peregrine bent over the limp form of his old nursemaid. Her eyes were shut, her face blanched of any colour. He crumpled up her shawl to try to staunch the flow of blood. 'Stiga,' he whispered. 'Don't worry. We'll find somewhere safe to stop and tend to you. Everything will be all right.'

She opened her dark eyes and looked up into his face. 'Stormlinn is betrayed, fallen to the blade.'

The world spun around. Peregrine kept his seat with difficulty. 'Mam? Father? Aunty Rozie and Uncle Zed?'

'All you love is taken, the castle is forsaken.' Her voice was such a thin thread he could barely hear it.

'Taken? Where?'

She shook her head. Her face twisted in pain.

'What happened? Can you tell me how?' he demanded. 'Please, Stiga. Who betrayed them?'

'They came in through the secret way, all the guards they did slay.' Her voice failed her. She shut her eyes.

'But how could they have known about the secret way? Who could've told them?'

She did not answer. He felt a strange tingling in his hands and arms where he held her. Then she was gone, and he carried in his arms a dead owl.

Peregrine buried Stiga under a cairn of rocks in a small copse of trees, saying in a low, choked voice: 'Go easy, beloved Stiga, fly once more in the moonlight, fly across moor and meadow, fly across forest and field, fly across the bright sea, let the waters carry you to the sun. Be at peace, faithful Stiga, and know I shall never forget you.'

Jack knelt beside him, passing the rocks to him in silence. Grizelda sat nearby, her arms wrapped about her knees, her eyes wide and fearful.

'The arrow just came from nowhere,' Peregrine said in a choked voice. 'I heard nothing. Nothing!'

'He must have been following us all the time,' Jack said. 'He must've crept up close, to hear what we were saying, maybe.'

'Why did he shoot her? Why, why?'

'She was attacking Grizelda,' Jack pointed out.

'But why?' Grizelda said in a small voice. 'I've done nothing. I warned you the soldiers were coming!'

'Perhaps it was enough that you are of starkin blood,' Peregrine said. 'Perhaps, in her simple way, she thinks you brought the attack upon the castle.'

Grizelda's voice shook. 'She always hated me.'

There was a long silence. Peregrine rested his head on his arms. He felt so sick and weary he just wanted to curl into a ball and never move again.

Jack watched the landscape behind them. The moon sailed high in a sky of piercingly bright stars. It was almost full. Nothing moved but the wind in the branches. 'He does not seem to be following us,' he said. 'Shall we ride on?'

Peregrine did not answer.

'Your Highness? Shall we ride on? I don't feel safe here. We're too close to the castle.'

Still Peregrine did not answer, his face hidden. Jack squatted beside him, one hand resting on his shoulder. 'My lord?'

Peregrine shook his hand away, standing up abruptly. 'Yes. We'll ride on. What else is there to do? My only hope now is to find the spear. We'll find the spear, we'll rescue my parents, and we'll wrest the crown from that malevolent old hag, I swear it! Come on, let's ride!'

They rode all night, keeping to the hedgerows, letting the tired horses plod. Once or twice Peregrine almost fell asleep in the saddle. He was jerked awake by the harness, which kept him from falling. Each time at the moment of awakening he remembered with a rush of black despair. Stiga dead, Stormlinn Castle fallen, his family taken captive. Surely he could rescue his parents if he found the spear? If only the spear was still there to be found . . .

As dawn approached, they hid in a small copse of trees in a valley, bounded on both sides by wide bare fields. It was odd to hear no birds singing. It seemed to unsettle Blitz, who was hunched on his perch, his hooded head turning this way and that as he strained to hear. Peregrine stroked him between his wings and gave him a small gobbet of meat from his wallet, then tied his jesses to the perch. He dared not risk a falcon being seen flying in these birdless skies.

They ate, then huddled themselves in their cloaks to sleep, taking turns to keep watch. Even though the daylight hours were so short that they did not need to hide for long, Peregrine still found the waiting difficult. He wanted to be up and moving. The road was busy this close to the castle, however, and it would not have been safe to ride on. Farmers' carts trundled up and down, a girl walked past with a flock of geese, a battalion of soldiers in silver armour marched by. Once a wedge of sisika birds flew over, and Peregrine shrank down beneath his grey cloak, hoping no betraying piece of metal from the horses' tack would catch the sun.

He slept for a few hours while Jack kept watch, but the sun stabbed through the thin, bare branches and his dreams were restless. At last Peregrine sat up, hunched in his cloak, and watched a farmer working nearby, laboriously mending a broken wall. He was a poor stick of a man, tattered as a scarecrow, with feet bound with rags. Once he came close enough for Peregrine to see that both his ears had been chopped off, leaving only ugly red scars. Peregrine flinched, sick with pity and horror. When he woke Grizelda in the dusk, he demanded to know what crime could possibly result in such a dreadful punishment.

She shrugged, her blue eyes unable to meet his. 'He could have listened to seditious songs or stories, or to slanderous lies about the queen.'

'They would cut off his ears for listening to *stories*?' Peregrine asked. When she nodded, he continued furiously, 'It is evil! This is your county, Grizelda! Your brother is Count of Zavaria, he is responsible for justice in this land. How can he be so cruel?'

'It is the law,' she said unhappily. 'The queen makes the laws.'

'I bet she would not lose her ears if she listened to gossip,' Jack cried.

'Shhhh!' Grizelda looked around her. 'Be careful how you speak of the queen,' she said in a much lower voice.

'Why? Will I lose my tongue if I say something nasty about her?' Jack said sarcastically, then stared in disbelief when Grizelda nodded.

A shrill, triumphant scream right overhead made them all jump as another wedge of sisika birds flew over. At once Peregrine and Jack froze, hoping their hooded cloaks were enough to hide them from view. Peregrine's heart was beating so hard it bruised the bones of his chest. The giant birds kept on flying, though. Peregrine gazed after them and then cried out in shock.

A net was suspended between two of the birds. People were crammed, struggling, inside. Peregrine saw arms, legs, bodies, heads, pressed hard against the crisscross of rope. Hundreds of wild birds soared around the net, screaming in distress.

His legs gave way. He sat down.

'Are you all right?' Jack whispered.

Peregrine nodded.

'What?' Grizelda said. 'It's only a load of prisoners being taken to the castle.' Then she realised. 'Oh no! Do you think . . . I'm so sorry! They're prisoners from Stormlinn Castle, aren't they? Those sisika birds belong to the soldiers that attacked you.'

'Including your brother?' Jack spoke harshly.

She nodded her head, looking frightened. 'He wouldn't have been able to do anything to help, though,' she babbled. 'The queen's commanders—'

'They're being taken to your castle, though,' Jack pointed out.

'It's the closest,' she answered defensively.

'Is there some secret way into your castle?' Peregrine demanded. 'A passage or hidden door?'

She shook her head. 'No. It's very well guarded, because of the rebels, you know. There's a moat around it filled with pikes and poisonous water snakes and blood-sucking leeches, and the only entrance is guarded night and day. And then, of course, there are the dogs. They'd tear any intruders to pieces.'

She paused for a moment, then her eyes brightened. 'I could get you in, of course.'

Peregrine sat staring at the castle, his hands clenched together.

'We can ride straight there. Oh, let's! We'll have a feast. My brother's cook is the best in all the counties. We'll be able to sleep in a bed. I can have a bath and change my clothes. Oh, please, your Highness . . . please, Robin.'

'We can't risk it,' Jack said anxiously. 'They are your enemies, sir!'

'I know,' Peregrine said. 'I'm sorry, Grizelda.'

She began to storm at him, striding up and down, alternating between ordering him to take her home 'right now!' and begging him like a child.

'Tell me, how well do you know Vernisha?' Peregrine's voice cut through hers, an odd note in his voice. His eyes were fixed on the tall white castle, banners snapping in the breeze.

'I've met her,' Grizelda said cautiously. 'She goes on progress in the spring and summer, you know, and stays with each of the counts in turn. It costs us a fortune!'

'So why do you think her flag is flying above your brother's castle now, in the very midst of winter?' Peregrine asked very quietly.

Grizelda lost colour. 'Well, she came . . . to demand my brother's help, you know. I told you! She wanted our dogs to pull the sleds.'

'So the queen is at your castle right now? And you tried to persuade his Highness to go there?' Jack was furious.

'I didn't know she was still there! And he would have been in disguise.'

'Until you betrayed him!'

'I wouldn't have! How dare you say that! It's so unfair. It's a big castle. No-one would need to know he was there!' Her voice rose higher and higher.

'If you don't shut up, I'll gag you again,' Jack threatened.

'You wouldn't dare!'

'Watch me!'

'How can you let him speak to me so?' she appealed to Peregrine. 'He's an ill-mannered lout!'

'He's right, though,' Peregrine said. 'You'll bring the soldiers down upon us. If they cut off somebody's ears for listening to gossip about the queen, imagine what they'll do to me.'

Grizelda bit her lip and struggled to control her temper. 'Please, Robin.'

He shook his head. 'They have my parents captive, do you really think I'd be so stupid as to let them get their hands on me too?'

He spoke so savagely that she said no more, though she kept glancing longingly at the castle.

'Well then,' she said, when they were all packed and ready to go. 'I might just head on home. You don't need me on this mad adventure of yours. I'll be quite safe between here and the castle.'

Jack had been expecting this. He came up close, glowering down at her. 'I don't think so. Do you think we're fools? You'll have the army out and hunting us down within minutes. No, you're coming with us, princess.'

'I won't! I promise I won't tell a soul.'

'No, you won't, because I'm going to make sure you don't.' Jack whipped out a long scarf that he had been hiding behind his back. Grizelda opened her mouth to scream, but Jack had his arm clamped about her neck and the gag over her mouth in seconds. She kicked and struggled but he was too strong for her, tying the gag tightly behind her head. 'That's better,' he said in satisfaction as he hauled her over to his horse. 'I think you can ride with me, at least until we get out of Zavaria.'

Oskar growled, his hackles rising. Jack said, dropping one hand to his sword, 'If your dog attacks me, I'll have to kill him.'

Grizelda at once flung up one hand, palm outward, and the dog subsided, though his lean body was still tense and ready for action.

'I'm sorry,' Peregrine said. 'Please forgive me. I wish there was some other way, but you must realise the risk is too great.'

'Mmmf-mmmf!' she mumbled.

'It won't be for long,' he promised. 'Just till we get away from here.'

They left the road behind them, riding cross-country through the fields, Oskar running close behind. As far as possible they kept to the shelter of hedgerows and trees, watching carefully for any signs of life. How Peregrine wished Stiga was flying before them, her keen owl-sight alert to any danger. His heart ached and his eyes were hot, but he set his jaw and would not let the tears flow. He had to get help for his parents!

Swartburg Castle glowed on its hill, all its windows flaming with light. No matter how the landscape dipped and rolled, the castle was always there, dominating the skyline. At last it began to dwindle, shrinking in the distance, and the dark mass of the Swartwood Forest came ever closer, offering the hope of refuge.

All the time he rode, leading Grizelda's horse and keeping Blitz tucked close to his chest, Peregrine wondered about the man who, he was sure, still followed quietly along behind them. *What did he want? Why did he follow so close he could shoot an owl down out of the sky, and yet not shoot at them?*

It seemed to make no sense.

CHAPTER 13

Vernisha the Vile

THE TIES OF THE NET WERE LOOSENED AND LILIANA TUMBLED out onto the cobblestones of the courtyard at the heart of Swartburg Castle. Seconds later, Rozalina rolled on top of her, with Merry and Zed falling helter-skelter behind.

It took them a few seconds to sit up and recover. Liliana examined one grazed elbow, then looked about her in dismay.

Grey walls towered all around, topped with steeply pointed towers. From each steeple long pennants hung, bearing the swan ensign of Vernisha the Vile.

Vernisha herself was waiting for them. Bloated as a body louse, she was barely contained within the broad spread of her throne, a massive carved and gilded affair carried aloft by two unhappy-looking hobhenkies, thick iron collars about their necks. Her face was as round and plump as a giant soufflé, her eyes peering from between the puffy slits like peeled goose-berries. Bracelets were embedded in the bulging fat of her wrists, and rings jammed onto every sausage-like finger. On her head she wore a silver crown, studded with sapphires and diamonds, with one blue diamond as large as one of her fat fists.

An obese pug dog was cradled in the crook of her arm, panting heavily, his bulging eyes watering. Both mistress and dog were dressed in identical green and cerise striped gowns, with orange fur mantles draped over their shoulders.

Vernisha clapped her hands at the sight of the four bruised and shaken captives. 'Look what we've caught ourselves! A bag of fools.'

The crowd gathered in the courtyard all laughed. There were about two hundred people crushed together, ranging from courtiers in fur robes and extravagant hats to pot-boys in thin rags, with curious, fearful eyes. Soldiers in silver armour with long halberds stood in stiff rows, the face guards on their helmets lowered.

Stiffly King Merrik got to his feet and helped Liliana up. Zed helped Rozalina to her feet too. Her face bore the crisscross imprint of the net. They were all shivering with cold, having been dragged from their beds at midnight and not permitted to grab a cloak or fur mantle before being herded into the net for the dreadful trip to Swartburg Castle. If Liliana had not banished the snowstorms and called warmer weather, it would have been four frozen blue corpses tumbling out of the net.

'Good evening, Vernisha,' King Merrik said with dignity. 'I would be lying if I said I was pleased to see you again. Twenty-five years has not been long enough.'

A mottled mauve colour crept up her fat cheeks, but Vernisha smiled. 'Well, speaking for myself, I haven't been so delighted in a long time. You should have been squashed like a bug years ago.'

'I rather think you've tried, numerous times, but failed,' King Merrik replied.

'Yet here you are, at my mercy.'

'Mercy is not a word I associate with you, Vernisha.'

She smiled. 'Nor should you. I've been planning my revenge for years now and, believe me, mercy has nothing to do with it. I'll make sure you die as slowly and as painfully as possible.'

King Merrik said steadily, 'On what charges, Vernisha? Where are my judge and jury? Or have you dismantled the law of the king's court along with the law of primogeniture?'

She waved one fat hand. 'Big words for a little man.'

He bowed. 'Indeed, I must seem small beside you. Small in stature does not mean small in spirit, however.'

She narrowed her eyes, her colour deepening.

King Merrik looked around the crowd. 'Let it be noted that I have been seized unlawfully and kept against my will. I am the rightful King of Ziva, being the grandson of Princess Drusilla, eldest daughter of King Zhigor the Sixth. Vernisha is nothing more than a tyrant and a bully. Do not permit her to lead you into murder and treason.'

'I am queen! Call me your Majesty!'

'You are no more the Queen of Ziva than I'm a fat flounder,' Merry said in a bored-sounding voice.

Vernisha's face turned the colour of an eggplant. 'Teach him how to treat his queen with respect!'

At once half-a-dozen soldiers rushed at King Merrik with clubs. Zed did his best to protect the king, but since both men were unarmed, barefoot and exhausted after the long, cramped hours in the net, the struggle lasted only a few minutes. King Merrik was knocked to the ground and kicked and beaten mercilessly. Liliana struggled to get to him, but was seized by a soldier who swung around to slap her across the face. Liliana's hand flew up and caught his wrist. For a moment, he stared at her in surprise. Then his eyes rolled back and he fell, dead. The other soldiers all sprang back with cries of alarm.

A hum of amazement and fear rose from the crowd. Vernisha's eyes bulged from her head. 'Witch!' she screamed. 'We'll burn you at the stake!'

Liliana knelt and cradled King Merrik's head in her hands. Slowly the blood oozing from his cuts ceased flowing and the grazes and bruises faded away. King Merrik sat up, gripping her hands, his face filled with sorrow. Tears crept down Liliana's cold face. It was a terrible thing to touch someone and stop their heart. Although Liliana had fought beside her husband for years, being as skilful with her longbow as any of his archers, she had never before killed anyone with her bare hands. It made her feel sick and unclean. Her Gift was meant to heal, not kill. Yet she knew she would do it again if she had to.

'It won't do any good,' he whispered.

'I could not stand by and watch them hurt you,' she replied in a low voice.

'We need to be strong. We must not lower ourselves to their level.'

'They drag us down,' she said, weeping harder.

'No,' he said passionately. 'If we are to die today, let it be with our heads held high.'

She nodded, pressing her wet face into the sleeve of her white linen shift.

'We must try to stay alive,' he whispered. 'Tom-Tit-Tot will have told the Erlrune by now. Help will be on its way.'

'Get me some firewood! We'll burn them all now!' Vernisha raged.

Rozalina stepped forward, her eyes blazing with anger. 'It is Yuletide! Will you break the truce?' Even in her thin chemise, with bare feet and ruffled black hair, she looked every inch a queen. 'I thought the starkin valued their honour? Is it honourable to beat a prisoner of war, a man who has done no wrong except to fight against tyranny and injustice? Is it honourable to attack an enemy's castle in the dead of winter? The twelve days of Yule have been a time of truce and a celebration of peace for as long as history remembers.'

A silence had fallen over the crowd. Even Vernisha had fallen under the spell of Rozalina's sweet, low voice.

'Yule is the lowest, darkest, coldest time of the year,' Rozalina went on, every word throbbing with conviction. 'I know it is hard, at times, to believe that winter will ever end.'

There was a faint sigh of agreement.

'It is easy to begin to despair when the hours of the night are so long and the hours of sunlight so short.' Rozalina leant forward persuasively. 'That is why the ancient law of chivalry forbids fighting and war during these days. We must have faith in the turn of the wheel towards warmth and brightness again. We must not allow our spirits to be dragged into evil!'

Somewhere in the crowd, someone sucked in a long, sobbing breath. Everyone gazed at Rozalina, transfixed.

'Am I to believe that those of starkin blood have forgotten honour and valour and courtesy? That your great lords care nothing for law and justice?'

'No!' a man cried. 'We haven't forgotten, Queen Rozalina!'

The use of Rozalina's title penetrated Vernisha's fascinated haze. She scowled and looked to see who had spoken. 'Seize him, whoever he is! I'm the queen! Me and only me!'

Soldiers looked around in confusion. Whoever had spoken had shrunk back, and people had been so spellbound by Rozalina's words that they had not noticed who it was. Everyone murmured and looked at each other sideways.

'And gag that witch! I'll not have her try to bewitch us with her evil tongue.'

Warily soldiers approached Rozalina, one tearing a linen cloth into strips.

'Think what you do!' Rozalina called. 'Think how you will be remembered. Are we of the wildkin to know more of chivalry than you great starkin lor—?' Her last word was cut off as the gag was roughly shoved into her mouth, and she was pushed down onto her knees. The other three were forced to kneel too, the cold stone striking up through their thin nightclothes. Sharp halberds were held to their necks. Someone hurried into the courtyard, staggering under a great load of firewood. Liliana's heart quailed within her.

'Say a word and I'll cut your throats,' the captain snarled.

Zed and Merry placed their arms protectively around their wives as a babble of voices broke out. A man with ice-blue eyes and two tall hound dogs at his heels approached the throne, bowing deeply.

'Your most honoured Majesty, surely we cannot allow a wildkin witch to know more of chivalry than us! We must not kill them. Not yet, anyway.'

Vernisha pouted like an obese baby, then shrugged her shoulders pettishly. 'Very well then, drag them down to the dungeons. There are only six days left till Yule is over. We can have some fun with them before we kill them!'

As the sun was coming up, Peregrine, Jack and Grizelda stopped in a small glade with running water so the thirsty horses could drink their fill. The snow was only thin on the ground, so they would be able to forage easily. This was a relief, since the horses had been ridden hard for days with only what meagre grass they could find and a double handful of oats each day. Already the panniers were almost empty.

Swartburg Castle could still be seen in the distance, rosy in the dawn light. Peregrine sat on his horse and stared at it, wondering where his family was, what was happening to them now. Were they in a dungeon somewhere? Were they hurt? The mild weather made him ill with fear. Surely his mother would be raging mad, and the weather with her?

Jack lifted Grizelda down from his horse and ungagged her. 'No point screaming, there's no-one for miles,' he warned her. 'And if you do scream I'll just gag you again.'

She stomped away from him, going to the stream and falling down on her knees to drink the icy water. She washed her face and hands, and then, keeping her back to the boys, snapped her fingers to Oskar. He came immediately, ears pricked, and she rotated one finger. At once he cocked his leg against a tree and released a stream of yellow urine.

Peregrine watched him, silent and morose. He did not answer when Jack spoke to him and did not eat when Jack put a piece of flatbread with pheasant stuffed inside it into his hand.

'What's wrong, sir?' Jack asked anxiously. 'Are you not well?'

'If I'm not mistaken this is the Swartwood Forest,' Peregrine said abruptly.

'Yes, it is,' Grizelda said. 'Why? What's wrong with that?'

'My mother's parents were murdered in this forest,'

Peregrine replied. 'They were led here by a man, a hunter, who told them he had heard stories of an ancient spear being found in the woods. He stole all their supplies and left them with only a loaf of bread. It was poisoned.'

There was a long silence.

'My grandmother survived just long enough to make it back to Stormlinn Castle. She ate only a slice. My mother wouldn't touch it, it was too hard and bitter. And so she survived. She was only a little girl.'

Again nobody spoke.

'Our hunter follows us still,' Peregrine said. 'I can sense him out there. He's baffled. He doesn't understand where we are headed. Yet somehow he manages to follow us.'

'We've tried not to leave a trail but it's hard. The snow is melting and the horses' hooves sink into the mud.' Jack spoke defensively.

Peregrine pressed his fingers against his eyes. 'Grizelda, tell me about the dogs.'

'I beg your pardon?'

'Those dogs the hunter has. Your family is famous for breeding dogs, you must know something about them.'

Grizelda answered reluctantly. 'Well, I suppose if you know that much about my family, you will know about our sleuth hounds. They're used for tracking game.'

'Game like us? Human game?'

'Sometimes.'

'They can track our scent?'

'They are bred for their noses,' she replied coolly.

Jack's eyes moved from face to face as he began to realise what Peregrine meant. 'You mean, those dogs belong to your brother! They've been tracking our scent all the way? But . . .

it was snowing ... the wind was howling ..' His voice was sharp with indignation.

'Sleuth hounds were bred to track over snow,' Peregrine said. 'Whoever thought all those geography lessons would prove useful? I remember reading that they can track a scent that is a week old. Only they need to know the scent to track it.'

Jack stared at him, then looked accusingly at Grizelda. She stared back at them, wide-eyed. 'You think *I* ..'

Peregrine nodded. 'I do. You may not have known it, though. I guess the hunter only needed a piece of your clothing—'

'And my bet is she has lots to choose from!' Jack said.

'And maybe the hunter wouldn't even need that. Grizelda's dog has marked our path every step of the way.' All three looked at the yellow stain in the snow under the tree. Peregrine went on, 'Remember how she told the dog to piddle when we got out of the secret passage? Even though she was blindfolded and gagged?'

'She wiggled her finger,' Jack said.

'Oskar had not been allowed to relieve himself for hours,' Grizelda said furiously. 'It would have been cruel not to give him permission.'

'He piddled against the door to the secret passage,' Peregrine said. 'And now I'm terribly afraid that is how the castle was taken. The secret entrance discovered and tunnelled through, my family attacked as they slept.'

'No,' Grizelda cried. 'I swear—'

'If I find out that was how the castle fell ..' Peregrine could not speak for the bitter rage that filled him.

Grizelda flung herself on her knees before him, grasping at his hand. 'Robin, I swear it's not true. I haven't betrayed you.

I'm sorry, I never thought that allowing Oskar to pee would endanger your family. I'm sure it has nothing to do with it!'

Peregrine frowned down at her, then looked questioningly at Jack. His squire shrugged.

'I know you are angry and upset, but you must believe me, I had nothing to do with the attack on your parents. I risked my life to warn you!' Grizelda's voice rang with sincerity.

Peregrine stood up abruptly. 'Let's ride on. I feel we don't have much time left to us.'

'But don't you believe me?' she begged.

'I don't know what to believe,' he answered wearily.

They rode on through the forest, following the long green tunnel that was all that was left of the old road. It led them down, down, down, through the slanting lines of sunlight that flickered over Peregrine's face. Flicker, flicker, flicker. He felt his head jerk forward, a spasm in his throat. He could not breathe. He cried out involuntarily, and then the world spun. He fell.

Dizzy, winded, he lay on the ground. Sable's velvet-soft nose nudged him questioningly. He heard Jack's boots hit the ground and run towards him.

'What kind of prince is he, if all he can do is fall off his horse?' Grizelda cried angrily.

Jack knelt beside him, cradling his head. 'The best of all princes! The kindest, the bravest . . .' He bent over Peregrine. 'It's all right, sir. You're just tired. You haven't eaten. Didn't I promise the king you'd eat? And I should've made sure you had your harness on. Are you hurt? Where does it hurt? Come on, let's make camp. You need to rest and have your medicine.'

Peregrine closed his eyes and did not answer.

CHAPTER 14

Into the Bog

As soon as it was dusk, Jack woke Peregrine and Grizelda so that they could ride on.

Peregrine refused to wear the harness, no matter how much Jack begged him. 'I will not fall again,' he said through his teeth. Jack could do nothing but hope he was right.

They trotted as fast as they dared through the forest, following the faint glimmer of the river under a night of bright stars. His prince had said, with a wry smile, that the river would lead them straight to the marshes of Ardian.

'To think that I complained at being made to learn the course of every river in Ziva,' Peregrine said. 'If I could, I'd shake Sir Medwin by the hand and thank him from the bottom of my heart.' The words made him feel terrible sorrow, remembering the way his tutor and all his bodyguards had died, and he sank into melancholy.

Searching for somewhere to hide in the grey light before dawn, they found a blackened and scorched ruin in which lay the charred skeletons of more than a dozen people, some no larger than children. Peregrine was so overcome with grief and anger that Jack feared he would suffer an attack of the falling sickness again. The prince galloped on, however, his face pale and set, with no sign of the dizziness that normally accompanied an attack.

Grizelda was pale, too, and unusually silent. She did not complain when Peregrine pushed on, even though the sun was rising and the smoke was beginning to uncurl from the chimneys of the cottages nearby. She did not even complain when Jack made her tuck all her hair up inside the hood of her cloak.

All she said was, 'I cannot help it if my hair shines, Jack. Do you think I am blonde on purpose?'

'Just keep your hood up,' Jack responded.

Several times over the course of that day, spearheads of sisika birds flew low overhead. Each time, Jack drew the two horses in under the cover of a tree, keeping a close grip on Argent's bridle so that she would not neigh and draw attention to them. Grizelda made no protest, nor any attempt to signal the starkin soldiers. She just watched them fly over, her face expressionless. At last they found refuge in a ruined barn, its walls blackened with fire, and then rode on again after a few hours' sleep.

Twilight darkened into night. It was so still and quiet, Peregrine could hear clearly the soft sound of the horses' hooves clopping. He felt an unbearable tension, sure they were still being followed. He dismounted and swaddled Sable's hooves with cloth, and made Grizelda and Jack do the same. Blitz crouched on his perch, shifting from foot to foot. It had been days since he had last been unhooded and let fly, and he was restive and unhappy and tired of old, bloodless meat. Mounting again, Peregrine stroked his falcon's back and tucked Blitz under his cloak, close to his heart, comforting him.

When dawn came, the world was swathed in mist. Peregrine did not search for shelter but rode on, listening for hoof beats behind him. Far away a sisika bird screeched. Peregrine's stomach lurched.

'Let's hurry,' he ordered.

'But the fog . . . we cannot see where we're going,' Grizelda protested.

'Follow the path!' Peregrine spurred Sable forward, letting him have his head; Jack and Grizelda followed close behind.

By midmorning, the mist had burnt away and they saw the fenlands unrolling before them. The sky seemed huge above them, the land so flat the horizon seemed to curve slightly. As far as Peregrine could see were patches of murky water, fringed by thick beds of rushes and sedges that rustled constantly in the wind. Occasionally willows dangled their bare branches down to the water, or there was a low hill where a few disconsolate-looking trees stood, rattling their twigs.

To the right was a spread of velvety green moss, the only colour in all the grey and dun landscape. There was little snow on the ground, though frost rimed the edges of the water that lapped sluggishly at the reedy banks.

'Now what do we do?' Grizelda said.

'I'll call someone to come and guide us through,' Peregrine said. He dismounted, leaving Sable to graze, and sat down cross-legged at the water's edge. He listened, glad to hear birdsong again for the first time in days. After a while, Peregrine drew out his flute and began to play a haunting tune, weaving into it all the sounds of the marshes—the wind in the rushes, the slow lap of the water, the monotonous *zrip, zrip, zrip* of the little birds in the reeds.

Swallowtail butterflies came and danced around Peregrine's head. An otter crept from the water and lay on its belly, listening intently. A group of mice sat by the prince's foot, swaying slightly to the music, while a water rat swam close, beady eyes fixed on his face. Two tiny birds fluttered down and perched on his knees. Grizelda drew in her breath in wonder.

From somewhere deep in the marshes came a strange, deep sound, like an ox lowing. Grizelda gave a startled cry, which sent the birds flying up and the mice scurrying away. Peregrine glanced at her quellingly and mimicked the sound. It came again, closer, and once again Peregrine answered.

The rushes parted and a man stepped out. He was skinny and long-limbed, dressed in mud-coloured clothes with a broad-brimmed hat of plaited rushes on his head. He wore a cape of some thin, sleek leather pinned at one shoulder with an unusual wooden brooch, cunningly carved in the shape of a long-beaked bird.

'Who is it who calls?' he asked in a low voice, looking suspiciously up and down the edge of the marshes.

'I am Prince Peregrine of the Stormlinn,' Peregrine replied. 'Will you please take us to Lord Percival?'

The man stared at them in surprise. 'Jumping Jimjinny! Are you tomfooling me?' He pushed back his hat to scratch his bushy grey hair.

A drumming sound came from behind them. Sable lifted his head and whickered softly. Peregrine glanced back and saw the grey hunter galloping towards them, his two great hounds loping at his heels. Behind him ran a whole battalion of soldiers, halberds thrust out.

'This is no trick! Please, we need to go now!' Peregrine unhooded Blitz and flung him up into the air, and the falcon soared high, uttering his sharp call. One of the soldiers fired an arrow at him, but Blitz wheeled and soared away over the marshes.

The man beckoned them urgently. 'Quick, now! You'll have to leave the horses, we can't take them in the marsh.'

Peregrine stared at him in consternation, then looked at his stallion with agony in his heart. 'Sable! I'll come back for you, I promise!'

'I'm not leaving Argent!' Grizelda cried.

'Then don't. Stay here and say hello to your brother's soldiers,' Jack said, slipping down from Snapdragon's back and giving his horse a loving farewell pat. The drumming of hooves came closer and closer.

'Halt!' the hunter commanded. 'In the name of Queen Vernisha, I order you to halt!'

'Quick! This way!' The man slithered back through the rushes. Peregrine was a few steps behind him. Jack swung his pack on his back and hurried after them. There were a few rough tufts of grass, making a kind of path through the rushes. Jack's foot slipped to the side and splashed into the water. It was icy cold.

'Come on!' Peregrine shouted, looking over his shoulder. Jack glanced backwards. Grizelda was hesitating, gazing at the galloping hunter and the phalanx of soldiers running full tilt towards them.

'Halt!' the hunter called again and raised high his bow, an arrow notched to his string.

'Grizelda, we cannot stay,' Peregrine said. 'Come with us now, else we must leave you.'

The hunter let loose an arrow. Jack ducked and the arrow sang over his head and straight through the fen-man's hat, knocking it off his head. 'Jumping Jimjinny!' The fen-man dove forward and out of sight. Jack leapt after him, seizing Peregrine's arm and dragging him away.

'Grizelda!' he cried.

'Good riddance to bad rubbish,' Jack said and propelled Peregrine forward. He heard another arrow being released and knocked Peregrine to the ground. The arrow whined over-head and clattered into the rushes. Together Jack and Peregrine crawled forward, seeing the fen-man beckon to them from a thicket of birches, their thin white trunks and bare branches shivering in the wind.

Grizelda dropped Argent's reins and ran to join them, slipping in the mud and falling. She scrambled to her feet and ran on, leaping from tuft to tuft, smashing aside the reeds with her hands. Oskar followed close at her heels, his tail between his legs, his ears raised anxiously.

Sable whinnied shrilly and kicked up his heels, galloping away as the hunter reached the edge of the water. The hunter did not pause but whipped his horse on. His grey gelding reared, whinnying in distress, but cruelly he forced it on, over the stretch of verdant moss and straight towards the small islet where Peregrine and Jack crouched in the long yellowish grasses. Jack's heart was hammering so hard he felt it would break free of the cage of his ribs. He kept one arm about Peregrine's back, trying to guard him as they slithered to where the fen-man crouched. He was watching the hunter with an oddly smug expression on his face.

'Bog'll get him,' he said.

Jack looked back. The hunter's gelding took only a stride or two before it began to sink rapidly. Within seconds it was up to its withers in black mud. It screamed in terror and struggled, but only plunged deeper into the bog. The rider cursed aloud and dragged one leg free. On the bank, his two great sleuth hounds whined and ran back and forth. The hunter managed, with a wrench, to drag his other leg free with a dreadful sucking sound. He knelt on his horse's saddle and leapt for the bank. The motion pushed his horse deeper into the bog. Only its head, its eyes rolling in terror, was still lifted above the bog. It took a few more agonising seconds for it to be sucked under.

The hunter, meanwhile, landed near the bank, his torso flat on the surface of the bog, his legs trailing behind him. He grasped frantically at the reeds, which snapped in his hands. Again and again he grasped, kicking furiously with his legs and hauling the broken reeds to his chest to give him some purchase. At last he was able to crawl out onto solid ground, caked in mud to his ears.

The fen-man slithered away through the rushes, following a faint, crooked path. More patches of velvety moss spread out on either side, edged with sedges and reeds and stretches of frost-rimed water. Jack and Peregrine crept after him on their hands and knees, their noses filled with the stench of rotting plants. Grizelda followed, her dress black with mud. She was gasping with tears. 'Poor horse,' she whispered. 'That poor, poor horse.'

'Shhh,' the fen-man hissed.

The path twisted and meandered, taking them back towards the bank. They all crept as slowly and carefully as they could, trying to copy the fen-man who moved so slowly and quietly that not a reed rustled.

They could hear the hunter cursing. Jack opened his eyes wide and grinned at Peregrine. He had never heard such imprecations.

Quietly the fen-man crept forward, and the three companions followed. Soon their whole bodies were plastered in mud, their limbs trembling with the cold and the strain.

'That was close,' Jack whispered, once the voices of the soldiers had dropped behind. 'I had not realised the hunter was so hard on our heels.'

'I knew,' Peregrine said. 'I felt him. I thought he would come when I called.'

'You called him?' Jack was incredulous.

'Not on purpose,' Peregrine protested. 'I don't know yet how to call only one thing or person. Aunty Briony is always telling me I need to learn control, but the lessons are so boring! You just sit there and try to think of only one thing at a time, and I can never do it.'

'But wasn't it rather a risk?' Grizelda said shakily.

'Well, yes,' Peregrine said, 'but so was sitting there on the bank waiting for someone to notice us!'

'Shhh,' the fen-man hissed again and they fell silent once more.

The path wound on, and at last led them to another tiny islet, crowned with birches. A long, flat-bottomed boat was pushed in among the reeds. The fen-man lay quietly for a long time, watching the sky and the shore. When he was satisfied they were unobserved, he wriggled into the punt and beckoned the others to follow. Jack did so gratefully. He was damp and cold and weary to his very bones, and one look at Peregrine's white face showed him his prince was even worse for wear.

An oddly shaped basket woven of rushes lay on the bottom of the punt, filled with sluggishly roiling eels. Jack was careful to keep away from them, sure they must bite. Grizelda made a face of disgust and clapped her hand over her mouth. 'They stink!' she said.

'So do you,' Jack retorted.

She cast a rueful glance down at her filthy, bedraggled clothes and then shrugged. 'What I wouldn't give for a bath!'

'Why did you come with us?' he demanded. 'You could be back at your luxurious castle right now, having a bath and a decent meal!'

She bit her lip. 'I don't know,' she said after a while. 'I guess I wanted to see it all through.'

Jack nodded in grudging respect and sat down, drawing the hood of his cloak over his face to shield his eyes from the sun, slipping towards the horizon.

CHAPTER 15

The Marsh King

Hours passed. Peregrine swayed in and out of sleep, the insistent whining of innumerable tiny midges in his ears keeping him from a deeper repose. Every few seconds came the sound of a slap, or a moan of irritation.

Occasionally a long stretch of water would open up on one side or another, but their guide kept close to the shelter of the reeds, crouching in the prow and poling the boat forward.

'Where are we going?' Peregrine asked, and some time later, 'Are we almost there?'

'Shhh,' was the only answer.

Then came the deep, booming cry that had so startled them earlier. Their guide sat up straight and blew on a wooden whistle that hung on a leather thong about his neck. The same eerie sound thundered out, so that Grizelda jerked and shrank down, hands over her ears.

'A-ha,' Peregrine murmured. 'I wondered if that was it.'

'What?' Jack whispered.

'The secret signal,' Peregrine whispered back.

'Shhh!' their guide hissed.

The punt slid out of the rushes and onto the hazy waters of a lake. An island floated ahead, wreathed in mist. Willows trailed their bare branches in the water, and Peregrine recognised the shape of chestnut trees, and the tall spires of poplars. The top of a round grey tower could be seen above the brown tracery of branches, and he could smell the tang of smoke in the air.

Above the island was an extraordinary panorama of clouds, mounting high into the sky in soft billows, blazing orange and gold with shadows of the most intense blue. Over the fenlands, the moon was hoisting itself above the horizon, the fattest, fullest, reddest moon Peregrine had ever seen. It looked bloated on blood, and a profound shudder ran all through him.

He gazed up at it, hardly able to breathe. It seemed the worst kind of omen. A golden pathway led to it across the water, glittering and scintillating. Peregrine felt a familiar brightness and clarity come over him, and the smell of rain on roses. 'No,' he whispered. He tried to steady his breath, clenching his fists. The colours in the water whirled and drew together. He saw a woman looking up at him from the water's surface. Her curly hair was streaked with grey, her eyes were black and fathomless. She was weeping. He stared down at her and saw she clutched a long knife in one hand. Blood dripped from her other palm. Her eyes widened as she recognised him. *Peregrine, where are you?* she called. He could barely hear her.

I go in search of the Storm King's spear, he answered silently and lifted one hand to point to the island drifting closer and closer.

Where? the Erlrune cried. *Where are you?*

'Where are we?' Peregrine whispered.

'That's the Isle of Eels,' their guide answered in a soft, reverent voice. 'That's where our king be.'

Peregrine could not speak. He gazed down at the Erlrune's face and saw her nod and raise her hand in a gesture of blessing and farewell. Then the vision blurred and dissolved away. Peregrine clenched his fists on the side of the boat, holding himself steady as the water and sky swung wildly around him. He tasted blood as he bit his tongue. For a moment he heard nothing, saw nothing, knew nothing. Then the whirl of colour steadied. He bent his head down onto his knees.

'Are you all right?' Jack asked, leaning forward.

Peregrine nodded, trying to calm his breathing.

'You're tired,' Jack said. 'We haven't slept properly in hours. You'll be fine once you've slept.'

'Yes,' Peregrine said.

'I'm looking forward to thawing out by a fire,' Grizelda said, sitting up. 'I'm completely frozen! My feet are like blocks of ice.'

'I'm starving,' Jack said. 'Let's hope they'll give us some grub!'

'There'll be eel stew,' their guide said, patting his basket of writhing eels. 'We'll just toss these beauties in a pot of water with some salt, and we'll be a-gobbling them down in no time.'

'Delicious,' Grizelda replied.

'Mighty good,' the fen-man agreed, not understanding she was being sarcastic.

Gradually Peregrine returned to himself. His temples pounded and he felt a little sick, but no-one had noticed and that made him feel better. He gazed up at the darkening sky. The moon was shrinking and fading as it rose. Outside it had been eerily quiet. Inside all was noise and activity. By the light of lanterns strung overhead, men chopped wood. Peregrine was comforted that the Erlrune knew where he was and what he was doing.

He could see no sign of Blitz's distinctive sickle-shaped wings outlined against the clouds. He pulled out his flute and blew his falcon's call note. Far away he heard a responding cry and put his flute away, smiling.

As the punt approached the island, they heard the deep, eerie boom of the secret signal ring out, and their guide at once responded, blowing on his own whistle. He poled the punt up to a muddy beach and leapt out. A few men came down to help him pull the punt up higher. Like the fen-man, they wore plain, rough clothes of brown and grey wool, with eelskin capes pinned at their shoulders with a carved wooden brooch. With their shaggy hair, bristling beards and broad shoulders, they all looked exactly alike, all except for their fen-man who was as skinny as a rake.

Peregrine was so stiff and weary he could hardly walk, but he made his bow and said, 'Thank you, sir, for your timely assistance. If you would be so kind as to take us to Lord Percival?'

'Liah's eyes, Fred, who's this babbling babe?' one of the men said.

'Says he be the prince, Ged,' the fen-man responded laconically. 'Had starkin scum on his tail, orright.'

The man's heavy eyebrows shot up. 'Prince, he say? Leeblimey!'

Jack stood at Peregrine's side, his hand close to the hilt of his sword. Peregrine shook his head slightly and Jack reluctantly fell back. Grizelda had drawn the cloak about her, its hood hiding her fair hair, and kept her hand on Oskar's head, keeping him still.

'Don't look much like a prince,' another man said, looking Peregrine over.

Peregrine straightened his back, lifted his chin, fixed the men with a proud glance and held out his right arm. Blitz came hurtling down and landed on his wrist with a thump.

The men all stared, speechless.

'I can assure you I am truly Prince Peregrine, son of King Merrik and heir to the Stormlinn,' he said. He lifted Blitz so they all might see the peregrine falcon, which only princes of royal blood were permitted to carry. 'Will you take me to your lord now, or must we remind you of the penalties of defying the expressed command of the prince royal?'

'Leeblimey,' one of the men breathed.

'Liah's legs!'

'Best take him to the king, eh, Fred?'

'Reckon so.' The fen-man they had met first pushed his hat to the back of his head and led the way up a rough track through willow trees. Small round boats, made of hide stretched over a lattice of willow twigs, were hidden here and there in the tangled undergrowth.

An old castle towered above the trees, built on the very peak of the hill. It was small and dour-looking, with two tall round towers springing from heavy battlements. A flag fluttered bravely from a flagpole. Peregrine did not recognise the ensign, which looked like a grey bird crouched among grey rushes on a grey background.

The path wound up through the trees and came out in the midst of a small village which had, at some time in the past, been attacked and nearly burnt to the ground. There was nothing left of the houses but blackened foundation stones and a few scorched walls. Peregrine noticed the marks of swords and axes in the walls and doorframes.

The men did not linger in the desolate scene, but hurried up the hill to the castle. Peregrine, Jack and Grizelda followed wearily, Oskar trotting behind.

The only entrance to the castle was a heavy oak doorway. Two men stood guard outside, helmets of boiled leather pulled down over their faces, halberds of shining steel in their hands. At the sight of the small procession, one stepped forward, his halberd thrust out.

'What's all this then?'

'Hey, Hal. This kid reckons he's the prince,' Fred said, jerking a skinny thumb at Peregrine. 'Reckon he oughter see Percy.'

'Leeblimcy! How'd he get here?'

'Knows the bittern call,' Fred replied. 'Liah knows how.'

Hal gazed at Peregrine thoughtfully, scratching his bristly beard. 'Orright, better take him in then. Hey! Better give me your bow and all those arrows. No weapons allowed.'

Peregrine stilled, his hand on his quiver of arrows. 'We mean Lord Percival no harm.'

The men all roared with laughter, slapping their thighs and bending over. 'Harm! The stripling thinks he could be a-harming our Percy!' One wiped tears from his eyes.

'I'm sorry, but we cannot surrender our weapons without some undertaking from Lord Percival that we shall have safe passage.' Peregrine stood firm, locking his knees so no-one could tell how they trembled.

'Liah's eyes, don't he talk pretty! Mebbe he do be a prince.'

'I am indeed a prince and your liege-lord,' Peregrine replied. 'Am I mistaken in my belief that the people of the fenlands have sworn fealty to my father, King Merrik, and promised to uphold his rule? For I promise you he shall forgive no transgressions against our person!'

'Leeblimey! Those are mighty big words from a mighty little fellow . . .' one began, but the man with the halberd held up his hand. At once all the men fell silent.

'No harm meant,' he said. 'You keep your bow but I warn you, prince or no prince, we'll kill you if you do aught to harm our king.'

'He is no king,' Peregrine said, holding the man's gaze. 'My father is the only true king and I bid you remember it.'

After a moment, the man inclined his head. 'Orright then. Lord Percy is what I mean.'

Peregrine nodded and, holding Blitz high, walked through the oaken door the man flung open and into the outer bailey.

It was a very different scene inside the high stone walls. Outside it had been eerily quiet. Inside all was noise and activity. Men chopped wood, or mended old boots, or cleaned out pigsties. Women were taking in washing that had been spread over rosemary bushes, or ground chestnuts in heavy stone mortars, or wove baskets out of rushes. Children played here and there, dressed in dirty smocks, their bare legs muddy to above their knees. An older boy was fishing in a round pool with a long-pronged fork, impaling wriggling eels. Another was hard at work whittling ash boughs into long staves. A girl about the same age as Grizelda was feeding a flock of white geese, which hissed at the sight of the intruders, their white, snaky necks darting forward indignantly.

As the small procession made its way through the crowded courtyard, everyone stopped and stared. The men laid down their tools and jostled close, whispering, 'What's all this then? Who's the dandyprat?'

Small houses of mud bricks had been built inside the shelter of the walls and thatched with reeds. Instead of glass, their windows were protected by carved wooden shutters, now open to let warm light shine through the cracks. Smoke trickled from their chimneys.

Another heavy oaken door was the only entrance to the castle itself. It was propped open with a boulder. A mob of children ran out, pots on their heads and wooden swords in their hands. They came to a sudden halt at the sight of the strangers, gawping at the falcon on Peregrine's wrist. Oskar growled menacingly, and Grizelda put her hand on his head.

Peregrine walked slowly and proudly through the archway and into the inner bailey. The ground here was cobbled, with archways all along one wall leading into stables and workrooms. Another wooden door at the far end of the courtyard stood ajar, allowing a glimpse of a garden. The castle loomed above, its only windows narrow arrow slits. A flight of steep stone stairs led up to the front door, which was reinforced with heavy iron bands.

A thickset man with a grizzled beard sat on a wooden block outside a long, low building of grey stone, a halberd leaning against the wall, his helmet of boiled leather at his feet. He was playing conkers with a grubby little urchin with tousled curls. At the sight of the newcomers, he dropped his conkers, grabbed his halberd and jumped to his feet, staring at Peregrine.

Once again there was low discussion and argument. By now there were about a dozen men in the procession, all of whom had something to say. Peregrine did not speak, just stood as straight as he was able, looking around him with interest. Jack and Grizelda stood close beside him, the starkin girl keeping the hood of her cloak shadowing her face.

The low stone building had two entrances, both framed by a giant horseshoe-shaped arch of curved bricks. In one, a green-painted door stood open, pots of herbs clustered close on either side. The other framed the village smithy, where sudden sprays of sparks illuminated the gloom. The ring of metal on metal came clearly over the sound of hens cackling, children playing and women gossiping.

'What! He's a-claiming he's the prince? The wildkin one?' The man who had been guarding the smithy stared thoughtfully at Peregrine, frowned, and went inside the smithy. All the men outside shifted uneasily from foot to foot, eyeing the travellers askance. Jack stared back at them belligerently, his hands on his belt. Grizelda kept her hand on Oskar's collar. The hound was growling deep in his throat.

The ringing sound stopped. An immense giant of a man appeared in the archway, bending his neck to avoid banging his head on the stone.

He had thick curly black hair and eyes like black coals under bushy, angry-looking eyebrows. His black beard bristled all the way down to his waist, and was tied up with a piece of ancient leather, presumably to stop it catching fire. What little could be seen of his face was as brown and weathered as ox hide, and he carried an enormous hammer in one enormous hand. His leather apron was pitted with small scars from burning sparks, and Peregrine noticed many similar scars all over his hairy forearms and hands. His frowning gaze travelled over them all and came to rest on Peregrine, standing straight-backed and proud in his dishevelled, muddy clothes, the falcon perched on his wrist.

'Your Highness, welcome to my home,' the Marsh King said and knelt in the mud, his head bent low.

CHAPTER 16

The Marsh King's Daughter

'THANK YOU, MY LORD,' PEREGRINE REPLIED, TRYING TO HIDE the rush of relief the blacksmith's words gave him.

'You look as if you've been a-travelling hard,' the Marsh King said, getting ponderously to his feet. Peregrine had to raise his chin sharply to look up into his face, else he would have been staring at the blacksmith's beard. 'Won't you come on in and have a sup of something with us?'

'We would be most grateful for some refreshments,' Peregrine said.

'My lassie will whip something up for you, quick smart,' the Marsh King said. 'Come through here.' He strode through the other horseshoe-shaped door and Peregrine followed him, hoping his legs would hold out until he found somewhere to sit down. His arm quivered under the strain of holding Blitz aloft. Jack and Grizelda followed, the crowd of big, bristly-bearded men pushing and shoving to get in after them, their hobnailed boots making a great clatter on the doorstep.

Within was a long, low room, its walls whitewashed, with a door at the far end. A fire smouldered on the floor at the other end, the wall behind it stained black. There were various pieces of beautifully carved and painted wooden furniture, softened with cushions and rugs of otter fur. Along one wall stood a tall dresser crowded with jars of preserved fruit, pickled onions, jellied eels and potted shrimps. Bunches of dried herbs and smoked fish were strung above the fire, and the dirt floor was brushed clean, hard and smooth as stone.

A tiny old woman sat napping in a wheeled chair by the fire, a marmalade cat asleep on her lap. Beside her sat a thin girl, quietly spinning. She looked up in surprise as her father led the trio of weary travellers inside.

'Ma, Molly!' her father roared. 'We have guests! They're cold and hungry. What's t'eat?'

The old woman in the chair woke with a jerk. She put up one hand to straighten her lace cap, saying loudly, 'Holy mackerel! Percykins, my lamb, must you make such a racket?'

'Sorry, Ma,' he said contritely.

'Have you washed your hands and wiped your feet?'

'No, Ma,' he replied.

'Then out you go, quicksticks! All of you!'

The Marsh King obediently turned to go, shepherding Peregrine, Grizelda and Jack before him. The twelve big, black-bearded men hastily fell over themselves to get out too, and stood by while they all washed their hands and faces at the pump outside, wiped their feet carefully and trooped back inside.

'There you are, right as rain,' the old woman said, beaming. 'Muddy as a duck puddle, you boys get, a-romping and a-rumbling out there. Come on in! Where's your hanky, Percykins? You're dripping water on my nice, clean mud floor.'

'Sorry, Ma,' the blacksmith said and pulled out a handkerchief the size of a pillowslip, mopping his face with it.

'That's all fine and dandy then. Mustn't forget your manners! Did I hear you a-saying you was hungry? Holy mackerel, the lot of you? Percykins, you know I don't mind you bringing your wee friends home for a bite of supper, but a woman needs a bit more warning! We haven't enough bowls for you all!'

The blacksmith looked around in surprise and saw the men crowding in the doorway, looking rather sheepish. 'Not you lot!' he roared. 'Go on, out you go! Hal and Hank, go close the gate! Fred and Frank, go mind my fire! Bill and Bob, go ring the bell! Will and Wat, go draw some water! Gus and Ged, go stand guard! Ty and Ted, climb the tower! And look sharp about it!'

Grumbling, the dozen men all clumped away, leaving the long room strangely peaceful and quiet.

'Sorry, Ma,' the blacksmith said. 'I sent those louts away. It's only these lot left.'

The old woman rolled her chair forward. It was an odd contraption, rather like a rocking chair but on wheels instead of rockers. Peregrine could tell her legs were thin and wasted under her luxurious otter-skin lap rug. She had a face like an uncracked walnut, with two beady black eyes and sparse white hair that curled under her cap, rich with lace and ribbons. She peered short-sightedly at Peregrine, who bowed to her politely. 'Holy mackerel! What a poor, dwizzen-faced young fellow! He looks like something the cat'd cough up! Where did you drag him in from?'

'He's the prince, Ma,' the blacksmith said gently. 'He's fair tuckered out, poor lad. Have we got aught for him t'eat?'

'I've got some soup all ready, Da,' the thin girl replied. One hand groped for a wooden crutch, which she hitched under her left shoulder before struggling to her feet. She limped forward eagerly, her crutch swinging.

Peregrine started forward, his bright eyes moving swiftly from the crutch to her thin shoulders, one hitched up because of the crutch under her arm, and then to her face. She was a skinny, freckle-faced girl, with a long plait of brown hair and green-brown eyes. She looked surprised at his close scrutiny, and her thin face turned rosy. Peregrine began to say something, then checked himself.

'That sounds wonderful, my lady,' he said instead. 'We are indeed hungry. May I introduce myself? I am Prince Peregrine of the Stormlinn and my companions are my squire, Jack, and . . .' He hesitated, looking towards Grizelda.

She drew herself up proudly and put back her hood, so the firelight gleamed on her blonde hair.

'I am Lady Grizelda ziv Zadira,' she said in her most aristocratic voice.

'From Zavaria?' the Marsh King roared.

'Holy mackerel!' the old lady exclaimed.

'A starkin lady,' the girl said, her voice sharp with surprise.

'She is our faithful subject and our ally,' Peregrine said sternly. 'I bid you treat her with respect.'

'Of course,' Molly said, limping forward. 'May I take your cloak, my lady?'

Grizelda let it fall from her shoulder and Molly caught it and hung it from a hook, beautifully carved in the shape of a bird with an open beak. The Marsh King glowered at Grizelda, his eyes almost hidden by his bushy brows.

'Please forgive us our intrusion,' Peregrine said, leaning unobtrusively on the back of a chair and wishing someone would ask him to sit down.

Molly gazed at him in wonder. 'Please, your Highness, it is no intrusion. You are more than welcome.' Her voice was sweet and light and rather childlike. Peregrine wondered how old she was. She smiled at him and he smiled back.

Grizelda tottered forward, one hand to her forehead. 'I am weary unto death,' she whispered. 'My lord, I feel faint!'

Peregrine turned and caught her as she slumped. 'Jack, quick,' he said. 'Help me. She weighs a ton!'

Grizelda's brows contracted sharply at his words but she did not open her eyes. Together the boys half-carried her to one of the chairs by the fire, a deep curved affair with a rushwork seat, its timber back softened with a patchwork cushion. Grizelda swooned into it, her hand still at her brow. 'So cold,' she whispered.

'Let me build up the fire,' Molly said and limped across to a stacked pile of peat in one corner.

'Here, let me help you.' Jack moved swiftly to assist Molly in piling more of the peat turves upon the fire.

'What's wrong with the girlie then?' the old woman said loudly. 'She got a bit of wind? Dose her with some cod liver oil!'

A pained expression passed over Grizelda's face but she still did not open her eyes. Peregrine swayed slightly and put out one hand to grip the back of the chair again.

'Here, your Highness, sit down. You must be a-weary too,' the Marsh King said gruffly. 'Molly, put the kettle on!'

Peregrine held his fist to the back of the chair and Blitz stepped daintily off. Peregrine shook his aching arm and sat down gratefully. He swiftly removed the falcon's hood, digging out a small morsel of raw meat from his leather pouch. Blitz accepted it eagerly, looking around him with bright, inquisitive eyes. The dog whined and Peregrine offered him a gobbet. Oskar did not take it, his lip lifting as he turned his head away.

'What a beautiful bird,' Molly said, coming back with a kettle she had filled from a wooden bucket in the corner. She clearly found it hard to carry the heavy kettle with her crutch, so Jack hurried to help her.

'His name is Blitz,' Peregrine said. 'I've had him from just a fledgling and trained him myself.' He stowed the leather hood away carefully in its pouch and sat down thankfully, holding his numb hands to the blaze.

'What sort of bird is he?' she asked, showing Jack where to hang the kettle from a hook suspended from the ceiling.

'He's a peregrine falcon. They're the fastest birds in the world.'

'You share a name!' Her smile lit up her narrow face and brightened her eyes to a vivid green-gold.

'Yes, that's why my father gave him to me.' Peregrine was about to go on and tell her some of the funny stories of Blitz as a chick, when Grizelda said in a faint voice, 'My boots are wet through and my feet are like ice. Will you not remove them for me . . . what was your name?'

'Molly,' she replied and limped over to Grizelda. She knelt with some difficulty, wincing in pain, then carefully drew off the sodden boots, so filthy they seemed black instead of red.

'They will need to be brushed,' Grizelda ordered, stretching her stockinged feet to the fire.

Orange flames were beginning to lick up the turves, spreading warmth and smoke into the room. By its sombre light, Peregrine could see the spinning-wheel had been most beautifully carved with a design of oak leaves. More carvings decorated the edge of the dresser, and on the wall hung a beautiful tapestry that showed the Isle of Eels floating in a blue mist, clouds above and water below. All sorts of birds and creatures crept and clung and flew about the edges.

'Yes, my lady,' Molly said. 'Da, could you throw me a towel?'

Her father was sitting on a stool nearby, jabbing at the fire with an ornate poker, a scowl on his face. Peregrine could not tell if this was his habitual expression or whether he was angry about something. The Marsh King reached up one brawny arm and swiped a linen towel from a hook behind the wash basin. He tossed it at Molly who used it to carefully dry Grizelda's feet, then tried to swab away the mud on the hem of her dress.

'It's no use doing that!' Grizelda cried. 'It will have to be washed. I should like a bath too. That is, if you have one.'

'We do,' Molly said quietly, struggling to her feet and limping across to drop the soiled towel in a wash basket. 'I'll ask the men to heat some water for you.' She put her head out the door and issued a soft request, and immediately there was the sound of hobnails on cobbles and a great clattering of buckets.

'Who's that toffee-nosed prig a-ordering our Molly around like she were some sort of slave?' the old lady asked indignantly. 'Don't she know she's the Marsh King's daughter?'

'Shhh, Nan, it's all right,' Molly said as she came back inside. 'The poor lady is all worn out, and not used to our ways. Don't fuss now.'

'Eh, bless your sweet eyes, my moppet,' the old lady said, dabbing at her own eyes with a tiny lace-edged handkerchief.

'You listen to your old nan now and tell that uppity young miss to wipe her own toes, else it'll be something else she'll be asking you to wipe all too soon, mark my words!'

At that, Grizelda sat up abruptly, saying, 'How dare you!'

But Jack and Peregrine both laughed, and Jack cried, 'If she hasn't got you nailed in the first five minutes!'

'I best warn you, young lady, that we're all free men here, who do our level best to treat all men and women the same, regardless of how rich or how poor they be,' the Marsh King said sternly. 'We'll have none of your fancy starkin ways in my house, thank you very much, else you'll be tossed out on your backside. Got it?'

'I'm sure I have no idea what you mean,' Grizelda said, and turned her attention to smoothing down her crumpled dress.

Molly bit back a smile but said shyly to Grizelda, 'It'll take some time to boil the water. Would you like something t'eat first?'

'Yes, please,' Jack put in. 'I'm fair famished!'

'I would indeed,' Grizelda said haughtily, giving the old woman a scorching glance.

'I'm sorry, it won't be very fine. Just what Da and I and Nan would usually eat,' Molly said.

'We've grown rather used to rough fare over the past week,' Grizelda said in a bored tone. 'Comets and stars, what I wouldn't give for a sliver of roast venison and some sugared figs.'

'I'm afraid all we have is eel stew,' Molly said apologetically. Grizelda sighed.

'I'm sure it'll be delicious,' Peregrine said, and Jack concurred heartily, casting a look of undisguised dislike at the starkin girl. The blacksmith had much the same expression on his face. Peregrine sighed to himself. He wished Grizelda would think before she spoke. He wondered what had caused her to behave like this, when she must surely know she should be careful. They were at the mercy of the Marsh King, who ruled the fenlands now the Count of Ardian had been overthrown. No-one came in or went out of the fenlands without Lord Percival's approval. He regarded her closely, thinking to himself, *I do not believe she's stupid* . . .

She sensed his gaze and threw him an angry look.

I do believe she's frightened, Peregrine thought and frowned a little. *But why?*

CHAPTER 17

Eel Stew

MOLLY LIMPED ABOUT, SPREADING THE TABLE WITH A SNOWY white cloth and setting it with round pewter spoons. From a shelf she lifted down two slender iron candlesticks, cunningly forged to look like stylised birds, and put them in the centre of the table. From another shelf she took a vase with a bunch of red berries, dried twigs and delicate hellebore flowers, which Peregrine's mother always called the winter rose as it flowered in the dead of the year.

'Pretty,' Peregrine said appreciatively and she flashed him a shy smile.

'It is so smoky in here, how can you stand it?' Grizelda complained, holding her bare hands to the fire. Her ring caught the low glare of the flames.

'Can't have a fire without smoke,' the blacksmith growled, poking the fire so violently black puffs of smoke belched up, stinging Peregrine's eyes.

'We are just so glad to be here in the warmth,' Peregrine said. 'We've slept rough the last week, and I swear I felt I would never be warm again.'

'But why?' Molly said. 'What are you doing here? Has something happened?'

'Let his Highness eat in peace,' the blacksmith said gruffly. 'We shall call a council meeting in an hour and his Highness can tell us then what ill wind has brought him to us.'

'I'm sorry,' Molly said contritely and began to ladle bowlfuls of a rich, brown, delicious-smelling stew. There were chunks of meat in it, strong tasting and rather rubbery, but they all ate greedily. It had been so long since they had eaten a hot meal. Molly had fresh baked bread as well, round and golden-brown, and some pickled green beans, and she brought out a black leather bottle filled with mead, the most delicious drink Peregrine had ever tasted. He complimented her on it and she flushed with pleasure, saying, 'I make it with honey from our own beehive. I'm glad you like it.'

'It tastes like summer,' Peregrine said, smiling and holding out his horn cup for more.

'I think so too,' Molly said. 'At this time of year, summer seems so far away. I just need to smell the mead and it makes me think of the orchard in summer, buzzing with bees and fragrant with flowers.'

'The stew's good too,' Jack said through a mouthful. 'I was so hungry! Can I have more?'

As Molly ladled out another generous helping, Oskar whined softly, looking hopefully at the pot.

'Quiet, boy,' Grizelda said. Immediately the dog stopped whining.

'Is he hungry?' Molly asked and half-rose, as if to fetch him some food.

'He will not eat from your hand,' Grizelda said disdainfully. She snapped her fingers at Oskar and at once he crept forward, tail wagging hopefully. She held up one hand and he sat at attention, and she took a lump of meat from her bowl and held it to his mouth. The dog's nostrils flared and he salivated, but he did not snatch the meat. Grizelda held it so close to his mouth he had to turn his head away to avoid it touching his lip. Then she said casually, 'Eat, boy,' and gratefully he took the lump of meat and swallowed it whole.

'Poor dog,' Molly said and went to the stove and ladled a generous serve of eel stew into a bowl. She put it down before him and said to Grizelda, 'Let him eat. We have plenty.'

Grizelda shrugged. 'Very well then. Eat, boy.'

The dog fell on the bowl as if he was starving.

The old lady had wheeled her chair to the table and was eating heartily. 'It's a wonder the dog doesn't bite her,' she said to Molly, in what she obviously thought was an undertone. 'I know I would!' Then she turned to the Marsh King, who was steadily shovelling down a truly extraordinary amount of food. 'Elbows off the table, Percykins! Wipe your mouth! Do try not to chew with your mouth open, dear.'

'Sorry, Ma,' the Marsh King answered, hastily removing his elbows.

'Lady Molly,' Peregrine began, but she blushed and said, 'Please, your Highness, just call me Molly.'

'If you will call me Robin,' he said, grinning.

She smiled but said, 'I'm sorry, sir, I don't know you well enough, and I'm sure your parents wouldn't approve.'

Peregrine sighed. 'Very well, then, *Lady Molly*, can you tell me . . . is there a blind boy here in this village?'

It was not a question she had been expecting. She stared in surprise, then answered, 'No, sir.'

He sighed in disappointment.

'Why, sir?'

'Oh, nothing. Just an old prophecy.'

Only when a blind boy can see and a lame girl walk on water shall peace come again to the land, and the rightful king win back the throne . . . Peregrine could not help being disappointed. As soon as he had seen Molly struggle to her feet with the help of the crutch, bright hope had flared in him. What if she was the lame girl of the prophecy? What if, somehow, she was fated to help his father win the throne?

A bell rang out and the Marsh King rose, cramming one last slice of bread into his mouth. 'The bell's a-calling us all to council. You eat and rest and when we're ready we'll send for you.'

He went out, bending his head automatically to avoid banging it on the low lintel.

'Don't you worry,' Molly said. 'Plenty of time to eat and rest, they'll be hours yet.'

Peregrine sopped up the last of his stew with the heel of his bread, something he would never have done at the castle, under the eyes of his mother and Queen Rozalina.

'That's my boy,' the old woman said affectionately. 'You're not so dwizzen-faced now, poor thing that you are.'

'Nan, why don't you go and sit by the fire and I'll bring you a posset?' Molly said. 'Lady Grizelda, the men will have filled the bath by now. I heard them go up the stairs with the buckets from the smithy. Would you like to go and wash?'

'Thank heavens!' Grizelda cried, rising to her feet. 'I do hope it's a hip-bath. Too much to hope for? Believe me, an old bucket will do!'

'Indeed it is a hip-bath, made by my father's own hands,' Molly said. 'Just up those stairs, my lady.'

Grizelda hurried out of the room, her dog raising his head and gazing after her anxiously, ears pricked. After a moment he laid his head on his paws again. Jack pushed his plate away with a sigh. 'That was just grand, my lady.'

'Oh, please, call me Molly,' she said. 'No-one calls my father lord except for his Highness.'

'Robin,' Peregrine said.

They both ignored him. 'Well, thanks then, Molly. Best meal I've had in days.' Standing up, Jack sketched her a brief bow, then asked, rather diffidently, 'May I have permission to go and look around outside? I'd like to make sure we haven't been followed.'

'My father will have men a-looking out, don't you worry,' she answered. 'But of course, feel free. I know you must feel responsible for his Highness's safety.'

Jack smiled in relief and nodded. Catching up his coat, he went out into the cold, grey night. Molly began to clear the dishes and Peregrine rather clumsily helped. Without a word she passed him a linen tea towel and began to wash up in the tub. Meanwhile, Blitz the falcon, Oskar the dog and the old lady all began to snore quietly.

'I was wondering if you could tell me what creature it is that makes that deep booming noise? The one that signals to your scouts that a friend is near?' Peregrine asked.

She glanced at him in surprise. 'How do you know about that?'

'It is how we gained access to the marshes,' he explained. 'I listened and mimicked all the noises that I heard, and when I made that noise, the fen-man came, and just in time too.'

Molly was silent for a moment, her hands stilling in the water. 'It is the call of the bittern. It frightens those who hear t, for it's so loud and strange. It's unbelievable that you should be a-mimicking it! It's a hard noise to make. I carve whistles for all the men to wear about their necks.'

Peregrine pulled out his long white flute. 'I can make any noise I want with this.' He lifted it to his lips but Molly reached out her hand to him.

'Oh, please don't! It's a warning signal! We'll have all the men of the town rushing upon us.'

'Hal and Hank, and Fred and Frank,' Peregrine said.

She laughed in delight. 'You have a good memory!'

Peregrine did not tell her he had been trained so. Instead he said, grinning, 'Bill and Bob, and Will and Wat, and . . . can I remember? Ged and Ted. But that's not right.'

'Almost,' she told him. 'We're not very imaginative with names here. Nothing like Peregrine!'

'Except for your father. Percival.' His voice rose at the end in a subtle interrogation.

Molly smiled and sighed. 'Yes. Poor Da. Nan was always determined he wouldn't be a run-of-the-mill Bill.'

'Is that why he rose up against the Count of Ardian? That can't have been easy.'

'It was, in fact. The old count was never here, and on the rare occasions when he did come back, to try to squeeze a bit more out of his tenants, he had no notion of any path through the marsh except the old causeway. All Da had to do was dismantle the causeway, take over the castle, set up the count's own mangonels against him and blow up the starkin's marsh-gas mines.'

'Easy,' Peregrine teased.

She smiled. 'It was a long time coming, believe me.'

He played a few sweet notes on his flute, mimicking the *zrip*, *zrip*, *zrip* of the little birds he had heard.

'Reed buntings,' she said. 'Amazing!'

Ping, ping, ping, he played.

'Bearded tits!'

Kekekekeke! He mimicked the high, shrill cry he had heard just before the hunter had galloped down upon them.

'A marsh harrier, calling the alarm,' she said.

'So what was the name of that other bird, the one that sounds like some immense and terrible monster?'

'A bittern.' She laughed. 'It's really a very shy bird. It keeps to itself, just like the men of the marshes. It's hard to spot, for its feathers are the same colour as the mud and the brown reeds. It has long legs, and can walk delicately over the tops of the marsh plants, leaving no trail. It hunts with great stealth, able to stand still for hours without moving, yet when attacked will fight to the death.'

'Is that why your father chose it as a symbol for his men?'

'How do you know this?' she asked, almost frightened. 'Is it your wildkin magic?'

'No. I just notice things. I was taught to notice things.' Peregrine leant forward and touched the brooch that pinned her shawl at her shoulder. Made of some hard, dark wood, it was carved in the shape of a long, thin bird with a long, thin beak, tucked down close to its breast.

'I carved it,' Molly said. 'I carve all the brooches for the men.'

'And the spinning-wheel and the dresser?' He waved his hand at the beautifully carved furniture.

'Yes. I like to make things pretty. And I can't go out much, not like the other children.' She jerked her crutch.

'The brooch is beautiful. What kind of wood is that? It's so dark it looks like ebony.'

'It's bog-oak,' she said. 'Wood that has been buried in the bog for thousands and thousands of years.'

Peregrine stared at her in sudden excitement. 'But how is that possible? Doesn't the wood just decay away?'

'No. The bog preserves it. We've pulled many a strange thing from the bogs. Barrels of butter, still perfect after centuries, practically good enough to eat. Wooden pendants carved with strange faces. Even bodies of men, near turned to wood themselves.'

Peregrine hardly listened. 'So the bog does not cause wood to decay, it actually preserves it.' He laughed out loud in joyous relief.

Molly was puzzled but pleased. 'Yes. It's hard to carve, it's as hard as iron! My father's men bring me lumps of it whenever they find it, digging peat for the fires. Here, look.'

She showed him a basket filled with dark, knobby lumps of wood. 'This is a piece I found myself just last week. It was floating on the lake, which is odd. Usually it sinks like a stone.'

She held in her hand a small, heart-shaped lump of wood. It had a naturally formed hole at its base, which once would have been a knot in the bole.

'It'd make a good ring,' he said, sliding it onto his own finger. He could hardly keep his face from breaking into a huge grin. *Perhaps the spear of thunder is still there, preserved in the bog, made harder and stronger, just waiting for me to find it . . .*

'Not for a girl,' she said. 'The hole is too big. At least it is for my fingers.' She held out her own hand, brown-skinned, slender.

'Your father?'

She laughed. 'He couldn't fit it on his littlest finger. Have you seen how big his hands are? It takes me forever to knit him a pair of mittens.'

He laughed in response and slid the lump of bog-oak off his finger to pass it back to her.

She turned it in her hand. 'I think it'll make something special. I found it on Midwinter's Eve, you see, that's a special day.'

'That's my birthday,' he told her.

Her gaze flashed up to his, then shyly dropped back down to the bog-oak. 'I'm holding on to it until it tells me what it wants to be,' she said, turning it over and over in her hands. 'I'll know it when it's time.'

Peregrine looked through the basket, exclaiming over some of the half-worked pieces inside. In one she had begun to carve the impression of a tree, its roots and branches reaching out like embracing arms. Another had been shaped into a statue of a woman, cradling a baby in her arms. 'What do you mean, the wood tells you what it wants to be? Surely you decide what you're going to carve?' he asked.

She flushed. 'I know it sounds strange. But sometimes . . . the wood tells me. I feel like . . .' she hesitated, then said, 'like I'm setting free the shape inside the wood.'

He reached forward and took the lump of bog-oak back. 'Really? How does it tell you? Not in words?'

'No, of course not!' Her flush deepened.

'But you have a feeling . . . you sense it . . . you see it in your mind's eye.'

'That's it exactly! How did you know? Do you like to carve wood too?'

'No. But it sounds like a Gift. You know, the Gifts of the Stormlinn. It is hard to describe how they work to outsiders too. I say I have the Gift of Calling, because I can call birds and beasts to my hand. Yet I don't call them by name, like I would a pet dog, or even with my voice usually. I sense them with my mind, I reach out . . . and they come.'

'How wonderful!' she cried. 'Oh, I wish I could do that.'

'I do like being able to do it,' he admitted. He glanced at the marmalade cat, asleep on Nan's lap, and silently called to it. The cat opened round orange eyes, rose gracefully, stretched out its front legs and then its hind legs, then jumped down and stalked over to sniff Peregrine's hand. The tip of its tail twitched slightly, but it permitted Peregrine to stroke it, leapt lightly into his lap, turned round, kneading its claws painfully, then lay down and went back to sleep.

'Oh, you are so lucky! What else can you do? Do you have other Gifts too?' she asked, wide-eyed.

Peregrine hesitated. 'You do not mind? I thought the hearthkin hated our wildkin Gifts?'

'I don't mind,' Molly said. 'We have heard how your mother has the healing touch and your aunt tells the most beautiful stories. And we know your father has power over birds, but a bird is our emblem too, we don't shoot them like the old hag Vernisha tells us too.'

Peregrine laid down the lump of bog-oak and picked up his flute, softly playing a few sweet notes. 'I have the Gift of Music, the Erlrune thinks, though it's tied together with the Gift of Calling. And maybe the Gift of Finding too. I'm always the one that finds my father's seal when he misplaces it, or my mother's thimble . . .' His voice choked suddenly, at the thought of his parents.

'Don't you know if you have a Gift?' she asked.

He coughed and cleared his throat, and said huskily, 'Not

always. The Gifts of the Stormlinn are strange, unknowable things, different for everyone, and often taking years to show themselves. Usually you only have one Gift, which reveals itself as you grow into adulthood. But when you have more, the Gift takes longer to reveal itself, and, well, sometimes it's hard to know if it is a true Gift or just luck, or a talent, or intuition . . .' His voice trailed away.

'So you have three Gifts?' she asked, awe in her voice.

He shrugged uncomfortably. 'Maybe. The Erlrune thinks so. She has three herself. It is very rare. That's why—or that's one of the reasons why—they fuss over me all the time.'

Peregrine was amazed he was telling her so much. Perhaps it was the darkness of the room, the soft glow of the peat fire, the way she leant forward, her eyes filled with sympathy. Perhaps he was just tired. He changed the subject rather abruptly, picking up the bog-oak, tossing it in the air and catching it.

'Perhaps it will be another bittern brooch? You could carve the beak arching over the hole, like in your candlesticks.'

'Maybe,' she said. 'Each brooch I carve for our Levellers is quite different from the others. Perhaps it will be a brooch.'

'Levellers?'

'Those who believe that all should be level,' she answered, fixing him with her grave eyes. 'Men, women, boys, girls, kings, serfs. We all should have the same rights. Love, justice, the right to work . . .' She bent to poke the fire, biting her lip, then raised her eyes to his. 'We are all Levellers here.'

'Is that why you do not live in the old castle? I must admit, I was surprised to find the Marsh King living in the castle smithy.'

Molly smiled. 'Oh no! I mean, not really. It's because of Nan.' She glanced at her grandmother, sleeping peacefully as a baby in her cushioned wheelchair. 'There are so many steps at the castle, and the cobblestones are so uneven. Here the floor is smooth, and Nan can roll herself about all she wants.'

Peregrine heard the sound of footsteps overhead, as Grizelda at long last roused herself from the bath. No doubt the water would be cold and dirty by now, no use to anyone else at all. He looked at Molly urgently. 'Please help me! What should I say to the council? I'm only a boy, but I need your father's help, really I do!'

She hesitated. 'Don't lie to them. They have had a lifetime of lies and false promises. My father values truth above all else.'

Grizelda appeared in the doorway, glowing golden and pink, wrapped in nothing but a length of damp white linen. Peregrine had forgotten how very pretty she was. She smiled at him. 'The bath was marvellous! I'm a different woman! But I have no clothes . . .'

'You may borrow some of mine,' Molly said colourlessly and limped out of the room.

Grizelda came to sit by Peregrine, all the glory of her fair hair tumbling down her back. 'Have you forgiven me?' she said.

'What for?'

'The hunter,' she said. 'I swear I did not know he was following us.'

'You saw him, the time he attacked us at the pool.'

She nodded. 'I don't know all my father's servants, though. The dogs looked like ours . . . but then we sell our sleuth hounds far and wide. How was I to know? I was too busy running.'

Peregrine considered this. 'You think your brother set him to guard you?'

She nodded. 'It makes sense. I mean, although your father is famed for his chivalry—'

'Or maybe he was set to follow you so you could lead him straight to the Erlrune.'

Her blue eyes opened wide. 'No! You think so?' For a moment she was silent and then she leant forward, touching his arm. 'If so, I didn't know. I swear it.'

She smelt clean and fresh and sweet, like spring flowers. He wondered where she had found the perfume here in the marshes in the dead of winter. Perhaps it was Molly's.

He got up and walked away from her, feeling hot and strange and bothered. 'I have to speak to Lord Percival and his council. What do you think I should say?'

'Oh, tell them whatever they want to hear,' she answered at once. 'Whatever you do, don't admit weakness. Men like that only understand brute strength. Promise them whatever they want. Else we might never get away from this damp and dreary place.'

CHAPTER 18

Tongue of Flame

QUEEN LILIANA CROUCHED IN THE FILTHY STRAW, HER cropped head resting on her manacled arm. She tried to breathe shallowly, for the stink of the dungeon made her feel ill. Rozalina lay beside her, struggling not to weep.

'Don't cry,' Liliana said. 'You know the Erlrune will be on her way. She'll fly down on her grogoyle and blast this castle to the ground. She'll bring an army of gibgoblins to skin that vile woman alive.'

Brave words, Liliana thought to herself. Yet she feared there was little the Erlrune could do. She was an old woman now, and if she flew down on her grogoyle the starkin soldiers would just shoot them down from the sky. There was no army of gibgoblins. Or, at least, not much of an army. The wildkin had been fighting side by side with King Merrik and his supporters for twenty-five years now, and they had all suffered terrible losses. Liliana felt tears welling up in her own eyes. It seemed a dreadful thing that all their bright hopes, their battle to overthrow the tyrant Vernisha, should end so tragically.

Rozalina could not answer her. Her head had been locked into a witch's bridle, a cruel contraption like a cage, which enclosed her head, an iron curb-plate pressing down on her tongue so she could not speak. Since Liliana's hands had been locked in steel gauntlets, she was unable to do anything to help her.

It was their second day in the dungeons and already they were sick and weak. In that time there had been little to eat or drink, and no concession made for their personal comfort. Their own clothes had been roughly stripped from them, and a pile of uncured animal skins flung in for them to try to cover themselves decently. 'What do you need clothes for? Wildkin animals,' the soldiers had shouted.

'It's a blessing really,' Liliana had said to Rozalina. 'These skins are warmer than our chemises.'

Rozalina had nodded and fashioned rough slippers for their icy feet, tying them up with leather thongs.

Liliana's weather witchery meant that snow was no longer falling, but the dungeons would be bitterly cold and damp even in the height of summer. The cold kept them awake and made them feel feverish and ill.

Once a day all four captives were dragged from their cells and paraded before the court. On the first day, they had appeared at suppertime. Hundreds and hundreds of roasted birds had been laid on immense silver platters, their aroma filling the air, torturing the prisoners' empty stomachs.

'Your little friends,' Vernisha had cried, waving a tiny roasted lark on a skewer. 'I have to thank you for calling them to your aid, we haven't eaten bird flesh in simply ages! Come and eat!'

King Merrik could not touch a mouthful, nor could Liliana, Zed or Rozalina, hungry as they were. The smell made them feel ill. Vernisha laughed in glee and said cruelly, 'What, you refuse the feast I've prepared for you? You'll eat nothing else until you've tasted your poor little feathered friends!'

So they had not eaten since, and their hollow stomachs were burning with pain.

Straw rustled near the cell door. Liliana's nerves tightened. She peered through the gloom and saw a large black rat dragging something under the dungeon door. She swallowed and clenched her swollen hands inside the steel gauntlets, ready to strike out if the rat attacked them.

Yet the rat only sat up and stared at them with the most piteous expression on its face, something bright dangling from its mouth. It crept closer and dropped the object at Liliana's feet with a clanking noise, then darted away through the door. Bemused, Liliana bent and picked it up. It was a ring of small keys.

'Rozie, look!'

She passed the ring to Rozalina who at once began to try all the keys in the lock of the manacles that circled Liliana's wrist, keeping the gauntlets fixed on her hands. In seconds, the lock was loose and the gauntlets thrown on the ground. Liliana gasped in pain as the blood rushed through to her fingers, and she shook her hands. She then found the key to unlock the witch's bridle and the shackles around their ankles.

Taking each other's hands, the two queens did a little staggering jig in the straw.

The straw rustled again as the rat crept in under the door dragging a parcel wrapped up in a white linen napkin. This time Liliana approached the rat without fear, bending to take the parcel and unwrap it. Inside were floury white buns, a triangle of soft white cheese, two thick wedges of bacon and egg pie, and a bunch of dried cloudberries still clinging to their stem.

'Thank you,' Liliana said to the rat, who gave a courtly bow and scurried away under the door again.

Never had any meal seemed so delicious. Liliana and Rozalina devoured every last crumb and berry, wishing only for something to wash it down with. As if in answer to their wish, the rat reappeared dragging a bottle in a wicker case. He had some trouble manoeuvring the cork out with his sharp rodent teeth, but at last it popped out and the two queens were able to take turns in drinking one of the finest drops of brandywine they had ever tasted.

Only then did Liliana and Rozalina feel strong enough to turn their attention to the rat, who had watched them eat and drink with an expression of smug pleasure.

'Tom-Tit-Tot?' Liliana asked hopefully.

In answer, the rat somersaulted forward into his usual hideous omen-imp shape, with black leathery wings, orange fur and a huge grin that showed a mouth full of fangs like a cat's. The omen-imp put one finger to his black lips and pointed at the door, then pulled out a tightly rolled note from a message tube attached to his leg.

My dear friends, do not fear. We know of your plight. Pedrin flies today for bargaining chip. Mags on her way. L & I will bring wildkin. Robin on own quest, may he be blessed with success, love, B.

Liliana and Rozalina read the message and then looked at each other with questioning eyes.

'Bargaining chip? What can that mean? And what does she mean, Robin is on his own quest? I thought he was safe with her?'

'Shhh!' Rozalina hissed as heavy footsteps marched past the door. She quickly drew the witch's bridle back over her head and crouched down in the straw. Liliana forced her hands back into the manacles, her heart in her mouth. A tiny grille in the door slammed open and one bloodshot eye stared through. Liliana dropped in a dispirited way, her body hunched over the precious note, the empty bottle of wine hidden behind her body. The grille slammed shut and the footsteps moved away.

Rozalina and Liliana grinned at each other in fierce excitement. Help was on the way!

The great hall of the old castle was packed with men and women and children, filling the cold, echoing room with a hum like bees in a summer garden.

The Marsh King sat on a dais at the end of the hall, with three men and women sitting on either side. Two were grey-haired and elderly, two were in the prime of their lives, and two were young, not much older than Peregrine himself.

Peregrine stood behind a lectern. He carried the falcon on his wrist as always, a visible symbol of his status. His knees were shaky and his stomach cramped. He looked down into a crowd of upturned faces, seeing Jack and Grizelda sitting next to Molly and her grandmother in the front row.

'Stormlinn Castle has fallen,' he said. A roar of distress rose up. Peregrine waited for it to die down. 'My father, King Merrik, and my mother, Queen Liliana, have been taken captive, as well as Queen Rozalina and her husband, Lord Zedrin. I do not know the fate of the hundreds of others who sheltered at the castle. I fear the worst.'

'Then all is lost!' someone cried out.

'Vernisha has won!'

'What are we to do?'

Peregrine held up one hand. 'All is not lost. As long as there is breath in my body I will fight to free my parents and restore the true king to the throne. I will need your help.'

The crowd muttered.

'Knew the lad wanted something.'

'A poor, dwizzen-faced lad like that, what can he do?'

'Don't know what he thinks we could do. Much use we'd be a-marching against the starkin!'

'I have a plan. It's not much of a plan yet, but it's something to begin with.' Peregrine raised his voice but could barely make himself heard over the buzz of people commenting and arguing. 'I've come here to the marshes in search of something, something that was lost long ago . . .'

Someone shouted out a ribald comment, and the Marsh King's mother seized Molly's crutch and banged it loudly on the floor till the noise quietened. 'Holy mackerel, you lot, where's your manners? Let the lad speak.' At last the vast hall was silent and she turned back to Peregrine, beaming. 'There you go, love. Speak up.'

Peregrine drew a deep breath. He let his eyes roam over the hall and waited till the thudding of his heart had steadied. 'Long ago, in the brave days of the Storm King, a magical spear was made that had the power to heal as well as to kill. It can bring thunder and lightning and storm, and raise the oceans, and shake the earth. It is said it can even harness the power of the wild magic that slumbers still in the secret places of the land. The spear of the Storm King never misses its mark, and it returns to your hand once you've thrown it. It was once the greatest treasure of the Erlkings of Stormlinn.'

He paused and took another deep breath, resting his wrist on the edge of the lectern so the effort of holding the bird's weight did not drain his strength. He looked intently at people in the crowd, willing them to listen, willing them to care.

'But it was stolen. It was stolen by the starkin prince, Zander the Cruel, and thrown by him into the bog. I believe it is still there. I believe that I can find it and use it as my ancestor, the Storm King, once used it, to bring peace to this poor land of ours. But I need your help to find it.'

'The bog's a mighty big place,' one man called out. Peregrine thought it was Frank.

'Yes,' Peregrine agreed. 'But we know it was thrown into the bog near a high hill, which has a lightning-blasted oak tree growing on it. Mistletoe grows in the tree . . .'

'Why, he means Grimsfell,' several voices cried at once. 'There's only one place where mistletoe grows in an oak . . .'

'. . . and fair cleaved it is too, right down the middle.'

'Yeah, it's Grimsfell he means.'

Relief made Peregrine giddy, his knees threatening to give way. He locked his legs in place, gripped the edges of the lectern and said, rather shakily, 'Grimsfell? You know where it is? Can someone guide me there?'

Dubious glances were exchanged. 'Eh, no-one goes near Grimsfell,' a man volunteered, possibly Frank or Fred.

'Nah, it's haunted!'

'Old Grim sneaks about there. He'll creep up behind you and strangle you with his bony hands!'

'They say you can look down through the water and see all the old bones lying there.'

'I can take you,' a clear voice said. Peregrine looked around gladly and saw Molly struggling to her feet, her crutch clamped under one arm. 'I'm not afraid. Isn't Old Grim a wildkin thing? And isn't his Highness heir to the wildkin throne?'

'Thank you,' Peregrine replied gratefully.

'Eh now, my moppet, don't you be saying that!' her grandmother said. 'No need to go a-meddling in other folks' business. You stay home with your old nan and let someone else do the showing.'

'It's all right, Nan,' Molly said. 'I know where Grimsfell is. I can show his Highness the way, if his squire will pole the boat for me. Haven't we promised to support the king and do all we can to help him win back his throne? It seems a small thing to do.'

'But the king's a prisoner now, and his castle taken,' said Bob, or maybe it was Bill.

'Queen Vernisha takes awful hard against people who stand up against her,' said Gus, or maybe it was Ged.

'Fred says there was a mort of starkin a-chasing the young feller. They'll know we've taken him in. They're sure to send soldiers to roust him out.'

'Last time they sent those nasty great birds of theirs, we were near all roasted in our beds.'

Peregrine listened in dismay as people began to rise and shake their fists, and suggest they turn him over to the pretender-queen. He threw a glance of appeal to the Marsh King, but he sat quietly, his brown eyes narrowed, letting his people have their say.

'If you give in to Vernisha now, she will crush you all!' Peregrine shouted. 'She is cruel and vengeful! Your only hope is to help me defeat her!'

'A boy? With nothing but an old spear?' someone jeered.

Shouts and catcalls rang out. Everywhere Peregrine looked were angry, frightened faces, shaking fists, booing mouths. An idea came to him. He slid his hand into his coat and pulled out his flute. Lifting it to his mouth, he played a deep, strange, booming call. It rang out through the great hall and everyone fell silent, turning to him with startled eyes.

'The bittern is a bird both brave and wise,' he said. 'It hunts with stealth and can stay hidden for hours. Its call terrifies all who hear it, for they know that the bittern will defend its territory fiercely, fighting to the death if need be. It is no wonder you of the marsh have taken the bittern as your badge.'

There was a long silence.

Peregrine's voice rang out strongly. 'Of all the hearthkin people, you are the only ones to have flung off the shackles of slavery. All over Ziva, your brethren are starving and in misery. People are punished for singing and telling stories, for asking for mercy and justice, for dreaming of a better way. Whole villages are locked in their barn and burnt to death for who knows what trivial crime. I have seen their bones lying in the ashes. Some were babies.'

He heard someone gasp.

'The swan symbol of the starkin no longer means faithfulness,' he went on, his voice gathering strength. 'Vernisha has turned it into a symbol of treachery and betrayal. And similarly, the eagle of the wildkin people no longer stands for power and strength and royalty. The Erlqueen is captured, her castle fallen. Her people are hunted down and murdered . . .' Peregrine's voice broke. He had to bend his head for a moment, mastering his grief.

'It is time we rose up out of the ashes, like a phoenix, and built a new life for ourselves. Starkin, wildkin, hearthkin, we must build a country where we can all live in peace, where justice and mercy are available for all, where an accident of birth does not determine whether a man or a woman is poor and weak, or rich and strong, where our children can grow and prosper in peace, and our old can die comfortably in bed. Is this not what you Levellers hold dear to your hearts? Is this not worth fighting for?'

'Yeah!' men in the crowd shouted, punching the air with their fists. Women cried and embraced, children laughed and pretended to wrestle, while Molly smiled at him with tears shining in her eyes.

'You all know my grandmother Mags, who has worked tirelessly all her life to make things better in our land. My grandfather said she would be "a crutch for the crippled, a shield for the meek, a voice for the speechless, a sword for the weak". Well, my grandmother is growing old now. I think it is time for me to take on her mantle. I hope that you will all stand by me and help me, because there is a lot to be done.'

'So what do you want from us, apart from a guide to take you to Grimsfell?' the Marsh King asked. His deep voice cut through the uproar, bringing with it a gradual silence.

Peregrine took a moment to answer. 'I want your continued support, your shelter here in the marshes as long as I need it, and then, if need be, arms and men to help me fight Vernisha.'

'And what do we get in return?' the Marsh King asked.

Peregrine took a deep breath. He saw Grizelda leaning forward, urging him with her eyes to promise the Marsh King anything he wanted. He saw Jack swallow and surreptitiously lay his hand on his dagger. He saw Molly cross her fingers.

'I hope what I give you will be a new world,' he answered. 'But in all likelihood, what most of us face is death.'

Grizelda dropped her head into her hands. Jack shifted till he was poised on the very edge of his stool, biting his lip. Blitz ruffled his feathers and hunched his back, sensing Peregrine's tension.

'Vernisha has a tight grip on the land,' Peregrine went on. 'She will not be easy to dislodge. I hope that I'll find the Storm King's spear, and that it will give me the power and strength to stand against her. But I don't know if it will, even if I can manage to find it. I can only hope, and fight, and do my best. It's all any of us can do.'

The Marsh King nodded. 'True spoken,' he said with approval. 'Well then, what do we all say?'

The six men and woman who sat beside him rose and went down into the hall, moving among the crowd, listening to all the people said. There was a lot of arguing and gesticulation. After a long time—so long Peregrine's legs ached—they came back to the dais and spoke to the Marsh King. He nodded, then looked at Peregrine. 'Tell us, how are we to know whether you or your father will be any better a ruler than this Vernisha?'

'You could help us,' Peregrine said wearily. 'Tell us what you want, what you think needs to be done. We could have a council, like you do here, with representatives from the hearthkin and the wildkin as well as the starkin. I promise you, I'll do my best to work out some system to keep things fair.'

There was a long pause, as the Marsh King ruminated, both enormous fists on his knees. Then he slowly nodded his head. 'Well, you're a bold boy, but I like a bit of boldness. Nothing ventured, nothing gained, I say. All right, laddie, we're all yours!'

CHAPTER 19

The Story of Old Grim

THE GLOW OF THE PEAT FIRE FLICKERED OVER THEIR FACES as they sat around its warmth.

Grizelda lay back in the chair, an embroidered cushion at her head, stroking Oskar's ears, her stockinged feet stretched towards the coals. Molly sat awkwardly on the floor, carving a lump of dark gnarled wood with a small knife. Nan sat in her wheeled chair, knitting with a fierce *clack, clack* of her needles. Jack roasted old wrinkled apples on the end of the poker, thrusting them deep into the orange heart of the fire, while Peregrine sat on a stool, making a collection of new arrows to replace the ones he had lost on the journey. He was fletching the arrows with feathers from the rooster in the courtyard, and using reeds for the shafts, the only straight, light timber he could find in abundance. The Marsh King was in the forge, making him a set of new arrowheads.

'Tell me more about Grimsfell,' Peregrine said, his hands so accustomed to his work that he barely needed to glance at them. 'Someone mentioned something about Old Grim. Do they mean Lord Grim?'

'Never heard him called naught but Old Grim,' Nan said. 'There's lots of stories about him round here.'

'Can you tell me some?' Peregrine asked. 'Because we have lots of stories about *Lord* Grim and I'd very much like to know if they are one and the same.'

'Well, then, I'll see what I can remember.' Nan laid her knitting down on her lap. 'What my nan told me is that Old Grim's a-sleeping under that high hill, with all his boo-bogeys and boggarts. He used to ride out regular like, and everywhere he went people would be a-shivering in their beds, too scared to put a nose above their counterpanes in case they saw him and his Gallop. 'Cause if you saw him you'd have to ride with him and whither you'd go no-one knew. All folks knew was that few ever came back again.'

Peregrine leant forward eagerly. 'Yes! Lord Grim's Gallop. It's the same story. So that's where he sleeps, under the hill with the lightning-blasted oak?'

'Aye, that's right. My old nan always said there was a battle there once, which Old Grim lost, and that's why he's bound to lie a-sleeping under the hill.'

'The Storm King defeated him,' Peregrine said exultantly. 'With the magic of the spear!'

'Didn't he make the spear to fight against Lord Grim?' Jack asked.

Peregrine nodded. 'Yes. In the old days, Lord Grim and his Gallop came riding out of the hill every winter, through a dark and secret gate from their own realm into ours, bringing with them shadows and coldness and death.' He looked about at the circle of faces turned to his, and let his voice fall into a natural storytelling rhythm.

'Wherever they rode, the world would change according

to their whim. Lakes would form in their horses' hoofprints, mountains would heave themselves up and cast themselves down, gardens would be blighted with frost. Wherever he passed, candles turned blue, fires sank and skin turned to gooseflesh. Lord Grim's Gallop brought nothing but grief and fear, for no-one ever knew what the world would do next.'

As he spoke, Peregrine remembered his mother telling him the old story that had been told to her by her mother, and felt raw grief tighten his throat. Where were his parents now? He dreaded what the pretender-queen might do to them now she had them in her grasp. He recalled the story of how minstrels had their entrails eaten out by rats and storytellers had their tongues cut out, and shuddered.

'So what happened?' Molly prompted him, looking up from her carving.

Peregrine pushed away his dreadful imaginings and went on. 'The Storm King was then just a boy called Wolfgang. He was the only son of one of the Crafty, and he never knew his father. He was a strange, wild child who hated to be kept confined and would sometimes just stare off into space as if he saw things that no-one else could see.' Peregrine had always felt an affinity with the wild boy Wolfgang, for he too was accused of staring into space. 'Sometimes he fell into such a fit of temper no-one could constrain him. He had Gifts but did not seem to be able to control them. He could whistle up the wind but could not whistle it down again, and the storms he called would rage for days, flooding rivers and tearing down trees.'

'This is all very interesting,' Grizelda said, yawning behind her hand, 'but I really don't see what use it is for us to know all this.'

'He made the spear,' Peregrine said sharply. 'He poured all of his Gifts into the spear—the Gift of Calling Storm, the Gift of Finding and, of course, the Gift of Healing.'

Grizelda frowned. 'But the spear is a weapon. Isn't it meant to kill people?'

Peregrine nodded. 'All the Gifts of the Stormlinn are double-edged, though, Grizelda. I can call and I can send away.'

'He once ordered a mob of bully-boys to go away and they weren't found for hours,' Jack said with a grin. 'They'd walked their feet bloody.'

'I didn't know what would happen. I've never done it again,' Peregrine said shortly. 'It's against the law of three.'

'Go on, though, laddie, tell us more. It's the best story I've heard in many a long year!' Nan urged.

'Well, Wolfgang's mother was badly hurt one day by the passing of Lord Grim and his Gallop,' Peregrine said. 'Wolfgang did not yet know he had the Gift of Healing. He was beside himself with rage and grief. He ran after Lord Grim and seized his stirrup, trying to haul him out of the saddle. Lord Grim just laughed at him, scooped him up onto his saddle and rode away with him. Wolfgang howled and fought with all his strength but Lord Grim did not let him go. In the end Wolfgang fainted dead away. When he came to, he was many miles from home. It took him a long time to find his way back again, only to discover his mother was dead.'

'Oh, that's so sad,' Molly said.

'What did he do, poor lad?' Nan asked, clasping her small gnarled hands together.

'Wolfgang travelled all about the land, seeking a way to exact his revenge. He went to every one of the Crafty he could find and studied with them. Everything he was taught he wrote down, eventually making what is now the Book of the Erlrune. Everywhere Wolfgang went he saw the ruin left by the wildest of the wild things, who knew no rules. He began to think how best to tame and bind and teach them. Slowly he began to make alliances and build Stormlinn Castle, but every winter Lord Grim would come and lay waste to what he had built that year, almost as if mocking his attempt to bring peace and prosperity to the world. It seemed as if Lord Grim and his Gallop were invincible.'

Peregrine paused to take a mouthful of warm spiced mead, looking around at the faces upturned to his. 'One day Wolfgang heard that Lady Grim had cast a spell of protection on her husband and each of her sons.' He lowered his voice and leant forward so the glow of the fire would flicker eerily upon his face. 'She had said:

Naught shall harm thee, so I swear
Naught that moves upon the earth
Naught that flies in the air
Naught that swims in the sea
Naught that grows in the soil
Naught that lies beneath it
Naught that is made from it
Naught shall harm thee, so I swear.'

'That's fairly all-embracing,' Grizelda said. 'Jack, are you cooking that apple or burning it?'

'Sorry!' Jack cried and pulled the apple out of the fire. It was looking rather burnt, but he cut away the blackened peel, rolled it in brown sugar and passed it up to her.

She took it gingerly, for it was steaming hot, and ate greedily. 'These are really good,' she said indistinctly.

'So what happened?' Molly asked, her hands busy with her knife and lump of wood.

'Wolfgang despaired for a long while, but then one day he went out at midwinter to cut the mistletoe, as has always been the custom among the Crafty,' Peregrine said. 'It occurred to him that mistletoe did not grow from the soil, but was rooted into the branches of a tree. It did not fly, or swim, or creep, or move upon the earth. The more he thought about it, the more he felt that he might have found the flaw in Lady Grim's spell.'

He looked round the circle of intent faces. 'You may not know much about mistletoe. I don't know if you hearthkin follow our wildkin customs anymore.'

'We hang it from our mantelpieces come midwinter,' Nan said with a toothless grin, 'and kiss anyone who stands underneath it.'

'It is sacred to us,' Peregrine said. 'It stays green in the midst of winter, when the tree it grows in is bare of all leaves. We call it the golden bough, for it often glows golden in the bare winter trees, and thunderbesem, for it is thought to offer protection against lightning, both in the air and ...' he hesitated and looked away, '... and in the brain.'

There was a moment of silence, then he went on slowly, 'Sometimes it is called all-heal, even though it is poisonous. A ring carved of mistletoe, or a sprig carried on your body, is thought to ward off illness and help wounds heal.'

Peregrine slid his hand into his pocket and drew out his own sprig of mistletoe and showed it to Nan and Molly. 'Queen Rozalina plucked it for me on Midwinter's Eve. She cuts it with a silver knife and does not allow any part of it to touch the ground. We think that is a custom left over from the day Wolfgang the Storm King cut mistletoe to make his spear.'

'So the spear of thunder is made from mistletoe?' Molly asked. 'He made it to get around Lady Grim's spell?'

Peregrine nodded. 'He spent all year thinking and studying, and the following midwinter he used his Gift to find a place where mistletoe grew from a lightning-blasted oak tree ...'

'Our Grimsfell,' Nan said, nodding her head.

'It must be,' Peregrine said. 'He cut a branch of mistletoe and carved himself a spear, engraving magical runes along its length and honing its point till it was as sharp as an arrow. He anointed the point with the poisonous juice from its white berries, which only grow at midwinter, and then he called Lord Grim.

'Although he was compelled to come by Wolfgang's Gift of Calling, Lord Grim came without fear, galloping through the sky with his great black-horned steed, all his hounds howling at his heels. Lady Grim rode beside him and his ten sons rode behind. Midwinter is the time of Lord Grim's greatest strength. He was arrogant and sure of his power, which would not begin to wane until the twelfth day of Midwinter.

'Wolfgang confronted Lord Grim and told him he must submit to law and order. Lord Grim only laughed.

'Wolfgang warned him that if he would not submit willingly, he would have to hunt him down and kill him. "Try to catch me if you can!" Lord Grim laughed and off they galloped, howling, shrieking, turning the sky black.

'Wolfgang threw his spear of mistletoe. Because it was made with the Storm King's Gift of Finding, it could never miss its mark. No matter how Lord Grim swerved and leapt and galloped and dodged, the spear sped ever closer. For twelve days Lord Grim and his Gallop rode, turning the whole land black with frost and shadows, but still the spear sped closer.

'At last Lord Grim and his Gallop began to grow weary. His horse began to stumble and droop its head. The dogs were panting and limping, the boo-bogeys were failing, and still the spear sped ever closer. Lord Grim's sons were sagging in the saddle, Lady Grim was white-faced and drooping, and still the spear sped ever closer. At last Lord Grim's youngest, who was only a child, could hang on no longer. He fell from the saddle and Lord Grim turned and caught him as he fell.

'It was then that the spear at last found its mark. It plunged straight through the body of Lord Grim's youngest son and into Lord Grim's heart. Father and son went tumbling down, down, down, and would have been impaled on the sharp peaks of the mountains below if Lady Grim had not swerved her steed to break their fall.

'The spear flew straight back to the hand of the Storm King and Lady Grim followed, the body of her youngest in her arms, her older sons bearing the body of their father. Her grief was terrible to see. Wolfgang's heart was touched, for he remembered his own grief at the loss of his mother. He made a bargain with Lady Grim. He would heal her son if she and all her sons would agree to go back through the dark and secret gate to their own realm.

'Lady Grim hesitated. "Only if you heal my husband too," she said. The Storm King was torn. He did not trust Lord Grim, but he was determined to bring peace to the land and wanted to make some grand gesture of his intentions.

'In the end he agreed to heal Lord Grim, but only if he submitted to being bound under the hill, to be roused in a time of desperate need, by the striking of the spear of thunder upon the rock under which he was bound. And the Storm

King said to Lord Grim . . .' Peregrine put on a deep, resonant voice: '"This I promise you! If Lord Grim should rise and help me and mine in the hour of our greatest need, then he shall be free to return to his own realm thereafter."'

There was a long moment of silence. Peregrine reached for his cup of warm mead to ease his dry throat. There was a little murmuring and stretching as the spell of the story began to wear off.

'Three times you need to strike the stone,' Nan said, to Peregrine's surprise, 'and then the old oak tree will grow green, the dry spring will run with water, and Old Grim and his Gallop will wake.'

'I hadn't heard that part,' Peregrine said.

'It's what my nan told me when I was just a lass,' Nan said. 'Round here, if we think something is never going to happen, we say: "Yes, when the old oak grows green and Old Grim rides again."'

'That was a marvellous story,' Molly said, lifting her chin from her knees. Her carving was tucked by her side, forgotten.

'His Highness tells the best stories,' Jack agreed, taking up his poker again and putting another apple to roast in the fire. 'Don't let him tell you a ghost story, he'll scare you out of your wits.'

'I don't believe in ghosts,' Grizelda said stiffly. 'Nor in this Lord Grim. I hope you don't have your heart set on rousing this old boo-bogey from the grave, Robin.'

'I plan to give it a go,' he replied coolly.

'You'll need to find the spear first,' she reminded him. 'Though I hate to be the one to remind you that the spear is bound to have rotted long ago.'

'But that's the thing,' Peregrine said, joy in his voice. 'The bog doesn't make wood rot, it preserves it! Molly says they find things in the bog that were flung there hundreds and even thousands of years ago.'

'No! That's impossible!' Grizelda stared at him.

'It's true,' Molly said. 'Look, this is bog-oak I'm carving now. See how hard and dark it is?' She told Grizelda about the bodies that had been found in the bog, corpses that turned to leather instead of rotting away.

'So the spear could still be there?' Grizelda sounded dumbfounded. 'That's . . . amazing.'

'It's wonderful!' Jack cried, leaping up and dancing a wild jig about the fire. 'I'm so glad! Oh, your Highness, you really think you'll be able to find it?'

'If it's there, I'll find it,' Peregrine answered. 'Did I not find the road? You know it's my Gift.'

Grizelda's eyes, huge and shadowed, were fixed on his face. 'And you think you can use the spear to rouse this old boo-bogey?'

'Of course I plan to rouse him!' Peregrine said. 'As soon as I heard the hill was called Grimsfell I began to hope it would be possible. And it's still midwinter. Lord Grim's powers are at their full. If he can cast mountains down, I should think he'll be able to help smite the throne of stars asunder.'

'I saw Old Grim once, when I was just a lass,' Nan said dreamily. 'The old king's son called him out of the hill.'

Peregrine and Jack exchanged quick, thrilled glances. 'Yes? What happened?'

The old woman shrugged. 'The prince came down the old road, a-swaying in a litter, with a girl they called a wildkin princess chained beside him. I remember her well, she was the most beautiful girl I'd ever seen, with hair as black as night and eyes a-shining like stars.' She nodded to Peregrine. 'You've eyes just like her, lad, I thought so as soon as I heard you were a wildkin prince.'

Peregrine gazed at her in wonderment. Nan was talking about Queen Rozalina's mother, his own great-aunt.

'The prince's men asked about Grimsfell and my cousin agreed to guide them there. He says the whole way the prince was jeering at the wildkin princess, a-telling her that he'd make sure that all her prophecies and predictions came to naught.

'We all got on with our work. It was late in the afternoon and a-getting dark when I heard a noise the likes of which I've never heard before. All the ground was a-shaking and a-trembling. We locked our doors and banged our shutters shut, and doused our fires, just in case. The prince came a-riding in an hour or so later, and his men beat on our doors with their swords till we all came out. He had Old Grim there in chains, with bells around his wrists and ankles, and paraded him around for us to see.'

Peregrine sucked in his breath. He knew, of course, that Prince Zander had captured Lord Grim before throwing the spear in the bog. His mother had told him how she had freed Lord Grim from the palace at Zarissa at the same time as Queen Rozalina was rescued. Wondering how he had come to be imprisoned, the Erlrune had asked the Well of Fates to show her. Old Nan's description seemed somehow more vivid and immediate, told here in the flickering glow of the peat fire, so close to Lord Grim's hill.

'Ooh, he was a terrifying sight,' Nan went on. 'Black as a sablefish, he was, with a great black cloak. As he passed us, all the lanterns went dim and blue, and the puddles froze over. Next day we found none of the hens had laid and the goats were all dry. They marched on after that, a-taking the wildkin princess and Old Grim away to the palace, to be put in the prince's wildkin zoo.'

'Yes, that's right,' Peregrine said. 'My parents rescued the princess's daughter, and set free all the creatures in the wildkin zoo, including Lord Grim.'

'That must've been when Old Grim came back,' Nan said. 'It was before you were born, Molly, my moppet. He came back in a gust of icy air, and all our spring crops were blighted and the blossom shrivelled on the apple trees and the berries died on the bramble. It was a bad year for us, the year he came back.'

'I'm sorry,' Peregrine said. 'But Prince Zander should never have captured him.'

'What will happen if you release him?' Molly said. 'Will he go back to his old wicked ways?'

'I hope not,' Peregrine replied, frowning. 'Surely he wouldn't? Because I would have the spear, to strike him down again. Besides, I think the agreement was he'd be freed from his bonds and allowed to go back to his own world.'

The door opened and the Marsh King came in, smelling of smoke and steel, his enormous hands filled with sharp-pointed, glittering arrowheads.

'Thank you!' Peregrine cried and jumped up to take them. He could not hold them all in his hands and had to pour them into a sack made from his cloak.

'It's late,' the Marsh King said. 'If you wish to be a-going to Grimsfell early in the morn, you'd best all be a-getting some sleep.'

'Yes,' Peregrine said. 'I'll just finish my arrows and then we'd best get some sleep.'

The Marsh King hesitated, then gave Peregrine such a hearty clap on the shoulder that he staggered forwards. 'You spoke well today, your Highness. You've won the fen-folk over. I just hope you can find this spear of yours and start a-smiting at the throne of stars, like you said.'

'So do I,' Peregrine agreed fervently.

CHAPTER 20

Attack from the Air

MOLLY WOKE FROM A RESTLESS SLEEP TO HEAR BELLS TOLLING frantically. She sat up with a gasp and looked around her. Everything was dark.

She swung her legs out of bed and fumbled for her clothes. Dragging her gown over her head, she called in a low voice, 'My lady! Wake up. We're under attack.'

There was a mumbled groan from the lump lying on the other side of Molly's bed, then Grizelda sat up. 'Wha . . . at?'

'We're under attack. It'll be starkin soldiers flying in on sisikas. You'd think they'd know better by now. Come on, get dressed, we're not safe here. One may drop a firebomb, or they may have found some fusillier fuel.'

Soon both girls were dressed and hurrying down the stairs in the darkness, Molly hobbling as fast as she could on her crutch. Oskar padded along silently at his mistress's heels.

The boys were already up and getting dressed by the low gleam of the peat fire. Blitz was flapping his wings and screeching in anxiety, and Peregrine lifted the falcon close to his chest to calm him.

'What's happening?' Jack cried.

'Sisika attack,' Molly said briefly. 'My da was expecting it. We would normally take refuge in the castle but I think it'd be better if we slip away while we can. Grab your packs and we'll go find a boat. Nan, will you tell Da we've gone to Grimsfell?'

'You be careful now,' Nan said anxiously, wheeling herself forward. She had slept in her chair by the fire, with the boys making up beds from soft otter skins on the floor. She had the marmalade cat, and her bundle of knitting, on her lap.

'I will, I promise, Nan,' Molly replied.

'It's cold out. Have you got your warm underdrawers on?'

'Yes, Nan.' Molly blushed.

'What about a shawl? And a clean hanky?'

'I've got everything I need, don't you worry, Nan.' Molly patted her bulging pack, which she had crammed full of provisions and other necessities the previous night.

'I'm your nan, I'm meant to worry!'

Jack helped Molly push Nan outside to the courtyard, which was full of people hurrying into the castle, baskets of food and bundles of belongings clutched under their arms. It was cold and Molly's breath puffed white before her face. She huddled her shawl tighter about her and looked up at the sky.

A phalanx of sisika birds soared overhead, their white wings in rigid formation, starkin lords crouched on their backs. Suddenly a spurt of blue fire from the top of the castle illuminated the scene. A sisika bird screamed and dissolved into ash. Simultaneously, there was a deafening twang. Giant arrows shot out from the ballistas ranged along the top of the battlements. Although a few arced away to fall into the lake, most hit their target, sending sisika birds tumbling down to crash into the lake or the marshes. Grizelda gasped, her hand to her mouth, her eyes wide with disbelief.

'You have fusillier fire?' Peregrine cried.

Molly grinned at him. 'Of course we do! The Ardian fenlands are the biggest source of marsh gas in the world. You think we wouldn't make use of it ourselves?'

Two of the big, bristly-bearded men were nearby, hurrying people along. They laid down their halberds so they could lift the tiny old woman in her chair and carry her up the stairs to the great hall. 'Holy mackerel,' she said. 'Gently now! Don't rattle my poor old bones about, else they might fall off.'

'Sorry, Nan,' the big men said, as abashed as little boys.

'This way,' Molly said, and began to limp away from the castle, going down the hill towards the water's edge. Peregrine, Jack and Grizelda followed close behind, Oskar slinking at their heels, his tail tucked between his legs. Peregrine kept the falcon tucked inside his cloak.

Overhead the battle still raged. The starkin lords on the backs of the sisikas were dropping pots of hot coals or shooting fiery arrows. In retaliation, the castle's giant crossbows twanged. Mangonels flung boulders and giant studded balls of iron. People shouted, the bell tolled relentlessly, and the sisika birds screeched. Smoke and ashes drifted in the air.

Molly led them through a grove of willows to where a long eel-boat lay concealed in the darkness under the drooping brown fronds. It was a broad, flat-bottomed craft with a small hut built upon it. The back of the boat was crowded with curiously shaped baskets and long four-pronged forks. There were also a few heavy, long-shafted spades.

'Will you pole the boat for me?' Molly asked Jack.

'Of course. Just tell me where to go.'

'At first we must stay as close to the shore as possible, so that the soldiers do not see us. Head to the left.'

Molly propped her crutch on the deck and swung herself over. She did not like boats. Her hip ached worse than ever in the damp air, and the way the boat rocked and swayed underfoot made her gait even more unsteady. Most of the other children on the Isle of Eels had their own small boats and would be out on the water from dawn to dusk, fishing and gathering rushes and setting eel traps. Molly was never allowed to go out on her own, though. She had tried once a few years ago, but her hip had given way while she was poling. She had fallen overboard and nearly drowned. Her father's boat had been found, drifting and empty, on the tide. The men of the Isle of Eels had searched the bogs for her all night, at last finding her crouched in the reeds, shivering with cold and cramped with pain. She had been sick with a fever for days, and her hip had throbbed with a low, deep, grinding pain that no amount of beaver fat poultices would fix. Molly was not allowed out on the eel-boat alone after that, her nan preferring to keep her under her watchful eye.

Molly had still been taught the secret ways of the marshes, though. At least once a month she went out with her father, who had rebuilt his punt for her comfort. There was a cushioned bench where she could safely lie, a brazier with a tin chimney to keep her warm, and with her father poling the boat along, she had no need to risk dislocating her hip again.

Still, it was an adventure to go out in the middle of the night, without her father to look after her. Molly had craved adventure all of her life. She tingled with excitement, her cheeks pink and her eyes glowing despite the bitter cold.

Peregrine handed Grizelda aboard, Oskar leaping after her, and then clambered onto the boat himself, Blitz on his wrist as always. It must be awkward for him, Molly thought, always carrying the falcon on his wrist. It meant he only ever had one hand to use. He didn't seem to mind, though. Perhaps he was used to it.

Slowly the boat began to inch along, keeping close to the island. Bangs and twangs and cries and screams from the battle concealed any sound they might have made. Eventually, though, the small boat had to strike out from the shore. Molly waited until the moon was covered by thick black cloud before giving Jack the go-ahead.

They were about halfway across the lake when the moon sailed out, illuminating the landscape with silver. At once a starkin lord brought his sisika bird around and down, zooming straight towards them. The giant white bird screeched, its claws out-thrust.

'Quickly!' Molly cried. 'If we can just make the rushes, we can hide.'

'We'll never make it!' Jack yelled back, poling as fast as he could.

Peregrine pulled out his flute and held it to his lips. A cacophony of notes rang out, shrill and harsh.

'What are you doing, you fool?' Grizelda shouted. 'Shoot your arrows!'

Still Peregrine played. It was a strange tune, filled with jarring dissonances. Yet the sisika bird shrieked in response and wheeled about, despite the yelling of the soldier on its back, despite the cruel whip and barbed collar yanking at the giant bird's throat. Away the sisika bird flew, over the lake, over the dim-lit marshes, away from the small boat where Peregrine sat cross-legged and played his long white flute.

Silence fell.

'You saved us!' Molly said. 'But how? What was that tune you played?'

'I don't know,' Peregrine said. 'I thought about compelling the bird to go away and played what came into my mind. It certainly wasn't a very pretty tune!'

'Amazing,' she said and shook her head in wonderment.

Other starkin lords came against them as they noticed the dark shape of the eel-boat against the shining waters of the lake. Each time Peregrine played his flute and sent the sisika birds far away.

'We should've just stayed at Stormlinn Castle and had you play your flute against all those soldiers,' Jack grumbled. 'We could have stayed snug and warm and had a good laugh watching them all run away.'

'I don't think it would work against an army,' Peregrine said. 'The soldiers would all need to be close enough to hear my flute, and I have a feeling that the song for each individual is different. Besides, how long would it take them to work out what I was doing and jam a bit of candle wax in their ears?'

Dawn came at last, the clouds turning softly pink, the water glimmering between black banks of stiff rushes. Molly swung a pot over the brazier, and made them tea from dried marshmallow flowers. There were only two horn cups on the boat, set in beautifully forged iron filigree, which they had to share among the four of them. The hot tea helped warm them, for it was very cold on the water, with a damp mist rising.

The day passed slowly. Peregrine and Jack took turns to pole the punt along, while Molly fished for their supper or carved her bog-oak. Grizelda rested, her dog at her feet as always. The starkin girl looked very different in Molly's homespun clothes, which were all grey or brown or cream, the natural colours of the wool. None of her clothes had dried in time, which made Grizelda irritable. 'They're so itchy,' she complained. 'How can you stand it?'

'I guess I'm used to it,' Molly replied quietly.

It was a long, slow journey through the winding maze of the fenlands. They ate bread and cheese and dried fruit at noon, then dropped anchor a few hours later as the twilight closed down over the marshes. Nobody wanted to risk negotiating their way through the bogs and quagmires in the darkness. Molly had caught some fish and had packed plenty of food, so they had a feast and then settled down to camp on the hard boards. It was surprisingly cosy with the brazier glowing away and plenty of otter skins to snuggle under, and Peregrine entertained them with marvellous stories of ships and faraway lands and strange creatures, till they at last grew drowsy and fell asleep.

As soon as it was light, they kept on going through the marshes. It was hard to keep a sense of direction in the early morning mist, but Molly knew each tiny islet, each moss-hung tree, and so the small boat slowly wound its way deep into the swamps.

Midafternoon, the tall grey peak of Grimsfell rose on the horizon. Like the Isle of Eels, it was an island that rose steeply from flat, briny marshes, its lower slopes covered with leafless, twiggy trees, its height bare except for one dramatic rock that stuck into the grey sky like a broken fang. Below the rock grew an ancient oak tree, cleaved in two. Even from this distance they could see the clump of mistletoe that grew in its bare branches.

'The lightning-blasted oak,' Peregrine said. 'Jack, can't we get along any faster?'

Jack flashed him a hot and bothered look. 'No, your Highness. Unless you'd like to lend a hand?'

Candles blazed in the great hall.

Vernisha sat on her gilded throne, scowling as King Merrik and Queen Liliana danced a joyous jig in the centre of hall. Both were dressed in animal skins, and the king wore a set of donkey ears with as much dignity as if it were the starkin crown. They were smiling at each other, apparently oblivious to the jeering crowd.

Zed was clapping along; Rozalina waved a stick of jester's bells. They were as calm and relaxed as if they were in their own great hall. Vernisha obviously found this disregard for their humiliation most aggravating, for she kept yelling at them to do something else. 'Juggle, you fool! Do a cartwheel! Sing us a silly song!'

The four captives only smiled and bowed and did as they were ordered. Since Merry was a fine musician and both men had been trained since birth as warriors, they put on as fine a show as any jongleurs, and soon the crowd was clapping and cheering them in genuine pleasure. Vernisha's bulbous cheeks turned magenta.

Lord Goldwin, the Count of Zavaria, sat beside her, toying with a dish of broiled boar's head. A tall, handsome man with a fair beard and ice-blue eyes, he was the one who had persuaded her not to break the Yuletide tradition of truce. As always, two lean white hounds lay at his feet, eating tidbits from his fingers. The pug dog hated them and was continually yowling and yipping at them from his seat on Vernisha's lap. The hound dogs ignored him, laying their heads on their long paws with a long-suffering sigh.

'Such a shame Tom-Tit-Tot can't change shape into a grogoyle,' Liliana said with a scornful glance about the hot, crowded, gaudy room. 'I'd love to have him fly through here, breathing fire and making everyone run and scream.'

'Yes,' King Merrik replied, turning her in a skilful spin. 'But you know he can only change into something his own size or smaller. He's been jumping around Vernisha in the shape of a flea, but I'm afraid if she gets any crosser she'll have us burnt alive before help arrives.'

'I'm not sure if it's the food or the hope that help is coming, but I'm finding it easier to bear now,' Liliana said.

'Yes, thank Liah for Tommy-boy!'

'Stop gossiping!' Vernisha screamed. 'This isn't meant to be fun! Stars and comets, when can I have them killed?'

'Just a few more days,' Lord Goldwin soothed her.

Just then the grand double doors swung open and the steward hurried up the hall. 'Your Majesty, a wicked winged beast is flying about the battlements!'

Vernisha smiled. 'So? Shoot it down!'

The four captives looked at each other in sudden excitement and dread.

'Well, we would have, your Majesty, but . . .'

'But what, you flocculating fool?'

'Princess Adora is being held upon its back by a warrior, your Majesty. If we shoot the beast down, she'll be killed.'

Vernisha's eyes boggled. 'What! My daughter? But . . .'

Lord Goldwin was on his feet in an instant, the white hounds tense and quivering by his side. 'Your Majesty! But how? We must save her!'

'Let's go see this winged beastie,' Vernisha said and seized a whip, laying it about the shoulders of the poor hobhenkies chained to her throne. With a groan, they hoisted the gaudy chair high into the air and carried it down the hall. 'Bring the prisoners!'

Liliana seized Merry's arm and hurried after the procession of servants and courtiers, Rozalina and Zed close behind. 'Is that what Briony meant by a bargaining chip?' Merry whispered to her. 'Vernisha's own daughter?'

'I thought she had been locked away in a tower,' Zed said in a low whisper. 'For refusing to marry again.'

'Poor Adora,' Rozalina said. 'I don't blame her, though. That vile woman has married her four times already, each time to an older and richer man. And none of her children lived past the age of three.'

There was deep distress in Rozalina's voice. Princess Adora was her stepmother, although there were only six years between them in age. She blamed Rozalina for the deaths of all her children since Rozalina had once said that no child of Adora's would ever live to inherit the throne of Ziva. Curse or prophecy, Rozalina herself did not know, but it was hard not to feel pity for the princess, once the most beautiful and celebrated woman in Ziva.

'Pedrin must've broken her out,' Liliana said. 'What a brilliant idea!'

Up, up, up the winding staircases they climbed, the hobhenkies labouring under the weight of the laden throne, until they came out at last onto the battlements.

A creature out of a nightmare wheeled about the towers, uttering a high, defiant, spine-chilling scream. Bat-winged, with the graceful golden body of a lion and the deadly curved tail of a scorpion, fire spat from its gaping jaws. On the grogoyle's back was a tall man with brown hair and a greying beard, dressed in a long twilight-grey cloak. Zed grinned broadly and waved his hand, for the rider was his own father, Lord Pedrin. His father was holding a slender, fair-haired woman before him, keeping her steady as the grogoyle spun and soared.

Vernisha said, 'Tell him to come closer. I want to see if it really is Adora.'

A chalk-faced soldier climbed up onto the battlement and shouted through a speaking-trumpet, 'Come closer!'

The grogoyle dived. Many of the lords and ladies screamed and threw themselves to the ground. The pug dog whimpered and burrowed under Vernisha's voluminous skirts. As the winged beast sped overhead, Liliana could clearly see the petrified face of Princess Adora, her red widow's veil whipping in the wind.

'I have liberated Princess Adora!' Pedrin cried. 'I will exchange her for the safe return of King Merrik, Queen Liliana, Queen Rozalina and Lord Zedrin.'

'Shoot them down,' Vernisha said. 'At last, some proper entertainment!'

'But your Majesty! Your daughter!' Lord Goldwin gasped.

'What use is she to me anyway?' Vernisha replied indifferently. 'Won't do as she's told, all her brats die. She's costing me a fortune in that tower of hers. Shoot her down!'

The soldiers ran forward, knelt and raised high their longbows. At a gesture, they fired. Arrows sprang towards the grogoyle, who twisted and dived. Adora screamed.

'Blazing balls, they missed! Fire again!'

'But, your Majesty . . . you promised me your daughter's hand . . . you said I'd be your heir!' Lord Goldwin was aghast.

She smiled coyly at him and reached out one squat hand to pat his cheek. 'Why marry her when you can have me? Perhaps we can make our own heirs, eh?'

Lord Goldwin turned so pale it looked as if he might faint.

Again and again the starkin soldiers fired, while the four prisoners watched in an agony of fear. The grogoyle adroitly swerved and ducked through the wall of arrows, then soared away, disappearing into the blue sky.

'Stupid soldiers!' Vernisha grumbled. 'Tell them to practise firing against each other! Now, my darling, let's go eat. I need to keep my strength up if I'm to give you an heir.' She smiled at Lord Goldwin and held out one ring-laden hand. Looking sick and shaken, he bowed and kissed it, then followed the swaying throne back down the stairs towards the banqueting hall.

Slumped with disappointment, the four prisoners shuffled after, their faces all turned back to stare to the small square of blue sky slowly dwindling behind them.

Chapter 21

The Seal Ring

THE EEL-BOAT SLOWLY NEGOTIATED ITS WAY DOWN THE river, through shallow channels of water surrounded on either side by reedy beds and clumps of tall grasses and marsh weeds. Many times the boat almost ran aground on mud, and the long-handled shovels were used to push the boat back into deeper water.

The sun was only a small red ball bobbing on the horizon when at last they came close to Grimsfell. Surrounded by marshy fenlands, bogs and quagmires, the island rose steeply from one small half-circle of solid ground, where trees and bushes grew in a tangle. A few broken walls and doorways showed the ruin of what once must have been a village. Peregrine saw the bare boughs of apple trees, the pale drooping catkins of a hazel tree, and the tangled hoops of blackberry brambles. At either end of the beach were two huge boulders carved into the shape of a woman standing upon a striped archway.

'Taramis, the goddess of the rainbow and the bridge between worlds,' Peregrine said. 'I wonder why someone would put a statue of her here, so far from anywhere. They look very old.'

'They mark the beginning of the road,' Molly said.

'The road?'

'Yes. A causeway once led straight through the marshes to Grimsfell. The Count of Ardian built it when the starkin first came a-marching into the fenlands. Grimsfell is the biggest island in the fens, you see, and the count thought to use it. Yet none of the hearthkin would ever stay here. They were afraid, you see, of Old Grim.'

Peregrine nodded in understanding.

Molly went on, 'But when the prince woke Old Grim and took him away, people thought it'd be safe. They came and built this village and carved those statues to guard and protect the road. For a while it all flourished. But then Old Grim came back and put a blight on the place, and everyone fled. The village fell into ruin and the road with it. And then my da broke the dykes and flooded the marsh again and the causeway was drowned. It'll still be there, though, under the water.'

There was a grating noise from the bottom of the boat.

'I think we might've just hit it,' Jack said with a grin. He poked overboard with one of the long-handled shovels and knocked on stone.

'I'm not sure we'll get any closer,' Molly said. 'The bogs are very treacherous around Grimsfell. That's why they built the causeway. We can probably wade ashore from here.'

'But our feet will get wet,' Grizelda objected.

'Never mind,' Molly said. 'We'll take off our boots and stockings and carry them, and then light a fire. I can make us some hot soup, we'll soon get warm again.'

'Eel soup, I bet,' Grizelda muttered but took off her boots

—shiny crimson once more—and looped up her skirt so her legs were bare. Peregrine unhooded Blitz and flung him into the air, and he soared far above them, his wings bent and black against the red-streaked sky. Jack dropped anchor—a boulder tied with rope—and then the four of them waded to shore through the icy water, their boots in their hands. The water was so shallow that it scarcely lapped at their ankles.

'It's too late to do anything now,' Grizelda said. 'Let's make that fire and have something to eat.'

Peregrine hardly heard her. He was staring at the narrow grey stone on the peak of the hill. At the base of the rock grew the oak tree, its broad, knobbly branches as thick as a strong man's torso, its ancient trunk wide enough to hide a draught horse. Long ago it had been cleaved in two by lightning. The few ragged brown leaves which clung to its branches showed the tree still lived, as did the great cluster of golden-green leaves hanging high in the heavy boughs, dangling small white berries.

'I can't believe we've found it,' he whispered. 'I can't believe we're actually here.'

He bent and hastily dragged his stockings and boots onto his wet, cold feet. 'Come on! Let's go and take a look.'

He bounded up the path, Jack at once close behind. Molly dropped the heavy pot and the sack of food and limped after them, finding it hard to manage the narrow rocky path with her crutch. Grizelda sighed, rolled her eyes and charged after them, pushing past Molly so she could catch up with the boys.

It was a hard slog and Molly's hip was aching by the time she reached the top. She paused to catch her breath and surreptitiously rub her hip. She looked up at the grey fang of rock looming above her, sharp against the darkening clouds. From the base of the rock ran the stony path of an old dried-up stream. Molly could see from the mosses on the rock where the spring must once have run.

'Here, Molly!' Peregrine cried.

He and Jack and Grizelda were all perched on the low, broad branches of the oak tree, gazing out at the view. Blitz crouched above them, his feathers ruffling in the cold wind. Whining, Oskar was standing on his hind legs, his paws up on the tree trunk as if wishing he could climb up and be with his mistress. Molly went to join them. She could not climb the tree but she leant against its ancient fissured trunk and looked out at the fenlands. As far as the eye could see, the peat-bogs stretched, a crazy pattern of mud and reeds and grasses, with the occasional winding snake of shining water, a few crooked trees holding up stiff, cold branches against the sky.

'He was here,' Peregrine said. 'Prince Zander, I mean. He came here with the spear and he banged it three times against the stone and roused Lord Grim. Then, as Lord Grim emerged from under the hill, the soldiers seized him and bound him with bells. Then Prince Zander mocked Princess Shoshanna and told her that he'd make sure her prophecy never came true. And then he threw the spear into the bog. He was fat and lazy. He can't have thrown it very far. Maybe a hundred steps.'

He stared out at the bog, his hands clenched into fists. Mist swirled about the bases of all the trees, making their branches look like black skeletal fingers. Birds called eerily. The sun slid further behind the horizon, and at once it grew colder and darker. Molly shivered, her feet like lumps of ice in her damp boots.

'How do you know all this?' Grizelda demanded.

'I've seen it in the Well of Fates,' Peregrine said. 'The Erlrune showed me. I wanted to know what had happened to the spear. He threw it that way.' He pointed towards the west, where the mud and marsh seemed thickest. 'I'll find it tomorrow,' he said, utter conviction in his voice.

'I'm cold,' Grizelda said. 'Let's go down and get that fire started.'

Peregrine helped her jump from the tree and then they scrambled back down the path to the beach below. Molly found it hard going but, to her secret pleasure, Peregrine stayed back and helped her down some of the rougher patches.

'Let's get that fire going!' Jack said, rubbing his hands together. 'Brrr, but it's cold!'

'We'll need a lot of firewood if we're to stay warm all night,' Grizelda said. 'It's bound to be damp and misty.'

Molly's heart sank. Her hip was hurting so much she wasn't sure she could walk on it much longer, let alone go scrambling about looking for kindling. Peregrine must have sensed her dismay, for he said, 'How about you and Jack go and get it, Grizelda? I'll get the fire started here so Molly can begin to make supper.'

Grizelda's lips narrowed and she cast Molly an angry glance, before stamping across the clearing and into the undergrowth, Oskar bounding beside her. Jack went the other way, leaving Molly and Peregrine alone on the shingle. Peregrine called Blitz down and tied his jesses to a branch, slipping the leather hood over the falcon's fierce, bright eyes so he would rest and be still.

'Here, this'll make a good table,' Peregrine said then, slapping a broad, flat rock. 'If you sit here, you can start preparing supper.' He pulled a smaller rock over and settled it so Molly could sit down. 'I can make a fire quickly enough. Just so we can get supper on. There's plenty of kindling about.'

The prince busied himself gathering twigs and rushes and breaking a dead branch over his knee while Molly lowered herself down awkwardly. She was glad he had not mentioned anything about her hip. Molly hated anyone to make a fuss of it, liking to pretend she was as agile and capable as everyone else. She opened her sack and drew out some leeks, a bunch of smoked haddocks, some rashers of streaky bacon wrapped in cloth, a bunch of withered purple carrots, and a small crock of dripping. She drew her knife and began to roughly chop the leeks and carrots.

Within minutes, the prince had a crackling fire going.

'Do you need water?' he asked.

She nodded. 'Don't fill it from the marsh, though; the water will make us all sick. There should be a well here somewhere.'

Peregrine found the well easily enough, and lowered the iron pot down on a rope to fill it. Soon it was boiling away merrily on the fire. Molly threw in the ingredients and then bent to draw off her boots and stockings, putting her icy feet close to the flames to warm up. Peregrine came to sit beside her, feeding the flames with handfuls of dry moss and driftwood.

'I've made you something,' she said shyly. Sliding one hand into her pocket, she drew out a ring made from bog-oak and passed it to him. It had been carved into the shape of a small shield, with a bird etched upon it, wings spread.

Peregrine bent his head over it. 'You made it from that piece of driftwood you found on my birthday,' he said in delight, sliding the ring onto his finger. It fitted perfectly. 'What's the design? It looks like some kind of bird.'

'It's a phoenix a-rising from flames. You know, like what you said to the council. That we should all put aside our old emblems and make a new one, a symbol of the new land that will be born out of the ashes of this one. I thought you could use it as a seal ring. You, know when you are king.' Her cheeks hot with embarrassment, Molly stopped talking and ducked her head.

'I see, it's been carved in relief. That's why it took me a moment to recognise the design. I'll get a candle out of my pack so we can try it out.' Eagerly Peregrine pulled his pack towards him and rummaged through it until he found the stump of a candle. He lit it, then dribbled a small blob of wax onto a scrap of parchment. He then pressed the face of the ring into the wax. When he drew it away, there was the perfect impression of a phoenix rising from flames.

'It's beautiful!' he said. 'Thank you so much!'

He seized her hand and drew her forward so he could kiss her cheek, then sat back on his heels, studying the bog-oak ring with delight. Molly turned back to her pot, feeling the warmth from his kiss spread all the way down her body to her bare toes.

'What's all this?' Grizelda demanded stridently. She stood just outside the circle of firelight, her arms filled with kindling, her narrowed gaze moving from Peregrine's face to Molly's. Oskar stood beside her, hackles raised.

'Look what Molly made for me!' Peregrine cried, getting to his feet. 'It's a seal ring with a phoenix carved on it. Isn't she clever? And it's made from bog-oak, the same wood that the fen-men's brooches are made from. It's hundreds, maybe even thousands of years old. It's a symbol of the new order. When I am king I shall seal every new law and proclamation with it, and when I do, I shall always think of Molly of the Marshes, who made it for me.' He smiled brilliantly at Molly, who blushed even redder and turned away, pretending to look for something in her sack, so no-one would see her face.

'Lovely,' Grizelda said flatly and dumped her load, practically on top of Molly's bare feet. 'Always assuming that you can find the spear, rouse the boo-bogey, vanquish all of the queen's armies and seize the throne.'

The light went out of Peregrine's face. 'I can but try,' he said quietly. He bent and drew a small silver bowl out of his pack. 'I'll look now and see if I can discover where the spear is. I'll never be able to sleep otherwise. Then I can go and retrieve it early in the morning.'

He filled the bowl with water and then sat cross-legged on the shingle, staring into the glinting liquid. 'What is lost must now be found, take my luck and turn it round, show me the vanished spear, let my vision be clear,' he intoned. His expression changed, growing more intent, then triumph and gladness flowered. 'I know where it is! I know exactly where it is! I need to dig, though, it's buried down in the peat.' He looked up, grinning broadly, and emptied the water over his shoulder.

'I have a scraw-cutter on the boat,' Molly said eagerly. 'That's a special spade for cutting down through the peat.'

'You should have brought it,' Grizelda said in an accusing voice. 'Robin will want to dig up his spear first thing, won't you, Robin?' She smiled at him, looking quite dazzling pretty, and he smiled back.

'I'll go and get it,' Molly said, her spirits suddenly and unaccountably low. With the help of her crutch, she got to her feet and paused for a moment, but the prince was busy describing to Grizelda exactly what he had seen in his vision. Molly sighed, looped up her skirts through her belt, and began to limp down the beach. Although the sun had set, the moon glinted on the water and showed the dark silhouette of the boat, rocking gently at anchor. She began to walk out to it, feeling her way forward with her feet, the rocks of the old causeway just below the surface of the bitterly cold water.

'Why, Molly!'

She heard Peregrine's call and turned back. He was standing by the fire, one hand stretched out to her. 'It looks . . . it looks like you're walking on water!'

She gazed at him in bewilderment, wondering at the joyous light in his face.

'It's a sign,' he said. 'Now I know all will be well.'

A smile leapt to her lips. She met his gaze and nodded. 'Yes. All will be well now.'

Then she turned and walked out to the boat, walking upon moon-silvered water.

CHAPTER 22

A Toast to Success

PEREGRINE TURNED BACK TO THE FIRE, SMILING. A GLOW OF happiness filled him.

Only when a blind boy can see and a lame girl walk on water shall peace come again to the land, and the rightful king win back the throne . . .

And he had just seen a lame girl walk on water. He had seen where the spear was hidden. He knew where Lord Grim slept. Tomorrow he would find one and raise the other, and set out to free his parents, and win back the throne for his father. He wondered briefly about the blind boy, and when that part of the prophecy would reveal itself, but trusted it would all become clear in time.

Grizelda had sat down by the fire, her skirts tucked up so she could stretch her long legs to the flames. Oskar lay beside her, his head on his paws. Slowly she unbound her hair, letting it fall down her back in smooth golden waves. Taking her comb from her pack, she began to draw it through her heavy locks in long, slow strokes. She smiled at him.

'So tomorrow you'll find your fabled spear. Do you really think you'll be able to use it to throw down Queen Vernisha and seize the crown?'

Peregrine frowned. 'I won't be seizing the crown, I'll be winning it back for my father, the rightful king.'

'Of course, I'm sorry.' She sighed. 'A lifetime of propaganda is hard to forget. I've only had a few days to learn the right way to think.'

He felt sorry for his sharp words. He came and sat down next to her, stirring the soup in the pot.

'What then, Robin?' she asked, leaning close to him, putting one hand on his arm. He could smell her sweet, heady perfume and wondered again where it came from. Had she carried a bottle with her the whole way? *Starkin girls*, he thought, and smiled to himself.

'What shall you do, when you have defeated Vernisha and won back the crown? You have been fighting so long, what will you do with peace?'

'Oh, there'll be plenty to do,' he replied buoyantly. 'New laws to make, and old ones to abolish. Like punishing people for listening to songs and stories! And the roads should really be fixed, they're a disgrace.'

'But what will you do for *you*,' she insisted softly. 'Surely you will deserve *some* reward.'

Peregrine glanced at her, puzzled. 'I suppose so. What, do you mean a new horse? I'd rather have Sable back again.'

'And you'll need to make new alliances. Forge new relationships.' She looked away, her eyelashes dropping to form perfect golden crescents on her cheeks.

'Yes, I guess we will.' Peregrine turned to look for Molly, wondering if she was all right.

'Your father will want to make new treaties,' she said, a shade of impatience creeping into her voice.

Peregrine shrugged. 'I guess so.'

She put both hands on his arm, looked him straight in the eyes and said, in a slow, clear voice, 'No doubt he'll want you to marry well, to cement these new alliances and treaties, and to ensure there's an heir to the throne, one that has the requisite bloodlines to ensure the support of the starkin lords.'

Suddenly her meaning became clear to Peregrine. He gulped, and stood up abruptly. 'Maybe. Probably. I'm not sure. Plenty of time to worry about that!' Blitz moved restlessly on his branch, bells chiming.

'Don't you think it would be better to plan for all contingencies now?' she said persuasively. 'The starkin lords only supported Vernisha because her blood was pure. If you could assure them that your heirs would be of starkin blood, it could make all the difference. Whatever happens tomorrow, you will need the starkin lords' support if you wish to rule all of Ziva.'

Peregrine took a deep breath. 'There is much in what you say,' he answered carefully. 'And I am sure my parents will consider how best to win the starkin lords' support once they have won back the throne. However, I know that my parents would never try to force me into a marriage for purely political reasons. You may not know that their marriage was a love match, and has been blessed with much happiness. They will want nothing less for me.'

She touched his wrist gently, smiling coyly. 'But such a union does not have to be for purely political reasons.'

He pulled his wrist away. 'No, it doesn't. But I certainly would not wish to promise marriage to anyone until I had fallen in love. Which I hope very much will happen one day.'

Peregrine hoped he had made his meaning clear. From the sudden anger on Grizelda's face, he thought she understood. There was a moment's awkward silence. Peregrine was trying to think of something to say to ease the tension when Grizelda drew a deep breath.

'Well then, that's that. I think we should drink a toast to the success of your mission.' She turned and rummaged in her pack, drawing out two delicate silver goblets and a black leather bottle.

Peregrine was dumbfounded. 'Is that Molly's mead?'

She smiled. 'I knew you liked it, so I thought to bring some for you.'

'Does Molly know?'

She flushed with annoyance. 'Well, no, but surely she'd not mind. She was happy enough for you to drink it last night.'

Peregrine gestured to the silver goblets, which she had set up on the stone table. 'Have you been carrying these around with you all this time?'

She smiled. 'Well, I wasn't sure if the Erlrune's would have all the necessary luxuries of life. I wasn't expecting to end up in a bog!'

Peregrine smiled rather absently. She uncorked the leather bottle and poured some of the sweet-scented golden liquid into the goblets. 'It does smell like summer, doesn't it,' she said, smiling into his eyes. He looked away, flushing.

'To better days!' she cried and passed him a goblet. He took it and she raised her goblet to his, and drank deeply. Peregrine looked down into the goblet. Did the mead seem rather cloudy? Did it smell rather rank? He did not drink.

'It's bad luck to refuse a toast,' she said lightly. 'Drink up.'

She drank another mouthful, keeping her eyes on his. Holding her gaze, Peregrine lifted the goblet to his lips, noticing how pale she had grown and the faint sheen of sweat on her brow. Her pupils dilated.

'No! Your Highness! Don't drink!' Jack sprinted from the grove of trees, dropping an enormous load of kindling and dragging his sword free of its scabbard. Startled, Grizelda spun around, her own mead spraying in a golden arc. Jack was only a few strides from her, murderous rage in his eyes, his sword swinging high.

'Kill, boy!' Grizelda screamed. 'Kill!'

Oskar launched himself forward, snarling, leaping for Jack's throat. At the same moment Grizelda turned on Peregrine and slammed her hand into the base of the goblet, smashing it into Peregrine's face. The mead sprayed into his eyes, burning like acid. Peregrine screamed in agony. Falling to his knees, he lifted his hands to his eyes, unable to see a thing.

Chaos all around him. Peregrine could hear the savage sound of a dog snarling, jaws tearing. He could hear Jack screaming hoarsely and Blitz screeching. A few hard thunks, and then a high-pitched yelp. 'Oskar!' Grizelda screamed. Then quick footsteps ran past him and he heard splashing. The pain in his eyes and face was intense. He struggled to his feet, trying to see, but his vision was nothing but a red haze.

'Jack! Jack!'

A low moan. A few whimpers. Silence.

The iron door to the queens' cell scraped open. 'Up you get, my lovelies,' the gaoler jeered. 'The queen is ready to pass judgement on you.'

'I am the queen,' Liliana said quietly. 'You would do well to remember that.'

'I wouldn't go saying that to her Majesty's face, sweetheart,' he replied, bending so he could haul her to her feet. 'She has a nasty habit of cutting out people's tongues.'

Liliana jerked her arm free of his grasp but said no more. She felt sick with fear. It had been hard to keep despair at bay after Pedrin had failed to convince Vernisha to swap them for her daughter. The six days were almost over and still they had not managed to escape their dungeons. Tom-Tit-Tot had tried to steal the keys to their cells, but had been chased with a halberd and had lost the very tip of his tail. Liliana had been able to heal his tail, but the indignity had upset the omen-imp, as had his failure to rescue his master. It was an impossible task, though. The castle was stuffed as full of soldiers as a Yule cake was stuffed with currants and candied peel.

Outside the cell, the low glare of the smoky torches made Liliana flinch and cover her eyes. Rozalina gripped her arm and together, shorn heads held high, the two queens made their slow way along the corridor, prodded from behind by sharp halberds. Another cell was opened by one of the gaolers, and Merry and Zed came stumbling out. Like their wives, they were dressed in animal skins and both wore rough hats with donkeys' ears sewed to them. They looked grey and exhausted, but did their best to walk with their heads high and their backs straight. They smiled at each other but were not allowed to speak or touch.

Up endless winding stairs the four prisoners clanked, the shackles and other cruel confinements locked again in place. They shuffled down the long corridor into the banqueting hall, where a crowd of courtiers were once again stuffing themselves on a gargantuan feast. Liliana saw roast boars' heads, venison pies, frumenty, a fricassee of baby kid and bacon, oat biscuits smeared with smoked fish, meatballs with onion sauce, gilded peacocks, cheese and quince dumplings, and a vast steamed stingray served with oysters. Her stomach growled loudly and saliva sprang into her mouth. Even though Tom-Tit-Tot had done his best to bring them food and drink, it had not been easy for him and it was many days since she had last had a full meal.

Soldiers poked and prodded them up the hall with the sharp points of their halberds. Liliana imagined she was wearing a sweeping gown of golden silk with cascading sleeves, and that she was having difficulty walking because of her high-heeled crystal slippers and the crown of glowing jewels upon her head. The stink that came up from her own body made this fantasy difficult to maintain, but she did her best.

Vernisha reclined on her throne, gobbling down oysters that Lord Goldwin was feeding her, a false smile pinned to his face. She was dressed in an extraordinary gown of purple silk, cut very low across her bulging décolletage and sewn with enormous purple flowers. Her pug dog was dressed the same, purple velvet slippers on his feet. Vernisha's hair had been styled in extravagant ringlets, which stuck out from under the dazzling starkin crown.

She leant forward at the sight of the four prisoners in their filthy animal skins, her fat cheeks creasing in a smile. She snapped her fingers at Lord Goldwin. 'Bring me my marchpane. My night is about to get much sweeter.'

Lord Goldwin frowned and gestured to a servant, who brought forward a platter of marchpane, formed into fanciful shapes and gilded.

She selected a piece shaped like a fire-breathing gro-goyle and crammed it into her mouth. 'Mmmm-mmm,' she mumbled. 'Delicious!' She swallowed it down and licked her fingers.

'Look, our guests have arrived! Don't they look fine? Not so high and mighty now.' She sniggered, and the crowd all laughed. They were as richly and extravagantly dressed as the pretender-queen, so perfumed and painted and jewelled it was hard to tell what their real faces would look like.

'Well, tomorrow is Twelfth Night and the end of that ridiculous, outdated period of peace. I must thank my darling Lord Goldwin, though, for really it's been much more entertaining keeping you alive a few more days. I've had time to refine my plans too. Burning you at the stake was much too quick!'

She selected another piece of marchpane, this time shaped like a jester with donkey's ears. She broke off the head and offered it to the pug dog, who wolfed it down, the stump of his tail wagging happily.

'Now, I won't keep you in suspense any longer. I know you must all be *dying* to know what I've got planned.' She sniggered again and the crowd tittered.

'Firstly, our not-so-lovely ladies. Both of them witches as well as traitors. The one who kills our brave men by the merest touch of her finger will have both her hands hacked off and the stumps left to bleed freely. If she still lives after seven days, she'll be weighted with stones and flung in the moat for the pikes to chew on.'

Despite herself, Liliana's breath caught. She tried to clench her fists but was unable to move her numb hands inside the heavy iron gauntlets.

'Now, what can I do to you, my dearest Rozalina? I've thought about this long and hard, I promise you. I don't mind you cursing my poor uncle so much. After all, I'd long wanted him dead. And if you hadn't cursed him, I wouldn't be queen now, would I? But my poor, dear daughter. You told her all her children would die, and now I haven't a single grandchild to dandle on my knee and comfort me in my old age. That I find hard to forgive.'

Vernisha's hand reached out, hovered over the bowl of sweetmeats and selected a lump of marchpane that had been shaped into the figure of a queen with a wreath of flowers on her head. Vernisha contemplated the marchpane figure through narrowed eyes, then swiftly bit off its head. She munched with evident enjoyment, then licked her lips.

'So, Rozalina, you'll have your tongue nailed to the pillory for six days and six nights, one for each of my dead grandchildren, and then it'll be torn from your mouth. If you survive, you'll be put to work cleaning out the cesspits at my palace. After all, you are my step-granddaughter, people might talk if I was to have you killed.'

Rozalina's eyes were filled with horror, but she lifted her shorn head proudly.

'Vernisha, what law gives you the right to pass judgement on the Erlqueen of the Stormlinn, or on my queen-consort?' King Merrik asked. 'You have no right to sit on that throne or wear that crown. You are a tyrant and a dictator. Are there no laws in this land to stop such unjust cruelty? By the truth, I swear—' The hilt of a halberd slammed into the pit of his stomach, and King Merrik bent over, gasping and choking with pain.

'As for you, Merrik Bellringer, son of the brigand and rebel leader known as the Hag, you will be hanged by the neck until you are almost dead, then you will be cut down and disembowelled, and your guts burnt on a brazier before your very eyes. Then a horse shall be tied to each of your four limbs and whipped till they tear you in quarters. Your head will be impaled above the palace gates for the crows to peck at, and the rest of you tossed to the city dogs. The same shall be done to you, Zedrin ziv Estaria, for you have betrayed those of your kind.'

Liliana felt the ground swaying beneath her feet. Her legs trembled and gave way. She fell to her knees, bile rising sharply in her throat. Rozalina knelt beside her, supporting her.

King Merrik was very white but he kept his gaze on Vernisha's bloated face. 'I warn you, Vernisha, that all you do in this life shall be returned to you threefold. By the power of three, let it be.'

Vernisha's face turned purple as a plum. 'Take them away! The sentences shall be carried out tomorrow, at sunset, when the twelve days of Yuletide are finally over! And, somebody, bring me some more marchpane! Pugsie-Wugsie and I are hungry!'

Liliana managed to stand up. Exerting all her strength of will, she straightened her back and lifted her head high. She could not see the seething crowd of courtiers for the tears in her eyes, but she walked out, her arms linked with those of her cousin and her husband.

If only I knew that Robin was safe, she thought. *Please, let him be safe!*

CHAPTER 23

Blind Boy

Peregrine crouched in the darkness, unable to hear anything except the uneven pant of his own breath and a strange, unsteady whooshing in his ears. He groped with his hands, trying to orientate himself.

'Jack?' he cried again. Nobody answered.

From behind him came the sound of splashing, like someone running towards him through the water. Peregrine drew his dagger. The hiss of metal on metal seemed very loud. He kept the dagger close to his side and turned towards the sound, trying to judge what was racing towards him.

'Your Highness, what happened?' Molly's voice cried. 'Oh, leeblimey! Your face . . . Oh, no, Jack!' Uneven footsteps ran past him and he heard Molly fling herself down on her knees, her breath catching on a sob.

'Molly,' he said rapidly. 'What's happened? Where's Grizelda?' He stumbled towards the sound of her voice and almost fell over something in his path. He reached down and felt fur, bone, blood. He snatched his hand away.

'Wait, your Highness. Jack! The dog attacked him. He killed it. Leeblimey, I've never seen so much blood.' Her voice shook.

Peregrine crawled past the dog and bumped into Molly, who was on her knees. He squatted down beside her. Reaching out, he felt Jack lying huddled on the ground. The skin of his face was slick and sticky. Peregrine's stomach twisted. It was hard to breathe. Then Jack moaned and moved slightly.

'He's still alive,' Peregrine said in a hoarse and shaky voice.

'I have my shawl over the wound in his neck.' Molly's voice was not much stronger.

'How . . . how bad is it?'

'It won't stop a-bleeding.' Molly sounded close to tears. 'What . . . what happened?'

'Grizelda tried to poison me.' Peregrine's voice gave out. He bent and laid his face against Jack's. 'I wasn't going to drink it, you idiot! How could you think I'd be so stupid?' Tears dampened his skin.

'We have to help him.'

'I can't see,' Peregrine said. 'The poison splashed in my eyes, I'm blind.'

'Here, put your hands here. Push down on my shawl, try to stop the bleeding. I'll fetch water to wash your eyes with.'

Peregrine did as he was told, pushing down on the sodden mess of her shawl, listening to her as she hurried, limping, to the well. She flung down her crutch and lowered the pot on its rope and then dragged it up again, the iron scraping against stone. She limped back, water splashing as she stumbled on the shingle. It was strange how clear all her movements were to him, when he could not see, only hear.

'Bend your head back,' she whispered. He felt cold water flowing over his face, wetting his hair and his collar. The pain in his eyes lessened. She gently wiped his face with her sleeve. 'Is that better?'

He opened his eyes, but all was a blur. 'I still can't see! I'm blind.' The words of Queen Rozalina's prophecy came back to him: *Only when a blind boy can see . . .*

He cried out in anguish.

'It's all right, it'll pass,' Molly said rapidly. 'We'll keep on washing your eyes, it'll be all right. Just stay there, keep your hands on Jack. I need to do what I can for him.'

He heard her uneven footsteps running this way and that, and then the sound of her petticoats being torn. Then she came and took hold of his hands, lifting them gently while she eased the sodden shawl away. She drew in her breath in a gasp, but was quick to replace the shawl with a pad of petticoat which she bound tight to the wound.

'I've made him a bed of your cloaks,' she whispered. 'Help me lift him.'

Together they managed to lift Jack. He moaned in pain. Peregrine felt in his pocket for the sprig of mistletoe and tucked it into Jack's pocket. 'It may help,' he said. 'It's meant to help heal wounds.'

'It's a very bad wound.' Molly's voice trembled.

'Do you think—?'

'I don't know! I hope not! Oh, if only we were home, we could call the Crafty to come and heal him.'

'If only my mam were here, she'd heal him in a trice.' Peregrine pressed both hands to his hot, throbbing eyes, tears choking him.

'We can't even take him back to the Isle of Eels—Grizelda took the boat.'

'Grizelda took the boat?' Peregrine repeated, unable even now to understand all that had happened.

'I was a-coming back from the boat with the scraw-cutter when she ran past. She just about shoved me over. I heard her pull the anchor up but I was a-coming as fast as I could to see what had happened to you and Jack. I should've tried to stop her.'

'She might've tried to kill you too.' Just saying the words shook Peregrine again. He gulped a breath.

'But why? Why did she try to poison you?'

'I don't know!' Peregrine dropped his head into his hands. His eyes felt sore and hot and inflamed. His head ached, and he felt dazed and bewildered. Everything had happened so fast. 'I need my eyes! I can't find the spear if I'm blind. If I had the spear, I could heal Jack and I could find some way to get us away from here. But I'm blind, I'm blind!'

'Shh,' Molly said. 'Let me wash your eyes again. There's nothing more we can do for Jack now.'

She brought more water and sat behind him, drawing him back to lean against her legs and gently pouring water over his eyes. He submitted gratefully, the icy water easing his pain. For a long time they were silent. The only noise Peregrine could hear was the *lap, lap, lap* of the water on the shale, the rattle of branches in the cold wind, the chime of the falcon's bells, Molly's soft breathing, and the occasional low moan from Jack.

'She wanted me to marry her,' he said.

'What?' Molly jerked, slopping the water.

'I think that's what she meant. She kept hinting about alliances, and how a marriage with a starkin would appease the starkin lords, that sort of thing.'

Molly muttered something under her breath.

'I basically told her that I wasn't interested and that was when she brought out the mead. I mean, how odd was that?

She had fine goblets with her, in her saddle pack, and a bottle of your mead!'

'So the mead was poisoned?' Molly's voice was indignant.

'It must've been. Except she drank it. She drank half a glass while trying to make me drink.'

'Maybe she just put the poison in your cup.'

'But we searched her and all her luggage at Stormlinn Castle. I mean, Stiga said . . . Stiga said she had venom in her hand and venom in her heart . . .' Peregrine could not go on, his eyes burning now with tears.

Molly stroked his hair from his brow, waiting for his breath to steady. After a moment she said, 'When we took over the Castle of Ardian, we found a collection of curious things in the count's dressing-room. One of them was a ring that unlatched to show a secret compartment. It had some kind of powder in it.'

'A poison ring! Of course, I've read about them. She was always twisting that big ring of hers on her finger. She must've added the poison while I wasn't looking.' Peregrine was disgusted with himself.

'It'd only take a second,' Molly consoled him.

'But why? I still can't understand why. She was the one who warned us about the ambush, she fled the castle with us, we've been travelling together for almost two weeks . . .'

'Perhaps she was playing a double game,' Molly said.

Peregrine nodded his head thoughtfully. His shock and distress was beginning to ebb, and the cold water was soothing his burning eyes. 'Yes. That makes sense. Really, she had nothing to lose from warning us of the ambush but she gained a lot.'

'She got into the castle, learnt all your plans, earned your trust,' Molly said.

'She was able to mark the entrance to the secret passage so the soldiers could creep in at night and take my parents by surprise,' he said bitterly. 'And then once we fled the castle, she made sure we left a trail so her hunter friend could follow her the whole way. She must have intended to lead him straight to the Erlrune.'

'She must've been furious when you went the other way,' Molly said with a faint smile.

'She was! She had a full-blown temper tantrum.'

'So why did she stick with you?'

'She was still playing her double game. What would happen if I did find the spear and my father won back his throne? Vernisha would be out of power, and all her supporters with her. But Grizelda and her brother would be the only ones with a foot in our camp. We'd be grateful, we'd reward them. Yet if I failed, they'd lose nothing because her brother was still with Vernisha, no doubt feeding her all the information that Grizelda managed to winkle out of me.'

'She was clever,' Molly said begrudgingly.

'What am I to do, what am I to do?' Peregrine beat his forehead with his hands.

Molly caught his hands, holding them both in hers. 'You need to find the spear.'

'But I'm blind! How can I find it when I can't see?' Even as he spoke, Peregrine heard the echo of words in his mind. He remembered the prophecy, spoken long ago by his own grandfather, Durrik the Seer, when he had been a boy much the same age as Peregrine was now.

Though he must be lost before he can find,
though, before he sees, he must be blind,

if he can find and if he can see,
the true king of all he shall be.

Peregrine drew in a deep, slow breath. He had often puzzled over those words, asking his mother, 'What does it mean?' Each time she had shrugged and said, 'The words of a Teller seem obscure but they always tell truth. Perhaps it just means that the third child of the prophecy will not understand the nature of his destiny for a long time. Perhaps it means he will grow from a blind, newborn babe to a man before he finds his way. Maybe it means that he will be blinded by love or by fear, and must learn to see clearly. I don't know what it means, Robin, but I'm sure we will understand it one day. And you know we are always looking out for blind boys, for one appears in Rozalina's prophecy too, as you know.'

'But aren't I the third child of the prophecy?' Peregrine had demanded. 'You and Aunty Rozie always say I am.'

Liliana had paused a while before answering. 'I think you are, Robin,' she said. 'I wish that you weren't, I fear what it might mean. But you are the only one who has wildkin and starkin and hearthkin blood in him, at least that we know about.'

Peregrine had not been afraid. He had been eager to be the one to smite the throne of stars asunder, to win back the throne. His mother had drawn him against her knee, ruffled his hair and said, 'You should be afraid, Robin. It's a terrible thing to have the weight of destiny bearing down on you.'

But Peregrine had only laughed.

'*I'm* the blind boy,' he said to Molly now, in a strange, choked voice. 'I've known the prophecy all my life but not once did it occur to me that I'd be the blind boy.'

'I don't know what you mean,' she said, sounding frightened.

He sat up and twisted around as if to look at Molly, but then remembered he was blind and slumped back against her bent legs. She stroked his wet hair back from his forehead with her hands.

'Long, long ago, my grandfather spoke a prophecy. He said:

Three times a babe shall be born,
between star-crowned and iron-bound.
First, the sower of seeds, the soothsayer,
though lame, he must travel far.
Next shall be the king-breaker, the king-maker,
though broken himself he shall be.
Last, the smallest and the greatest—
in him, the blood of wise and wild,
farseeing ones and starseeing ones.
Though he must be lost before he can find,
though, before he sees, he must be blind,
if he can find and if he can see,
the true king of all he shall be.

'My grandfather was the first child, the sower of seeds, the soothsayer. Then came my Uncle Zed, who fell from the tower while rescuing Aunty Rozalina and broke his back and his legs. And then came me. The prophecy says I had to be lost before I can find—well, I was lost in the forest and now I'm lost again in the marshes. And it said I must be blind before I can see. Well, now I am blind and I can see nothing, *nothing*!' He groaned and flung one arm over his eyes.

'Is that why you asked me if there was a blind boy at the castle?' Molly asked. Her voice was soft and low.

Peregrine nodded. 'I saw that you were lame . . .' Somehow it was easier to talk to her of her affliction when he could not see her. 'Aunty Rozalina said peace would not come until a blind boy could see and a lame girl walk on water.'

'And I have walked on water, so now, if peace is to come, you must see.'

'But how?' Peregrine stretched his eyes wide but could see nothing but a dim red haze where the fire was.

'I don't know. Washing your eyes has not helped?'

'A little. They feel better. I still can't see, though!'

'If you find the spear, you'll be able to heal your eyes too.'

Peregrine sat up. 'Yes! Of course!' Then he subsided. 'But how can I find the spear when I can't see?'

'Is there not some other way? Like . . . when I see what shape is trapped inside the wood, I see it in my mind's eye, not in my real eye.'

'I could try,' he whispered, then shook his head. 'No, I must try. But how?'

She got up, shaking out her skirts. 'Sit and rest awhile, and I'll check on Jack and make us some supper. You must be hungry, your Highness.'

'Please, call me Robin.'

'All right . . . Robin.'

He heard the blush in her voice. That amazed him and gave him hope. If he could hear a blush, surely he could use his other senses to find what he had always used his eyes for.

CHAPTER 24

Corpse Candles

MOLLY HUNCHED BY THE FIRE, STIRRING HER SOUP. SHE WAS shaking with cold, her shawl now a sodden, bloodstained ball discarded on the shingle.

Jack lay nearby. His hands and face and throat all showed deep lacerations that still oozed blood. He was hot, and the wounds she had not been able to bandage were weeping and inflamed. The corpse of the dog still lay beside him, its blood staining the grey shingle black.

Peregrine sat next to Molly, his face turning from side to side as he strained to make sense of the eerie night noises of the marsh. An intense red rash spread over his face, and his eyes were puffy and swollen almost shut. Molly suspected a plant like marsh spurge was the source of the poison, for she had once seen a boy come up with a similar rash all over his hands after plucking the weed. Her spirit quailed inside her.

She raised her face to look at the frosty-white stars, spread across the dark sky. The night was clear and Molly thought she had never seen so many stars. The moonlight glimmered on the still water, and the flames of the fire leapt towards the sky like strange beasts from a fairytale. Sparks whirled.

What would it be like to be struck blind? Molly's heart twisted with pity for the poor prince. Imagine never being able to see the stars again. Imagine never seeing again the sun shining through new leaves, never seeing again the first marsh-marigolds springing out of the shrivelled brown of frost-bitten grasses, never seeing again the Isle of Eels floating in a blue mist. She pressed her hands together and hoped and wished with all her might that it was only a temporary blindness, and that Prince Peregrine would see again.

Robin.

She blushed again and began to ladle the thin soup into two horn cups. She brought them to him and knelt before him so she could press one into his hands.

'Be careful, it's hot,' she whispered.

'It smells good,' he answered, trying to smile, then wincing as the movement hurt his face.

She told him about the boy who had hurt his hands plucking marsh spurge. 'He was fine in a day or two. Maybe your eyes will be too.'

'Maybe.' He nodded. 'I can't wait, though. I can hear Jack is getting weaker, he barely makes a sound anymore. As soon as we've eaten, I'll try to find the spear. What does it matter if it is dark, I can't see anyway.' His voice was bitter.

'I can see quite well. The stars are bright and the moon is shining. If you tell me what to look for, maybe I can guide you.'

'All right.' Prince Peregrine lifted his horn cup to his lips and drank. Molly drank too. The hot, savoury liquid gave her strength. She was tired, but did not see how she could possibly sleep with the life slowly ebbing out of Jack and the corpse of the dog lying so still on the sands. Of all the things that Grizelda had done, Molly thought she hated the starkin girl most for the way she had so casually sacrificed her hound to save herself.

Peregrine finished in a few mouthfuls and sighed, as if wishing for more. 'Molly, I thought I saw a hazel tree growing next to one of the ruined cottages. Did you see it?'

'I think so,' she replied.

'Can you see well enough to cut me a forked branch from it?'

'I'll try.' Molly got out her knife and, crutch under her armpit, limped slowly across the shingle to the ruins of the village. She had to use her crutch to help her find rocks and holes and other hazards. She dreaded falling and wrenching her hip. She would be no help to the prince at all if she fell.

The pale buds of the hazel tree floated in the darkness like tiny glowworms, and relief rushed through her. She felt along the branches until she found one with a fork in it and cut it carefully. Limping, for her hip hurt badly, she made her way back to the fire and put the forked branch into Peregrine's hand.

'Hazel is one of the sacred woods,' he said. 'I have read it can be used for divination and for finding water. Let's try it and see what happens.'

Peregrine held the two prongs of the hazel branch in his hands and bent his head over it. In a low, weary voice, he said:

By the truth, let me find what is lost
The spear that in the bog was tossed
And ever since cannot be found

To my will let it be bound.
Tell me where to find the spear
Let me know when I am near.'

Then he rose to his feet. 'I felt it twitch! Come, Molly, let's see where it leads us.'

As Molly laid down her crutch and picked up the shovel, propping it under her arm, Peregrine knelt for a moment beside Jack's body, feeling for the pulse in his wrist and telling him, in a low murmur, to hang on. 'I'll be back soon with the spear, and then we'll heal you,' he promised. He then stood and turned, looking blindly for Molly. She was there in an instant, laying her hand on his thin shoulder.

'I'll guide you,' she said. 'Careful, the dog is just there, poor thing. Come around. Now, which way? To the west?'

Step by slow, stumbling step, the lame girl guided the blind boy into the marshes. On either side stretched bogs and quagmires, black and menacing under the silver radiance of the round moon. Molly listened to the frogs, smelt the wind, felt the quake of ground beneath her feet and, barely able to take a breath, found him a path.

'It's close,' he whispered after a long while. 'It's very close.'

The hazel branch was jerking in his hands, leading them closer and closer to a deep blackness where no grasses shivered in the cold wind, where no frogs sang their peculiar song.

'It's here!' he cried, and Molly clutched him close as he would have stepped out into the very heart of the bog.

'Stand back,' she warned. She tiptoed past him, testing the surface of the mud with her boot, then grasped a handful of bulrushes and leant forward, trying to dig one-handed. Some of the bulrushes broke and Molly lurched forward, only just managing to save herself by grasping another handful.

Will-o'-the-wisps danced before her eyes. At the Isle of Eels they were called corpse candles and were a premonition of disaster. Resolutely Molly turned her face away from the eerie ghost-blue lights and took the shovel from under her arm. She began to scrape at the mud. It smelt like a grave.

Hours passed. Molly was filthy and exhausted. Gnats whined about her head, biting her mercilessly. Peregrine strained forward beside her, balanced precariously on the edge of the inky blackness. Impatiently he directed her, and she did her best to obey him, throwing down handfuls of bulrushes as they broke to give her a slowly sinking platform on which to stand.

The darkness began to seep away. Pink flushed along the horizon. A bird called, and then another. Molly took a long, sobbing breath and brushed back tendrils of hair with her mud-dripping arm.

Suddenly her shovel clunked against something. Molly flung herself on her knees and began to scrabble. Heedless of the shifting ground, Peregrine dropped down and dug too, throwing gobbets of mud behind him.

'I have it!' he cried. He came upright, gripping a long dark thing in his hand.

Commonsense told Molly it was just an old branch. Yet it was so slim and straight. Foolish hope told her it was the spear of the Storm King.

They were both waist-deep in the bog, sinking fast. Molly leant upon the shovel with all her weight, hauling herself upright, and then, clinging to bulrushes and heath bushes, dragged herself out of the bog. 'Grab my shovel,' she told Peregrine and pushed the end into his chest. He seized it and, with the last of her strength, she dragged him free. They fell together into the reeds, then lay there for a moment, too exhausted to move.

Molly kept still, Peregrine's slight body lying against her, his heaving chest against hers. She looked up at tiny rosy clouds floating in the arc of pale sky, and smiled. After a moment Peregrine sat up, pushing his hair away from his face. The rash had subsided, but his eyes were still puffy and half-closed. He held out the long, slim thing to her.

'I cannot see. Is it the spear?'

Molly sat up and took it from him. It was light and well balanced in her hands. At one end was a sharp point. At the other, the wood flared into wings, like the fletching of Peregrine's arrows. She carefully rubbed it in her skirt. It was made of a twisted length of silvery-pale wood, with strange shapes inscribed all along its length.

A smile burst onto her face.

'It's the spear,' she said. 'We've found the spear!'

Slowly Molly and Peregrine trudged back to the camp, both so weary it was hard to put one foot in front of the other. They were both filthy, every inch of their skin smeared with mud.

'I can see a little,' Peregrine said. 'Just shapes and shadows. Do you think my sight is coming back?'

'I hope so,' she answered.

'Let's hurry. I'm worried about Jack.'

Blitz was calling frantically, flapping his wings, his bells clashing angrily. Peregrine whistled to him reassuringly. 'It's all right, boy. I'm coming, I'm coming. Just let me check Jack first.'

His squire had not moved, but still lay by the ashes of the fire, wrapped in his cloak. Molly gently folded back the grey cloth and felt her stomach twist at the sight of the wet red rag at his throat. Her petticoat was completely drenched with blood. Awkwardly she knelt beside him, feeling for a pulse in his wrist. Dread chilled her.

'How is he?' Peregrine asked anxiously.

'I don't know ... I can't tell ... Oh, Robin, I think he's dead!'

Peregrine fell to his knees beside her, groping out with his hands. 'No, no, he can't be!'

'I can't feel his heart beating.' Tears scalded her eyes.

Peregrine laid his ear against Jack's still chest. 'I can hear it! It's slow, but I can hear it.'

'Are you sure?'

'No!' he wept, burying his face against Jack's bloodstained clothes. 'No, I'm not sure. Is it just the sound of my own blood beating in my ears? I can't tell. Jack! Jack!'

Molly looked around wildly, panting, unable to catch her breath for the sick dread that filled her. She saw the silver goblet Grizelda had dropped lying in the shale. She seized it and wiped it clean on her dress, then held it above Jack's mouth. A faint mist appeared on the silver surface, then faded away, then reappeared.

'He's a-breathing! It's all right, Robin, he's a-breathing.'

Peregrine lay for a moment longer, his face hidden against Jack's chest, then he sat up. 'The spear. I don't know how to use it. What do I do? Do I just touch him with it?'

'I don't know,' she answered wildly. 'How am *I* meant to know? You're the wildkin prince!'

Peregrine felt out with his hands till he found the spear, which he had dropped nearby. He laid it against Jack's cheek. 'Is he better?'

Molly looked hopefully, but there was no change in Jack at all. Bitter disappointment filled her. She shook her head, then, realising Peregrine could not see her, whispered, 'No.'

Peregrine heaved a breath. He sat back on his heels, the spear clutched so tightly in his hands his knuckles were white. 'We have to take him to the oak tree. I'll rouse Lord Grim and make him tell us how to use the spear. After all, the Storm King healed both Lord Grim and his son. He must know how it was done.'

'How are we to get him up there?' Molly stared at him in dismay, remembering how hard it had been for her to make the climb on her own yesterday. Now she was utterly exhausted, and the pain in her hip was sharp. Peregrine was as worn out as she, and blind and in pain. How could they possibly manage?

'We'll make a litter,' Peregrine said. 'He's already lying on his cloak. We'll slide sticks through the seams of his cloak and carry him. You'll have to go in the front, as I can't see the path.'

For a moment Molly sat, unable to make a move, the enormity of the task weighing on her like chains. But then she breathed in deeply, struggled to her feet and went in search of two long sticks. Luckily the bundle of firewood Jack had brought the night before still lay scattered on the ground. She was able to find two long sticks, fairly straight, and bring them back to where Jack lay.

Meanwhile, Peregrine groped his way towards where his falcon was tethered, cheeping anxiously and flapping his wings. Working by touch alone, he unhooded the bird and then unknotted his jesses so Blitz could fly. The falcon launched straight up into the air, screeching in joy.

Picking up the edge of Jack's cloak, Molly found the end of the seam and unpicked the threads with the point of her knife and slowly inserted one of the sticks. To her surprise it slid in easily all the way to the end, not snagging on any knots or twigs or getting stuck, and out the other end of the seam. The other stick slipped in as easily, and suddenly Jack lay on a litter.

'Well, that was easier than I expected,' she said.

Peregrine gave a strained smile. 'It's the Erlrune's magic, helping us. She wove these cloaks, you know, and her magic is powerful. I think we would have died of cold in the forest if it had not been for her cloaks, and no doubt we would have been seen when we were riding through Zavaria.'

He laid the spear next to Jack, in the hope it would help him, and then felt his way down to the end of the litter, taking both sticks in his hands. 'All right, heave!'

To Molly's surprise, Jack did not weigh nearly as much as she expected. 'The cloak again?' she asked.

Peregrine shrugged and smiled, a quick flash of his old cheeky grin. 'If only I'd known I'd have used it for a sack instead of hauling my pack all through the marshes. It nearly broke my back!'

'Let's put the packs on the litter too,' Molly said. 'We'll want something to eat.'

'Good idea,' Peregrine said. 'Here, let me lay my bow and quiver beside Jack. My mother gave them to me, I'd hate to leave them behind.'

When the litter was laden, they once again heaved it up and began to carry it along the steep, slippery path to the height of Grimsfell, Blitz flying overhead. Even with the weight eased by the magic of the cloak, it was a hard scramble. Both Molly and Peregrine stumbled many times so that their knees were bloodied and grazed and their arms and faces scratched by the time they reached the top. Black spots danced before Molly's eyes and her hip hurt so much it was all she could do not to sob aloud with every step she took. Peregrine was in as bad a state as she was, for he was constantly bashing into rocks or stumbling into brambles, and their last meal was many hours behind them.

At last they reached the top of the hill and collapsed in the shade of the oak tree. Blitz came to rest above them, head bent to watch them curiously. Molly was so hot and thirsty she would even have drunk a cup of marsh water.

Jack moaned, a faint sound that caused them to sit up and look anxiously towards him. He must have been jerked painfully all through that difficult climb, and Molly adjusted the blood-soaked pad over his throat and wished she had another petticoat.

Peregrine pushed himself to his feet and groped for the spear. 'Molly, will you show me where the rock is?'

She took his hand and led him to the base of the rock. Her heart began to slam in loud, uneven bangs. Peregrine steadied himself on the rock then raised the spear and rapped it sharply on the stone, once, twice, thrice.

Gradually a low rumbling rose from deep in the hill. The ground trembled. Birds took to the air, Blitz among them. A few dry brown leaves scattered from the oak tree. Then a crack appeared in the rock. It split in half and, with a terrifying roar, gaped wide open. A gust of stale earth blew out. A tall, bent figure loomed over them.

'Who dares wake me?' a deep voice snarled.

CHAPTER 25

Lord Grim

'I DO. I AM PRINCE PEREGRINE, DIRECT DESCENDANT OF THE Storm King, and son of King Merrik and Queen Liliana who freed you from the starkin tower so long ago.'

Peregrine spoke proudly, his head tilted back, his hands clenched by his side. Molly stood as close to him as she dared, offering him what little support she could.

Lord Grim was twice as tall as her, and wrapped in a long dark cloak that smelt of mildew. His hands were bony and black, his back hunched. Deep scars ringed his wrists, a legacy of the bells that had once bound him. A hood was drawn over his face, shielding him from the light of day, but his eyes glittered with a strange unearthly light.

Unexpectedly, a hollow laugh shook him. 'You look like a mud-troll.'

'We had to retrieve the spear of thunder from the bog,' Peregrine replied with dignity.

The glittering eyes moved to Molly. 'And who is this?'

Peregrine waited a moment, as if expecting Molly to speak on her own behalf, but she was too awestruck and afraid, so he answered for her. 'Lady Molly, daughter of Percival Smith, Lord of the Marshes.'

Lord Grim frowned. 'I thought Ardian was ruled by Count Malcolm ziv Zardian.'

'It was. But then my da and the fen-men rose up against him, a-booting him out,' Molly said, her voice rather high.

One thin black brow rose at the sound of her accent. 'I see. So what do you want of me, Prince Peregrine of the Stormlinn?'

Peregrine took a deep breath. 'I want to raise high the spear of thunder and smite the throne of stars asunder! Your wife promised the Storm King that, if he saved the life of you and your son, you would rise for his descendants in the hour of our greatest need. Well, we need you now! My parents are held captive, the crown is in the hands of a vicious tyrant, our castle is ransacked, our people are kept in slavery. And I need you to help me learn to use the power of the spear. As you can see, my squire is dying. I need to save him!'

'Is that all?' Lord Grim sounded amused.

'I . . . I've had poison thrown in my eyes. I'm blind, I cannot see. I'd like to use the magic of the spear to heal my eyes.'

'You ask a great deal of me. Three boons you may have. What is your choice?'

'Three? Three only?' Peregrine clenched his fists upon the haft of the spear. 'Very well. First, I want to master the power of the spear. Second, I wish to ride against Vernisha the Vile and rescue my parents. Third, I wish to throw down the throne of stars and win the crown for my father.'

Lord Grim chuckled. 'Well chosen. Somehow you've managed to cover all contingencies. Very well. Let us begin with the spear. Do you realise that the spear, like all magical artefacts, is only as powerful as the one who wields it? The spear draws upon your own strength and your own talents. You are only a boy, and a thin, weak one at that. Do you really hope to have the strength to smite down the starkin?'

Anger flared in Peregrine. He was so sick of everyone telling him he was too young, too small, too weak. He hefted the spear high and flung it with all his strength towards the sound of Lord Grim's voice, aiming a little to the left. In his mind, he thought, *Smite that rock asunder!*

A moment later came the loud *craaaack* of rock splitting, then the echoing rumble of a giant boulder rolling and tumbling down the hill. Peregrine held up his hand and the spear returned swiftly to it.

'Impressive,' Lord Grim said, when the thunder at last died away. 'Particularly for a blind boy.'

Peregrine did not explain that he remembered exactly where everything was on the hill. 'I have many gifts,' he replied quietly.

'I thought, when I saw that foul, fat spider Zander throw it into the bog, that the spear was gone forever and I would be enslaved eternally. How did you retrieve it?'

Peregrine told him quickly, all the while conscious of Jack lying on the litter behind him, his breathing faint and laboured.

'You do indeed have many gifts,' Lord Grim said when he had finished. 'Who would ever have thought that the spear could be found by a blind boy led by a lame girl? Very well. You wish to heal your friend? First wash the spear clean in the spring, and then dip its winged end into a cup of water. Use that water to let him drink and wash his wounds. Then do the same for yourself.'

He stepped forward and gestured with his bony hand to the spring of water, which now burbled down the old stream bed. Molly blinked at it in surprise. She had been so focused on Lord Grim and Peregrine that she had not noticed the water begin to well. She glanced over her shoulder and saw, with amazement and joy, that the old oak had indeed put out a wealth of fresh green leaves.

'Robin!' she cried. 'The old spring is running, the oak tree has turned green.'

She knelt before it, hurriedly filling one of her horn cups with the cold, clear water. She brought it to Peregrine and helped him dip the handle of the spear into the water, then she limped to Jack's side and lifted the cup to his lips. He managed to swallow a few mouthfuls, and she used the rest to wash his wounds. Twice more she filled the cup, and twice more Peregrine dipped the spear into it. The third time Molly brought the cup to his mouth, Jack swallowed greedily, leaning up on one elbow.

'He's awake!' she cried. 'Robin, he drinks! His eyes are open.'

Peregrine squatted beside him, groping for Jack's hand. 'How could you be such an idiot? Didn't you trust me? I wasn't going to drink! I was trying to find out what her intentions were.'

'I'm sorry,' Jack croaked in shame.

'You should be. You almost got yourself killed!'

'Well, I think we found out what her intentions were,' Molly said caustically, filling the horn cup again. She brought it to Peregrine and, when he had dipped the end of the spear in the water, gave it to him to drink. She waited, hands clasped tight before her to stop their trembling, as the prince swallowed a mouthful, then poured some water into his hand and washed his face and eyes. He looked up at her, his face clear of all blemishes, his eyelashes spiky. He smiled broadly. 'I can see!'

She laughed in delight. Jack grinned, leaning up on his elbow. Peregrine passed her the cup, smiling. She turned it so she could place her lips where his had touched, lifting it so she could drink deeply. The healing water tasted like summer. As it flowed down her throat, she felt all her bruises and scratches heal. The deep, grinding pain in her hip faded away. Jubilation filled her.

Molly looked up and met Peregrine's eyes. Her face burst into a smile. Gladly Peregrine held out two hands to her. She grasped them, and he whirled her away in a wild and joyous dance, Jack clapping and cheering them along. Lord Grim watched in amusement, his hood laid back so they could see his long-boned, weary face with its hooked nose and slanted eyes. Molly had never danced before, but she spun and leapt as gracefully as if she had danced all her life. At last, breathless and laughing, they came to a halt, Peregrine still gripping her hands. Molly blushed hotly and drew her hands away.

'I can dance,' she said, then blushed even redder at the thought of how idiotic she must sound.

But Peregrine only smiled and said, 'You're cured! And Jack's alive, and I can see. I can hardly believe it. The magic of the spear is amazing. To think we found it, after all these years.'

'Sir . . . Robin . . . maybe if you drank a cupful of the enchanted water, you'd cure yourself of the falling sickness,' Jack said eagerly.

Peregrine looked troubled. 'Do you really think so? Mam would never cure it; she said the lightning in my brain was as much a part of me as my blood and my bone. I'd like to be free of it . . . but then, sometimes, it seems to help me too.

I see things . . . I *understand* things I don't think I'd see or understand otherwise.'

'You have lightning in your brain?' Lord Grim asked urgently.

'Yes,' Peregrine answered briefly, bracing himself for the inevitable plea to be careful, to not do anything dangerous, to keep close like a child.

Lord Grim smiled broadly. 'So too did the Storm King. He told me himself it made his childhood a misery, yet he went on to become both the first Erlking of the Stormlinn and the first Erlrune. Perhaps it is because you too have lightning in your brain that the spear called to you and was able to be found?'

'Maybe.' Peregrine gave Jack and Molly a crooked smile. 'I don't think I should drink any more of the enchanted water. What if I should cure myself of my Gifts at the same time? I think Mam is right, and the lightning in my brain is a necessary part of me. Without it, I'd be a different person.'

'And we don't want that,' Molly said softly.

Peregrine smiled brilliantly at her and took the spear in his hand, examining it closely, running his fingers over the runes carved along its length. Exalted, he could not keep still. He danced about, holding the spear in his hand, pretending to throw it. 'I knew I'd find it! I knew it wasn't lost!'

Emotion overcame him. He stood still, his head bent over the spear. 'So, at last, it is time.'

He raised high the spear again, hefting it in his hand. 'I, Prince Peregrine of the Stormlinn, claim the right to wield the spear of thunder. By the power of the blood and bone of my body, the light and life of my soul, the wit and wisdom of my mind, I swear I will wield the spear with truthfulness, compassion and courage. By the power of three, so let it be!'

He turned and flung it at the oak tree, and it sped from his hand and buried itself deep in the trunk. Then Peregrine held out his hand to it, and the spear wrenched itself free of the wood and returned, swift and straight, to his hand. He shook his head in wonderment. Again and again he flung it, aiming at a different place each time, and each time the spear flew true and returned easily to his hand.

'What a mighty weapon. To think I've found it, after it being lost for so many years.' His voice thickened with emotion.

'Well, I don't know about you but I could do with a wash and a feed,' Molly said, wanting to lighten the moment. Peregrine smiled radiantly at her, making her heart catch.

'You know, you really are a very useful person to have around,' he said as she brought out a muslin facecloth and a cake of homemade soap scented with honey.

'Why, thank you, kind sir,' she answered with a shy smile.

Together they washed themselves in the bubbling spring, laughing and splashing each other. Jack came to join them, his legs rather wobbly, the scars on his throat and arm pink and shiny. They all drank deeply of the cold, delicious water and, feeling greatly refreshed, rubbed themselves dry on the Erlrune's cloaks and dressed in clean clothes, Molly going behind the oak tree to change.

Then she raided her pack, putting together a rough meal of bread, soft goat's cheese, vinegary herrings and spiced pickled pear. To her surprise, Lord Grim sat down with them and ate with great enthusiasm.

'Best meal I've had in eons,' he said at last. 'May I have that last pear? I'd hate it to go to waste.'

At last nothing was left but crumbs. Molly heaved a deep breath. 'All right then. What now?'

'We strike the throne of stars asunder!' Jack and Peregrine said together, grinning at one another.

Deep within his hood, Lord Grim smiled. He reached under his cloak and pulled out an ornately decorated hunting horn made from bone, lifting it to his lips. When he blew, the most extraordinary sound rang out, high and sweet and long. It made Molly shiver, her skin rising in goose-bumps all over her body.

On and on the note rang out. Birds rose, shrieking, and wheeled about the cloud-smeared sky. All over the marsh, bitterns bellowed. Molly could not tell if it was the true call of the marsh bird or the warning signal of her father's men.

Blitz screamed and launched himself away, soaring so high he was soon a mere speck in the sky.

To the north, a smut of darkness on the horizon swelled until it was a fierce thunderhead. Its shadow fell over the fenlands, dousing the dawn colours reflected in the endless maze of stream and pool and creek and puddle. Closer and closer the dark cloud raced, until Molly realised it was not a thundercloud, not a storm, not an eclipse.

The Wild Hunt galloped towards Grimsfell, neighing and barking, shouting and hullabalooing. Giants with icicles in their beards and lightning in their fists strode on the flanks. Ghouls with black holes for eyes and icy bones for fingers crept below. Tall winged horses with fiery eyes and sharp horns hurtled in front, steam gusting from their red-rimmed nostrils. Giant hounds raced before and grey, shaggy wolves slunk behind, their ears laid flat, their eyes like coals, their fangs like ivory daggers. Giant birds wheeled overhead, leathery wings flapping with a sound like a thousand ancient, creaky bellows. Occasionally they screamed. The sound made Molly cower.

'Do not fear,' Lord Grim said softly in her ear. The chill of his breath, the graveyard smell of his skin made her shudder, but slowly she forced her spine to straighten, forced her eyelids to open, forced herself to look at him. He smiled at her jubilantly. 'Once again we shall ride! How I have longed for this day! At last I am to be free of my living death and allowed to return to my home.'

'My lord!' a woman's voice called. Molly looked up and saw a tall, statuesque woman riding a black-winged horse. Her face was dark and haughty, and her long dark hair whipped wildly about her, her coal-black eyes glowing with triumph. 'The day has come at last!'

'My lady,' he called and held out his hand to her. 'A glad day indeed.'

She bent and kissed him, embracing him close. When at last they moved apart, there were tears on the tall woman's dark face.

Ten broad-shouldered, black-haired men rode behind her, armed with heavy swords and clubs. They bowed from the waist, calling greetings. 'My lord father! Well met!'

'Well met, my sons! We ride now at the prince's command. Let us wreak what havoc we can and then I shall ride home with you at last!'

'At last!' his sons cried. 'Let us ride!'

Lord Grim reached up and seized the writhing mane of a gigantic horse with twin horns as sharp as scorn. With a single, swift motion, he was astride the beast and once again blowing on his horn. Molly flinched, despite herself, for the sound pierced her to her very entrails.

'Take my bow and arrows,' Peregrine said, thrusting them into her hand. 'Do you know how to shoot?'

She shook her head.

'I'll teach you one day,' he promised, making her heart glow. She swung the quiver over one shoulder, and the longbow over the other. He gripped the spear in one hand and then reached up. By standing on tiptoe, he was just able to seize the mane of one of the black-winged horses. He leapt up and managed to get his leg astride. Swapping his spear to his other hand, he reached down for Molly.

She did not hesitate for a second. Grasping his hand, Molly scrambled up behind him, wrapping her arms tightly about his waist. The quiver dragged at her shoulder.

Jack was seconds behind them, jumping onto the back of another giant winged beast, his square face alight with excitement. He had unsheathed his sword.

'Let's ride!' Peregrine shouted.

What a noise! What a racket! Shrieking and screeching and yelling and yelping, the Wild Hunt rode through the sky, hail rattling behind them, bolts of lightning sizzling ahead. Blitz screamed with joy, riding the tumultuous winds, his sickle-shaped wings spread wide. Molly laughed. In a scant few strides, Grimsfell was lost behind them. Before them spread the curving panorama of the fenlands, the shining waterways slowly being engulfed by the shadow of the Wild Hunt.

The miles melted away below them. In hours they covered all the long, weary distance that Peregrine and Jack had ridden so doggedly. By midafternoon, the fenlands were far behind and the Wild Hunt was flying above the river, following its sinuous curves through the Swartwood Forest, dark, tangled, brooding. Sometimes Lord Grim would swoop down close enough to the rushing water for his heel or the hem of his cloak to touch. At once ice spread out across the water, turning the cataracts hard and white. Lord Grim would laugh and soar high into the sky, hailstones clattering behind him.

It was a wild, exhilarating ride. Molly had never experienced anything like it. Her breath quickened, her heart pounded. Occasionally she let out an exultant cry that made Peregrine turn and grin at her.

By sunset, they could see the white towers of Swartburg Castle rising on its hill. Peregrine had begun to play his flute of swan bone, calling, calling. Hearthkin labouring in the fields looked up at the sound. With their shovels and axes and billhooks held like weapons, they began to run after the Wild Hunt. Horses tore free of their traces, galloping in their shadow. Pigs broke free of their pens, goats leapt the walls of their gardens, hens and geese were swept up in the whirlwind. The sound of bleating and neighing and honking added to the hullabaloo.

The sky darkened. Thunderclouds filled the sky, growling and rumbling with rage, their undersides flickering with lightning. From a small gap in the west, the last rays of the sun glared upon the river, turning it red as gushing blood, even as the sun was swallowed whole by the weird shadow of the Wild Hunt.

'The rivers will run red and the sun shall turn black,' Peregrine cried gleefully. Molly laughed and squeezed his waist, pressing her face against his back.

'Look!' said Peregrine. 'The castle! We're almost there.'

CHAPTER 26

The Gallows

DRUMS ROLLED OMINOUSLY.

Slowly King Merrik and Queen Liliana hobbled through the great oaken door and into the inner bailey, the shackles about their ankles clanking. Queen Rozalina and Lord Zedrin stumbled behind. All four were now dressed in the loose red robes of convicted criminals. Donkey's ears were set upon King Merrik's head.

The courtyard was filled with people, all richly dressed in heavy furs against the bitter cold. Although it was sunset, the gloom under the storm clouds was so intense that flaming torches had been lit all round the square. Liliana swept her eyes over the crowd, recognising many of the starkin lords. She met their gaze defiantly, determined to show no weakness. Inside, she prayed: *Let the Erlrune come! Let an army of wildkin rescue us!* But she was afraid it was impossible for help to arrive in time.

Vernisha sat on her throne, wrapped in leopard fur, her pug dog sitting splay-legged and panting on her lap. He too was bundled up in leopard fur, with matching leopard-fur booties on his tiny feet.

A scaffold had been set up in the middle of the courtyard, with two pillories standing on either side of a gallows where two hangman's nooses dangled. Men in black leather hoods and breast plates were busy heating up tools in an orange-glowing brazier. The smell of the smoke made Liliana feel sick. She swallowed and tried to lift her head proudly, but her knees trembled so much it was difficult.

Then she saw a tall, fair girl standing near the back of the crowd. She was gorgeously dressed in turquoise-coloured brocade, which deepened the extraordinary hue of her eyes. Her face was as pale as the white fur of her muff; her pale golden hair cascaded down her back from beneath a tall, conical hat.

'Look, Merry, Lady Grizelda,' she whispered through stiff lips.

Her husband scanned the crowd and saw Grizelda shrinking behind the broad figure of Lord Goldwin, her brother. The two lean white hound dogs were at his feet, as usual, and a tall, grey-clad man with hair and beard the colour of dust stood by his shoulder, whispering in his ear. At his feet were two more hounds, great slobbering beasts with red-rimmed eyes and drooping ears.

Liliana felt Merry stiffen.

'If Lady Grizelda is here,' Liliana managed to say, 'where is Robin?'

'If Vernisha had got her claws on him, we would know,' he said quietly. 'She'd have paraded him for the court to see, like she did us.'

'Maybe she's been saving him up as a last-minute surprise,' she whispered back, hunching over the agony of fear in her stomach. 'Oh, Merry! Where is he? I should never have let him out of my sight!'

He did his best to support her as the grey dusk and the flaming orange torches whirled together in a giddy kaleidoscope. 'Be brave, darling. Keep your head high.'

Liliana managed to straighten her back and lift her chin, though she shot Lady Grizelda a look of such burning reproach and accusation that the girl shrank back even further.

Slowly the four condemned prisoners mounted the steps to the scaffold. A few starkin children, so bundled in furs they looked like mothballs, threw rotten fruit at them. Rozalina raised her hand and pointed at them, fingers spread wide. At once they squealed and dived behind their parents. Rozalina smiled grimly. She was still wearing the witch's bridle and so had no power to curse them, but the starkin feared the wildkin queen so much they dreaded her smallest gesture.

'Oh, goody, goody,' Vernisha said. 'I am looking forward to this. Rozalina, I think you should go first. We've got a red-hot nail all ready to hammer through your tongue. Then you, wildkin witch. We'll chop off your hands and then leave you to watch while we gut your husbands. It should all be very entertaining.'

'How can you be so cruel?' Merry cried. He turned to the gathered crowd, huddled together for warmth before the scaffold. 'Is this the kind of land you want? Where innocent women are tortured? Vernisha is a vile murderess and traitor to me, the rightful king. Her rule has brought nothing but a harvest of bitter sorrow. I implore you all to seize this moment and stand against her. Do not be a party to her wickedness!'

As he spoke, lightning flashed brilliantly overhead. Thunder clapped.

The crowd stirred, muttering. Vernisha yawned widely and waved one fat hand at the rows of soldiers standing along the walls, weapons at the ready. 'Fighting words, my dear cousin. I assure you that anyone who listens will be joining you in a traitor's death. Now, enough chitchat. Let's get the show on the road.'

Rozalina was seized and dragged towards one of the pillories. She was forced to kneel, her head and hands thrust through the holes and padlocked in place. One of the hooded men reached into the brazier with a pair of tongs and pulled out a long nail, glowing orange. Another hefted a heavy mallet. Rozalina was white and trembling, hardly able to believe what lay ahead for her. The hangman with the hammer ripped the witch's bridle from her head and began to prise her jaws open. She bit him, and he cursed and sucked his finger then threatened to smash her jaw with the hammer if she did not open her mouth. Her jaw set firmly, Rozalina defied him. He raised high the hammer.

'Wait!' Liliana cried. 'What's that sound?'

Far away, the haunting howls of dogs and wolves rose into the dusk. Then came strange yelps and shrieks, the call of hunting horns, and the triumphant shouts and hullabaloos of hunters.

Vernisha sat upright, spilling Pugsie-Wugsie to the ground. 'Quick, do it!' she screamed. 'Kill them all!'

The hooded men ran to seize hold of Merry and Zed, but at once they began to fight back. Zed smashed one over the head with his manacles and then wrapped his chain about another's throat, throttling him. Merry kicked one in the face then spun and ducked, tripping another attacker. Liliana smashed her iron fist into the face of the hangman with the hammer. As he fell back, hands to his bloody face, she seized the hammer awkwardly with her bound hands and began to wield it fiercely against the padlocks that held Rozalina trapped in the pillory.

'Stop them!' Vernisha cried.

The soldiers ran forward, swinging their swords and halberds. Liliana smashed the last padlock just in time, seizing Rozalina's hand and jumping off the scaffold into the crowd. Zed and Merry fought back to back, all their anger and frustration at last released in action.

The crowd screamed and began to panic. Lords and ladies scrambled everywhere, treading on each other in an effort to escape.

'Kill them! Kill them!' Vernisha shrieked.

Liliana clambered off the fat woman who had broken her fall, shoved her into the path of a soldier and hammered at the shackles that bound her ankles till they snapped free. Another soldier sprinted towards her and Liliana hurled the hammer, hitting him square between the eyes. He went down like a collapsing wall.

Beside her, Rozalina was struggling with another leather-clad hangman. Liliana clasped her hands together and brought them down sharply on the back of his head. As he crumpled, she seized the hammer again and with a few desperate blows, her arms aching, managed to release Rozalina from her chains. Rozalina gathered her strength and aimed a precise blow at Liliana's bonds, the gauntlets falling to the ground. Then Liliana threw the hammer to her husband, calling, 'Merry!' He caught it and at once began to strike at his own shackles, Zed standing over him and keeping the soldiers away.

The wind howled. Hail clattered down, bouncing off the soldiers' helmets. The eerie yowling and yelping grew ever louder. Liliana had no time to look up. She was fighting desperately against two soldiers, using a sword she had wrenched away from the soldier she'd knocked down with the hammer. Beside her, Rozalina had been seized and was now pinioned by two strong arms, a sword held to her throat. Up on the scaffold, Merry fell to one knee, only just able to block a sword that would have swept his head from his shoulders. Zed had his back to the gallows, fighting off three soldiers at once. He seized the dangling rope and swung high, kicking one of them in the face.

A dark shadow fell over the courtyard. The last feeble rays of the sun were swallowed up. The only lights were those few torches still flaring and streaming in the blustering wind. Ice needles stabbed at Liliana's face. Someone screamed hysterically. Liliana scrubbed away the frost blinkering her vision, glanced up and gasped.

The Wild Hunt poured over the battlements of the castle, howling and ululating. All the remaining torches blew out as if with a single breath, and only flash after flash of lightning lit the courtyard. People screamed and struggled to escape, pushing against the soldiers who were doing their best to repel this eerie and unexpected attack. Liliana fell to her knees, exhausted and bewildered, unable to fight anymore.

'Hey, Mam!' a dearly beloved voice called.

Liliana looked up and saw Peregrine astride an immense horse made of shadows and fire and smoke, its eyes glowing, its mane and tail writhing like vipers. Behind him clung a girl with wind-tossed brown hair, a quiver of arrows on her back.

'Robin!' Liliana cried. 'What are you doing here?'

'I found the spear,' he called back and lifted it high in his hand, aiming it at the gilded throne where Vernisha cowered, shrieking in terror. The spear was illuminated from tip to tail in golden fire, shedding radiance all over the courtyard. For a moment he hefted it, aiming carefully, then it flew from his hand like a blazing comet, shedding sparks.

Vernisha screamed and threw herself back so violently the throne toppled over. Only her fat legs in striped stockings could be seen, kicking wildly in the air. The spear struck the underside of the throne, splitting it in two with a loud *craaaaccck!*

Vernisha screamed again, turning topsy-turvy and thumping heavily to the ground, her legs over her head, revealing her flouncy lace-trimmed knickers. Her legs thwacked down to the ground and she struggled to sit up, purple-faced and indignant, the crown tipped over one ear.

'I'll take that!' Peregrine cried. The glowing spear flew back to Peregrine's hand and he brought the winged horse down to the ground, steam gushing from under its hooves. Jack's winged mount landed lightly behind him, and the squire jumped down, sword in one hand and dagger in the other.

Vernisha scrambled away, wheezing in terror. Peregrine slid off the horse and held up his hand for the brown-haired girl. She landed clumsily, catching at Peregrine for support. He steadied her.

'Mam, this is Molly!' he called. 'Will you look after her? Molly, give her my bow and arrows!'

Liliana leapt forward, pushing aside panicking courtiers, servants and soldiers to reach the brown-haired girl, who was being shoved from every direction. She seized the bow and quiver of arrows without a word, and with a few quick motions had deadly arrows flying into the crowd. One took out a soldier ready to murder Rozalina. Another zoomed through the throat of the soldier about to split Merry's head in two. A third zipped through the soldier duelling with Zed.

Liliana took a deep breath of relief. 'Stay behind me,' she said to Molly tersely, fitting another arrow to the bow.

Molly ignored her. Peregrine had raced after Vernisha, but her pug had latched on to the hem of his cloak, growling deep in his tiny throat as he was swung this way and that. Molly reached forward and snatched the pug away. 'Now, hush, else you'll be trodden on,' she said sternly. The pug dog subsided at once, rolling his bulging eyes up to her face then tentatively wagging his stump of a tail.

Molly put the dog down and seized a broom, the only weapon to hand, and whacked it as hard as she could on the head of a soldier about to slash Peregrine with his halberd. The soldier crumpled and fell, and Molly hit out at another. The soldier turned to strike at her, but the pug darted forward under his boots and the soldier tripped and fell heavily. Then the pug latched triumphantly on to the soldier's ear with his sharp teeth, snarling and worrying away at it. 'Ow!' the soldier cried.

Liliana bit back a sudden, hysterical laugh and shot down a soldier about to sideswipe Molly. The brown-haired girl smiled gratefully, then her expression changed. Uttering a bloodcurdling war cry, she hit the head of a soldier about to stab Liliana, giving the queen time to whirl about and shoot him down.

Soldiers boiled about, trying to protect Vernisha, kill the prisoners and fight off the Wild Hunt. It seemed as if there was no end to the broad figures in silver armour and helmets pouring out of the guardhouse and the castle, their weapons swinging.

The two hobhenkies had joined the fray, using their chains to knock the enemy flying. Lord and Lady Grim were fighting with long daggers of ice. Many of the hearthkin servants had seized the moment to fight against their starkin oppressors, wielding wooden buckets, mops, brooms, saucepans and frying pans. To make things worse—at least for an archer trying to take aim in the melee—a hundred animals had suddenly materialised, coming to fight at Peregrine's side. Ignoring the shrill whistles of Lord Goldwin and his sister, a pack of long-legged hound dogs tore into the soldiers with their sharp teeth. Pigs charged, squealing. Cats hissed, striking out with unsheathed claws. Rats writhed through the crowd, squeaking and biting. Geese flapped their strong white wings and snapped at soldiers with their sharp orange beaks. Blitz was diving at the soldiers' heads, striking viciously with his talons. Then someone crashed backwards into the stables, and whinnying horses galloped out, trampling the screaming crowd under their hooves. Among them was a magnificent black stallion, plunging through the crowd towards Peregrine.

'Sable!' he cried in joy, but had no time to do more than pat the stallion's satiny side before he had to turn back to the fray. Sable kicked down one starkin soldier and trampled another as Peregrine fought his way towards the scaffold. Jack's brown gelding, Snapdragon, beside him fought with heavy hooves and strong teeth.

The Wild Hunt was chasing soldiers and courtiers all over the castle. Some ran for the cellars and were chased back by packs of hungry rats, led by a particularly large and nasty-looking brute that kept somersaulting into new and terrifying shapes. Others fled towards the battlements and were hunted down by howling wolves. Others crept under furniture, only to have Lord Grim's sons drag them out by their heels.

The scream of a grogoyle split the night as the great winged beast soared overhead. Its fiery breath turned the massive gate to ash in a second. Pedrin waved jubilantly to Merry and Zedrin as an army of wildkin burst in through the front gate, led by the Erlrune and Lady Lisandre, both mounted upon river-roans and wielding silver daggers. Behind them marched a ragged crowd of hearthkin, fiery torches in their hands, and a charging herd of wild deer come from the forest.

At once the tide of the battle turned. Soldiers began to throw down their weapons; servants fell to their knees, begging for mercy. A few still fought on, grim-faced and wild-eyed, but the cracking of the whips of grogoyles, the eerie singing of the lake-lorelei, the bellowing of the hobhenkies and the fierce faces of the hearthkin convinced them to surrender. Soon three hundred soldiers were all on their knees in the courtyard, heads bowed in a gesture of submission.

CHAPTER 27

The Starkin Crown

'WHERE'S ROBIN?' MOLLY AND LILIANA CRIED TOGETHER. They cast each other a wild glance, half-laughing, half-frightened, and turned as one to search the crowd.

Peregrine had taken the brunt of the attack, but with Jack protecting his back, Blitz soaring and diving about his head, and Sable and Snapdragon kicking and rearing by his side, he had managed to fight his way through to where Vernisha cowered behind the scaffold.

Peregrine raised the spear high.

'No, please don't kill me,' she begged, fat hands held up in supplication. 'Here, take the crown! It's yours!' She seized the crown from her head and flung it at Peregrine. He put up his hand and caught it. As he gazed down wonderingly at the glowing blue diamond, big as a goose egg, she snatched up a fallen halberd and brought it around with a shrill squeal of victory.

Liliana screamed. Time seemed to slow as she watched the sharp blade swing towards Peregrine's stomach. Then Blitz plummeted from the sky, shrieking with rage. The falcon clawed at Vernisha's face and head. Screaming, trying to protect her face, Vernisha dropped the halberd. Her face went plum-red. She choked, clutched at her chest, and fell to the ground. One heel kicked wildly, then subsided.

Peregrine looked up from his contemplation of the starkin crown to find the pretender-queen lying dead at his feet.

'Uh-oh,' he said and knelt beside her. There was no pulse. 'I guess her heart just gave out,' he said and looked for his mother.

Liliana knelt by his side, drawing him close. 'It wasn't your fault, Robin-boy.' She gently drew the dead woman's mantle over her face to hide her dreadful staring eyes.

'I'm just amazed she actually had a heart,' Molly said.

Peregrine smiled wearily at her, leaning on the spear, the crown dangling from his hand.

Suddenly a shadow fell over the three of them, taking them unawares. It was the grey-clad hunter, the knife in his hand plunging down towards Peregine's back. Liliana cried out but there was no time to nock an arrow to her bow. Molly twisted and dropped the pug dog, who immediately flew for the hunter's ankle, closing his tiny jaws on his boot. The hunter kicked him, head over heels and yelping, into the shadows. Molly flung herself before the knife, arm held up.

The knife tore through her sleeve, drawing blood. It was seconds away from piercing the flesh of her breast when suddenly the hunter was dragged upwards by the scruff of his neck, legs flailing, high into the dark sky.

'Let's hunt!' Lord Grim shouted. He held the kicking, squirming hunter with one strong hand. The dagger spun away to clatter harmlessly on the cobblestones. Peregrine caught Molly in one arm.

'Are you alright?' he demanded anxiously, bending over her.

Molly smiled up at him. 'I'm fine. It was only a scratch.'

Together they watched as the hunter was borne away into the lightning-racked sky. Peregrine watched them go, waving the spear joyously. Lord Grim turned back to wave and salute. The hunter struggled and fought but could not break free. The Wild Hunt soared after Lord Grim, snatching up soldiers, fat courtiers and screaming ladies as they went, the hounds baying with hellish joy. As they disappeared into the snowstorm, the yelping and howling gradually faded away.

The torches slowly spluttered back to life, glinting on the rows and rows of starkin soldiers, still kneeling in the icy slush. The hearthkin serfs began to cheer, waving their tools. The two hobhenkies danced a tumultuous jig. The dogs waved their plumy tails and pressed close to Peregrine's legs, looking up at him with adoring eyes.

Peregrine's gaze dropped to the starkin crown, which he still held in his other hand. Then he looked round the crowded courtyard and saw his father on the scaffold, the noose that was to hang him swaying in the breeze. Peregrine smiled and began to shoulder his way through the crowd, Blitz flying above his head.

As he passed her, Grizelda curtsied deep to the ground, her head bent. Lord Goldwin bowed. The rest of the starkin lords and ladies stiffly followed their lead. Peregrine held the starkin crown in one hand and the glowing spear in the other. He shone as if with starshine.

King Merrik, dishevelled and exhausted, was leaning on

his sword. Peregrine knelt before him in the muddy snow and held up the crown.

King Merrik dropped one blood-smeared hand on Peregrine's unruly brown head and said hoarsely, 'Thank Liah you're alive! We were so afraid for you.'

Then he let the sword fall with a clatter. He took a deep, steadying breath and took hold of the crown with both hands, lifting it and placing it on his brow.

'All hail King Merry!' Peregrine cried jubilantly.

'All hail King Merry!' Jack and Molly shouted.

Zed stepped up beside Merry, bowing low, and then slinging one arm about his shoulder. 'All hail the king!'

Grizelda knelt ostentatiously, her turquoise skirts billowing around her in the wind. 'All hail Merrik, the true king of Ziva!' she cried, bowing her head so low her ringlets fell into the mud.

Her brother dropped to one knee. 'All hail the king!'

One by one, the lords and ladies dropped to their knees in the filthy snow. A ragged shout went up, calling King Merrik's name. Rozalina and Liliana both ran to embrace him, their faces shining through their tears. Then the Erlrune was there, hugging Peregrine, hugging Liliana. Lord Pedrin and Lady Lisandre rushed to join them, the grogoyle soaring above, bugling triumphantly, breathing great spouts of flame through the frosty night.

'Welcome to my humble abode,' Lord Goldwin said with a sweep of his fine feathered hat. 'Thank heavens I can at last offer you the hospitality you deserve.'

King Merrik laughed. 'What, no more dungeons, Lord Goldwin?'

'I'll have the finest suite of rooms prepared for you and your lovely wife,' he said, snapping his fingers for a servant.

When nobody responded, he looked around, raising a haughty eyebrow in surprise. The servants were all too busy laughing and celebrating, though, to pay him any attention. 'My sister and I shall make everything ready for you with our own fair hands,' Lord Goldwin assured the king. 'Grizelda!'

Grizelda swept the king a graceful curtsey, saying sweetly, 'I am so glad that the House of ziv Zadira shall be the first to welcome you, your Highness.'

'Father, she tried to poison me!' Peregrine cried. 'She ordered her dog to kill Jack and she was the one who marked the secret entrance to Stormlinn Castle. And her servant shot Stiga!'

Liliana went white, tears springing to her eyes. 'Oh, no! Stiga? Stiga is dead?'

'She tried to poison you?' King Merrik said. 'And she marked the entrance?'

'An unfortunate misunderstanding,' Grizelda said through stiff lips.

King Merrik stepped towards her and she flinched at the look on his face. 'Hundreds of my people are dead, murdered in their sleep or cut down as they tried to defend their home. Hundreds more are hurt and wounded. You broke bread with us, you shared the Yuletide feast with us. How could you do such a thing?'

'I . . . I . . .' Tears rose in Grizelda's eyes. She looked around at the crowd of cold, implacable faces. 'I didn't know what would happen. I swear it! How was I to know?'

She saw Peregrine and took a step towards him, her hands flying up in appeal. 'Robin! Tell them!'

'Don't call me that,' he answered, arms folded across his chest, his face stony.

'Please, Robin . . . Don't be angry.'

'Don't be angry? You tried to poison me! Your dog almost killed Jack. You blinded me!'

'You must understand how hard it was for me,' Grizelda said. 'I was all alone. I didn't know what to do. Nothing had gone as I planned.'

'Hmmph,' Molly said and gave the broom she still held a little shake, as if wishing she could give the starkin girl a good whack. The pug darted forward and tried to bite the pointed toe of Grizelda's shoe, and she kicked him away so she could come and stand close to Peregrine, smiling up at him. The sweet scent of her perfume drowned out the smell of smoke and sweat and blood.

'I did warn you about the soldiers, didn't I, Robin? I put myself in danger to warn you. And I could have poisoned you a thousand times. I put it off as long as possible.'

'What's the starkin punishment for a poisoner, Molly?' Peregrine asked.

Molly looked at him in sudden horror. 'To be boiled alive in a giant iron cauldron.'

Grizelda took a step back. 'You wouldn't!'

'No, of course I wouldn't!' he said bitterly. 'We don't boil people! Or rip out their tongues, or cut off their hands.'

King Merrik said in an icy voice, 'I think, though, that we may offer Lord Goldwin and Lady Grizelda the same accommodation they offered us. Take them to the dungeons.'

'No!' Grizelda screamed. 'No, you can't do that! How dare you?'

The two enormous hobhenkies lumbered towards her, happy grins splitting their faces.

'Get your filthy hands off me! I won't go, I won't, I won't!' Grizelda kicked at one hobhenky's ankle but only succeeded in bruising her toes. Hopping on the other foot, she screeched and cursed and shouted, but the hobhenky simply picked her up and tucked her under his arm, carrying her away towards the castle, both her legs kicking wildly behind her.

'Noooooo!' she howled. 'Rooooobin!'

'Don't call me that!' Peregrine repeated softly. 'Only people I love can call me that.' He glanced at Molly and she blushed as red as a wild rose.

'King Merrik, I must remind you that I am Lord Goldwin, the Count of Zavaria, and that this is my castle!' Grizelda's brother said rapidly, backing away from the second hobhenky.

'Which is why you simply must spend a little time getting to know it better,' Queen Liliana said. 'My guess is you really have no idea what a horrible, filthy, stinking place your dungeon is.'

'If you did, you would have cleaned it up long ago,' Queen Rozalina said, smiling.

'It's cold down there,' Lord Zedrin advised him. 'Luckily, though, we left you a pile of animal skins. They help keep out the cold—a little, anyway.'

'I must protest . . . you have no right . . .' Lord Goldwin cried.

'No right? If I remember correctly, the penalty for treason is being hanged, drawn and quartered,' King Merrik said coldly. 'So which would you prefer? Your so-called queen's justice, or mine?'

'Yours, your Majesty, of course,' Lord Goldwin said with an exaggerated bow, before sweeping grandly after his struggling, squealing sister, the hobhenky trotting behind him, looking rather disappointed he did not have a struggle on his hands.

'Whatever are we to do with them?' Peregrine asked, staring after the odd little procession.

'There's a lot of work to be done now Vernisha's gone,' Molly said. 'Children left without parents, poor old people left starving, the sick and wounded to care for. There's plenty they could do to help.'

'Good idea, Molly! Really, you are a very useful person to have around.' Peregrine gazed at her with warm admiration. She blushed.

Peregrine heaved a deep breath and took her hand. 'It's over,' he said.

'Not yet,' she answered, gesturing at the crowds of people still milling about the courtyard. 'Look at them all! What on earth are we to feed them?'

CHAPTER 28

Twelfth Night

'THEN YOU DROP IN A GOLDEN COIN,' PEREGRINE SAID, MIXING the batter for the Yuletide cake in a bowl with a wooden spoon, 'and whoever finds it is the Lord of Misrule.'

'I haven't got a golden coin,' Molly said. 'Have you?'

'No.'

'Well, you'd better hurry up and find one, because this cake is almost ready.' Molly wiped her brow with a floury forearm.

'Jack will have one,' Peregrine said. 'I'll find him in a minute.' He passed the bowl to Molly, who began to scrape the currant-studded dough into a deep floured pan while he sat on the edge of the table, falling into a moody silence. Molly glanced at him once or twice, but Peregrine did not notice, frowning as he stared at the glowing coals of the fire.

'Are you ... are you upset about Grizelda?' Molly asked diffidently.

Peregrine glanced at her in surprise. 'Well, I could wish she hadn't tried to kill me! And that she and her brother had really been on our side. We need some allies among the starkin lords. But otherwise, no. I'm too glad at the way everything has turned out to hate her.'

'It was a terrible thing she did, playing a double game like that!' Molly said indignantly.

'Yes, but if she had not come to Stormlinn Castle I'd never have set out on this adventure,' Peregrine said, turning towards her. 'And I'd never have met you.' Taking all his courage into his hands, he leant forward and kissed her on the mouth.

'Well, we can't exactly boil her in oil for that, can we?'

Peregrine smiled at her and shook his head. 'No, though I do hope Mam sends her to work in a hospital a long, long way away.' He kissed her again.

'Mmm-mmm,' she agreed, lifting one hand to push his hair behind his ear.

Just then Jack came bounding in. He looked more handsome than ever, the scar on his throat giving him a rakish, dangerous look. 'What's this? Canoodling in the kitchen?'

'I'm helping to cook.' Peregrine picked up the wooden spoon and waved it to prove his point, sending cake batter flying.

'Well, your father wants you,' Jack said. 'That looks good, can I lick the spoon?'

'Do you have a gold coin?'

'Well, yes,' Jack said in surprise. 'Do I need to pay to lick the spoon?'

'We need it for the Yule cake,' Molly said, laughing, as Jack tossed her the coin.

Peregrine gave him the dripping spoon, mouthed an apology to Molly and went back up to the banqueting hall.

All his family were there, bathed and dressed in clean clothes, and busy trying to bring order to the chaos. King

Merrik and Lord Zedrin were deep in conversation with the Erlrune and the leaders of the hearthkin villages, including the Marsh King and his council, who had been experimenting for some time with the use of marsh gas as a way for propelling horseless carriages and had found, to their surprise and joy, that their invention worked quite well. They were all rather wind-blown, with blackened faces and singed beards, but overjoyed to see Peregrine with the spear of the Storm King thrust nonchalantly through his belt.

'Where's my Molly?' the Marsh King demanded after he had shaken the prince's hand so vigorously Peregrine was afraid his arm would be jerked off.

'Cooking,' Peregrine said with a shrug.

'That's my girl! We're mighty hungry, aren't we, lads?'

A roar of approval met his words.

Hobhenkies were blundering everywhere, moving tables around in an effort to fit everyone in. Wood-sprites flew about, draping evergreen wreaths from the rafters. Tom-Tit-Tot was excitedly turning somersaults midair, changing shape from an omen-imp to a black rat to a weasel to a cat, which made all the hobhenkies scream and run in terrified circles. Liliana, Rozalina and Lisandre were sitting by the fire, deep in conversation with a small, thin woman with short grey curls and shrewd hazel eyes.

Peregrine recognised her at once. 'Grand-Mags!' he shouted.

His grandmother turned and grinned at him. 'Leeblimey, Robin, what've you been up to? The tales I'm hearing!'

Peregrine ran to embrace her. 'What are you doing here?'

'You expected me just to wring my hands and weep when I heard that old hag had hold of my boy Merry? Hayhead! Of course I got here as fast as my skinny old legs could carry me. I brought my men with me,' she waved one hand at a group of tall, bearded, rough-looking men who had been among the hearthkin to storm the castle, 'and we were trying to figure out a way to get into the castle when we saw you a-coming! Leeblimey, but it was a sight to freeze your blood!'

'I'm so glad to see you,' Peregrine said happily.

'Me too, laddie. But come! We all want to hear about your adventures.' Mags cupped both hands about her mouth and yelled, 'Hey, Merry-me-lad! Come talk to Robin.'

Merry and Zed and the Erlrune at once came to join the family group around the fire, bringing chairs and stools to sit on. Peregrine gazed around in great satisfaction. He could not remember the last time he had had his whole family together in the one place.

'Now, Robin,' his mother said, waving one finger at him in mock exasperation. 'You have some explaining to do. You were meant to be safe and sound at Briony's, not galloping off on some wild adventure. How did you end up in the fenlands instead of at Evenlinn?'

The Erlrune smiled at him with eyes as warm and green as a forest pool. 'When you didn't arrive, I looked for you in the Well of Fates. Oh, but I saw such terrible things! I saw you blind and lost and betrayed . . .'

'Well, yes, all that happened.' Peregrine nodded.

'What! How? What happened?' his family demanded.

'It's a long story,' Peregrine began.

Everyone laughed. 'It always is,' Pedrin said, 'but we've all the time in the world, my boy.'

'Thanks to you,' Merry said. 'I don't think I'll ever forget the sight of you riding through the storm with Lord Grim's Gallop!'

'You arrived just in the nick of time,' Rozalina said. 'Another second or two . . .' She shuddered.

'Tell us how you found the spear,' Zed said. 'I bet you a bag of gold coins you've had some wild adventures.'

'Let the poor boy talk,' Lisandre said, reaching forward to pat his hand.

So Peregrine found himself sitting on a stool in the centre of a circle of eager, fascinated faces, describing all that had happened in the past twelve days. As he spoke, he felt the giddiness of his relief and joy passing into something much warmer and deeper. His family was safe, the future was bright, the land at last had a chance of true and lasting peace. He had found the Storm King's spear, won the starkin crown for his father, and had a new phoenix ring wrought for him, symbol of the cycle of life and the new world that might be made from the ashes of the old. He dug in his pocket and found the bog oak ring to show his parents, and they marvelled at the exquisite workmanship.

'Molly made it,' he said proudly.

'Is that the girl who rode with you and the Wild Hunt?' his mother asked at once.

He nodded. 'I couldn't have found the spear without her, Mam. I was lost and blind and in despair. She gave me the courage to go on, and then guided me through the bog. She was lame, you know. I was blind and she was lame.'

'I must thank her,' Liliana said quietly. 'Where is she now?' She looked around, but the banqueting hall was so crowded with wildkin and starkin and hearthkin it was impossible to see anyone.

'She's cooking supper. There's a lot to do, to feed so many, and most of the servants are too busy raiding the castle's cellars and celebrating.'

'Well, thank heavens someone thought about food,' Zed said. 'I'm starving!'

'Me too,' Merry said. 'I can't remember the last decent meal I had.'

'Well then, let's go down to the kitchen,' Liliana said. 'We can't let the poor girl do all the work!'

Everyone jumped up. 'Great idea!' Merry said. 'I want to meet this girl myself.'

'Don't overwhelm the poor thing,' Rozalina said anxiously. 'Does she really want to meet everyone all at once?'

'Just Robin and I will go,' Liliana said firmly. 'The rest of you can meet her at the feast. She can sit at the high table with us.'

She drew Peregrine's hand through her arm as they went slowly down the steps to the cavernous kitchen at the back of the castle. 'Oh, Robin, I was so afraid for you when I saw Lady Grizelda here at the castle. I can't believe she wore a poison ring! And that she actually tried to murder you.'

'We should have listened to Stiga. She told us Grizelda carried venom in her hand.' Peregrine's voice was bleak. 'Maybe if we'd listened to her, Stiga would still be alive.'

Liliana nodded. 'But we searched Grizelda and found nothing. And she was so young! How could any of us suspect her capable of murder? We're not to blame, Robin.'

'I suppose so,' he answered. 'If only we hadn't ridden out! It was all a trick, Grizelda saying the starkin had fusillier fuel, Mam. They didn't use it against us, not once.'

'No, they didn't,' Liliana agreed. 'Not even against the grogoyle.'

'If we'd stayed inside the castle, Grizelda could never have shown the soldiers where the secret entrance was. Her dog piddled on the entrance, you know, and the sleuth hounds tracked his scent. That's how the soldiers knew how to break in.'

Liliana shook her head in amazement. 'So . . . so clever. So cold-blooded.'

'She was both of those things,' Peregrine replied. 'She looked me in the eye and lied to me, Mam. And I believed her. And then she set her dog on Jack and tried to poison me.' His tone was incredulous.

'It's all my fault,' Liliana said. 'It's because I sent you away. I should've kept you close.'

'It was Grizelda who lied to us and tried to murder me, it's her fault and no-one else's,' Peregrine said. 'Besides, if I hadn't ridden out I'd never have found the spear. So, even though I'm very sorry about Stiga and everyone who died at the castle, in the end I'm glad Grizelda came to Stormlinn Castle and tricked us into fleeing. Because otherwise we wouldn't have found the spear or roused Lord Grim or won the starkin crown. It was all worth it, Mam!'

'In the end, it was!' Liliana hugged him close. 'I . . . I'm sorry, Robin. I was afraid for you. I wanted to keep you safe. The lightning in your head frightened me, upset me.' She hesitated, then plunged on bravely, 'Yet it is who you are. Look at what you've achieved! You found the spear of thunder, you won the crown for your father, you . . . you saved us all from a horrible death. I . . . I was wrong, I should've trusted you.'

'That's all right, Mam. Just don't do it again!'

Liliana laughed ruefully.

They came into the warmth of the kitchen where Molly was busy stirring a great pot of soup. Her freckled face was flushed, her brown hair was in disarray, and there was flour on her cheek.

Peregrine grinned. 'Hey, Molly. This is my Mam. Mam, this is Molly.'

Molly looked up, gasped in dismay, and at once dropped into an awkward curtsey. 'I'm sorry, your Highness . . .' she began.

Liliana swept forward and embraced her warmly. 'Thank you!' she cried. 'Robin has told me all you've done. Come, take off your apron, put down your spoon! I'll send the hobhenkies to finish up, they love to cook. Come and meet the family!'

It was nearly midnight on Twelfth Night, and everyone was having as good a time as it was possible to have.

Wildkin were dancing with hearthkin, starkin with wildkin, and hearthkin with starkin. On Twelfth Night, tradition demanded that servants were on an equal footing with their masters, and so the fat cook was dancing with a starkin lord, a farmer with a lady's maid, the Erlrune with a hobhenky, Queen Rozalina with a shyly smiling pot-boy, and Peregrine's grandmother Mags with Tom-Tit-Tot. A radiant Princess Adora was whirling in the strong arms of the Marsh King, while Hal and Hank and Fred and Frank and Bill and Bob and Will and Wat and Gus and Ged and Ty and Ted had all found dancing partners, ranging from goose-girls to grand starkin ladies.

King Merry, Lord Pedrin and a motley orchestra were playing their instruments as well as they could for laughing at the sight.

Jack had found the golden coin in the cake and so, as Lord of Misrule, was leading a riotous procession around the banqueting hall, singing, banging pots and pans with wooden spoons, dancing jigs on tables and swinging off the chandeliers.

Molly and Peregrine had been dancing for hours but, hot and breathless, had found a shadowy corner in which to throw themselves down on a cushioned bench and gladly gulp at their goblets of golden elderflower wine. 'What a night!' Molly cried.

'Twelfth Night is always wild and merry and out of control,' Peregrine said. 'It's the end of Yuletide, you see.'

'It seems a shame,' she said. 'I like to see starkin and hearthkin and wildkin dancing and feasting together like this, everyone happy and joyous.'

'We might need to think of a new name for all our people,' Peregrine said. 'I mean, what am I? I'm all of those things and none of those things. And if all goes well, I'll not be the only one whose blood is mingled.'

Molly looked at King Merry, the starkin crown pushed back rakishly on his head as he played a rollicking tune that just forced your toe to tap and your fingers to drum. 'What about the merrykin?' she suggested.

Peregrine's eyes blazed with excitement. 'Molly, I love you!' he cried and leant forward to kiss her full on the mouth. Molly slid her hand into his unruly curls and kissed him back with all her heart. They only broke apart when Tom-Tit-Tot hurtled down to land on the back of their bench, hooting, 'Ooooh, aren't they sweet? Ooooh, feel the heat!'

Molly turned crimson, but Peregrine only batted him away, saying, 'Go and bother someone else, Tommy-boy!'

The omen-imp shot off as fast as a speeding arrow to tease Princess Adora and the Marsh King, who were dancing a steamy *estampida* in the middle of the floor.

'You might need to rescue your father,' Peregrine said.

'Oh, I think he'll be fine. It's your starkin princess who needs rescuing! My father looks ready to sweep her right off her feet.'

'That's Twelfth Night for you,' Peregrine replied, fanning his hot face with his hand. 'Don't worry! Life returns to normal tomorrow.'

Some of the light went out of Molly's face. She sighed. 'I don't really want it to. These last few days have been so marvellous! I mean . . . apart from you being poisoned and Jack almost dying and the battle . . .'

Peregrine laughed. 'I know what you mean. I think the last few days have been marvellous too.' He couldn't resist kissing her red mouth once more.

'I guess the adventure had to end sometime,' she said wistfully, a long moment later.

Peregrine smiled and seized her hand. 'There'll be other adventures,' he promised. 'But until then, let's dance!'

Kate Forsyth
THE WILDKIN'S CURSE

Next shall be the king-breaker, the king-maker,
though broken himself he shall be.

Zedrin is a starkin lord and heir to the Castle of Estelliana.
Merry is a hearthkin boy, the son of the rebel leader.
Liliana is a wildkin girl, with uncanny magical powers.

They must journey on a secret mission to rescue a wildkin
princess from her imprisonment in a crystal tower.

Princess Rozalina has the power to enchant with words—she
can conjure up a plague of rats or wish the dead out of their
graves. When she casts a curse, it has such power it will
change her world forever.

Set in a world of monsters and magical creatures, valiant
heroes and wicked villains, *The Wildkin's Curse* is a tale of
high adventure and true love . . .

The dazzling companion to *The Starthorn Tree*.